GAY
ACTIVISTS
ALLIANCE

The Night G.A.A. Died

Jack Ricardo

St. Martin's Press
New York

THE NIGHT G.A.A. DIED. Copyright © 1992 by Jack Ricardo. All rights reserved.
Printed in the United States of America. No part of this book may be used or
reproduced in any manner whatsoever without written permission except in the
case of brief quotations embodied in critical articles or reviews. For information,
address St. Martin's Press, 175 Fifth Avenue, New York, N.Y. 10010.

Design by Tanya M. Pérez

Library of Congress Cataloging-in-Publication Data

Ricardo, John.
    The night G.A.A. died / John Ricardo.
      p. cm.
    ISBN 0-312-07752-1 (hc)
    ISBN 0-312-09353-5 (pbk.)
    I. Title.
  PS3568.I24N54   1992
  813'.54—dc20
                                            92-856
                                            CIP

First Edition: June 1992
First Paperback Edition: June 1993

10 9 8 7 6 5 4 3 2 1

The
Night
G.A.A.
Died

Stonewall Inn Mysteries
Michael Denneny, General Editor

DEATH TAKES THE STAGE
by Donald Ward

SHERLOCK HOLMES AND THE MYSTERIOUS FRIEND OF OSCAR WILDE
by Russell A. Brown

A SIMPLE SUBURBAN MURDER
by Mark Richard Zubro

A BODY TO DYE FOR
by Grant Michaels

WHY ISN'T BECKY TWITCHELL DEAD?
by Mark Richard Zubro

THE ONLY GOOD PRIEST
by Mark Richard Zubro

SORRY NOW?
by Mark Richard Zubro

THIRD MAN OUT
by Richard Stevenson

LOVE YOU TO DEATH
by Grant Michaels

THE NIGHT G.A.A. DIED
by Jack Ricardo

SWITCHING THE ODDS
by Phyllis Knight

For Joe Eisenbeiser

Acknowledgments

I'd like to thank the Gay Activist Alliance of the early 1970s for being there when I needed them. They aroused the militant side of my nature. They helped me believe the words I shouted from the barricades: Say it loud, Gay is proud.

The
Night
G.A.A.
Died

Chapter

1

I hopped onto and into the back of the truck. The night was quiet, humid, the air sticky. A dog day of autumn. Inside, the truck was dark but not empty. I could see outlines, silhouettes, a midnight forest of men seen only by moonlight reflected off fading metal. There was a slight but sharp aroma of dirt and sweat and amyl nitrate.

I walked toward a familiar figure. He had preceded me into the gaping open-air sex den. His black leather vest made a V to his breastbone. The pale skin of his arms and his neck was scarcely visible. He was waiting for me. He knew I'd be there. I stopped in front of him. I couldn't see his face, but I could hear and feel his breathing.

My mouth was only inches from his. Like a magnet on the verge. Neither of us spoke. We used our hands, gauging the texture of a cotton shirt against a chest, the sleekness of leather, sweaty and exhilarating, against warm skin; measuring the excitement of blue denim against white cotton against growing flesh. We used our lips, tentatively, pecking, not devouring. Our playful passion neither increased nor decreased. It stayed on an even plane. We played for five minutes. Like virtuosos.

I spoke first, less than a whisper, into the ear that was snuggled next to my cheek. "Let's go outside and have a smoke."

We jumped down from the back of the truck, leaving the others to more serious sexual pursuits. We weren't abandoning ship, merely charting our own course.

I had already known what he looked like, having followed him for the last three blocks. He was taller than I was, but not by much. His hair was long, curly and brown, and rather shaggy. Very much in fashion, if you were into fashion. I wasn't.

He didn't wear a shirt, not even a T. Only his vest and dungarees. The calendar said fall, but not tonight. The Indians had given us one last summer night before they were going to allow Jack Frost to continue on his way.

The vest, without the shirt, was appropriate for the hot evening. And the black of the leather against his body was a magical lure. His stance was masculine, his body small. A curly-headed Romeo in blue denim. And he knew what I looked like. A blond mustached honor guard in Levi's, slim and strong and sexually ready.

"Max Harmony," he said, not extending me a hand to shake. Under the circumstances, the gesture would have been not only redundant but ridiculous. Our hands had already touched in the darkness of the truck, as had our bodies.

I offered him a cigarette. He refused and loosened one of his own from his vest pocket. I lit his first, then mine. "Archie Cain," I said. Our eyes met in flame.

"It's not very crowded tonight," I noted. Men were milling around and behind and inside the parked eighteen-wheelers backed into the loading zone. But the men were few, less than a dozen, by my automatic count.

"It's early yet," Max said.

He was right, it was barely past midnight.

"Were you at the meeting?" he asked.

"What meeting?"

"G.A.A."

A group of three rather effeminate men, obviously together and joking more loudly than the atmosphere allowed, sashayed past us to join in, or make fun of, the hidden activities of the trucks. The cheerleaders of sex. Each said a hello or a hi to Max by name, or blew him an exaggerated kiss. Max gave each an acknowledgment, a smile, and a nod in return.

I quickly stepped out of the darkness and onto the sidewalk. Max followed. "That's what I dislike about coming down here," I said. "You never know what you're going to grab on to. Or what's going to grab on to you."

"You sound like a bigot," Max said.

We turned the corner and walked a few steps to the concrete loading platform that faced the quiet street. To the east, and not many blocks distant, was the life of the city. The neon lights and the honky-tonk. To the west were the decaying and unused piers, long abandoned by shippers but a bustling hive of nighttime male activity.

"If I wanted to have sex with a woman, I'd go find one and not some poor imitation," I told Max and propped my hands onto the cement dock behind me, hopping up for a seat.

"We have to learn to be tolerant," Max said, standing in front of me but glancing up and down the street.

"Do those queens turn you on?" I asked him.

Max looked up at me and smiled. "You turn me on," he said, laying his hands on my knees, bending his face over my denim crotch to give it a wet kiss. I looked around to see a man walking toward us from the waterfront. With both hands, I gently lifted Max's face from my Levi's. "Watch it," I warned, nodding at the upcoming interruption.

Max glanced at the interruption, decided that the approaching man was safe—one of us—and turned his body around to rest his back between my legs. I took a last drag on my cigarette and flipped the butt into the street. By the time the man passed, my fingers were giving Max's shoulders a massage. Max clutched my knees in satisfaction.

"Hi, Max," the man said when he passed. "Where's Davie tonight?"

"What you say, Tony," Max answered in greeting, not answering his question. He snaked his arms under my knees, kneading my calves.

The man didn't stay and chat. He gave me the standard evaluating once-over, then surreptitiously veered off into the shadows of the trucks. Another man walked out. He saw Max and sidled over to us.

"The firehouse was jammed tonight," the second guy said.

"Probably broke a record," Max agreed. He introduced me to Johnny. I smiled automatically. Johnny gave me a quick but inevitable glance, then returned his attention to Max. Max swiftly turned his back on Johnny and his attention to me.

"You have to be careful. The fire inspector can close us down," Johnny said, running a hand through the bristles of his hair. His hair was brown, thin, and neatly crew-cut. Johnny was white, thin, and cute. Not handsome, cute. His hair would have been appropriate in the 1950s, and he looked like Johnny College, I thought. He wore dungarees, of course. But they weren't Levi's. In five years, he would probably be just as comfortable, and just as awkwardly sexy, in a three-piece suit. All sorts visit the trucks—from aging hippie to retired accountant, from frivolous drag queen to lusty leatherman.

"The firehouse committee is checking into it," Max said, flipping his words off his shoulder. "Trying to find out what legal capacity the place can hold. But like everything else we do, the goddamn city agencies aren't exactly a help." He snapped his head toward Johnny. "What the hell are you doing here?"

Johnny seemed surprised at the question. "The same thing you are," he said. His tone was appeasing.

"I doubt it," Max said.

He gave Johnny a side-glance that would have stopped me in my boots. It didn't stop Johnny. "So what's the agenda for Thursday?" Johnny asked, changing the subject, his voice too friendly.

4

"Not tonight, Johnny," Max said, pushing himself up from my crotch and away from my knees. "Leave me alone. I told you that. The meeting's over." He again turned his back on Johnny and faced me, placing his hands on my knees, leaning over and giving me a nibble of a kiss. "Let's go," he said, smiling. "Find us some privacy."

Max stepped back and I hopped down. He grabbed my hand and aimed me toward the river. He didn't say good-bye to Johnny.

Before I walked off, I offered a small smile to Johnny. He didn't nod or smile in return. If Max hadn't come along first, Johnny might have been a strong contender, I thought. But if you go by types, Johnny wasn't mine. Still, he had a look, an innocent look that was compelling.

Max and I strolled hand in hand to the river.

"Are you involved in G.A.A.?" I asked. A silly question, I realized. But conversation starts somewhere.

"I'm vice president," Max answered.

There were shadows of men on the street, alone or in twos, leaning into indented doorways. Max turned around. I turned, too. Johnny had taken our place and was sitting on the dock, alone, peering in our direction. We continued our walk. "Johnny's a member, but he's not an officer," Max said.

"Do all your members come to the trucks after the meeting?" I asked in jest.

Max gave off a soft laugh. "No, not all, but most. Hell, some nights the executive committee could hold their meeting down here." He laughed again. "But Johnny rarely comes to the trucks." There was a sadness to his words. I didn't question him, but Max added, "Johnny's the virgin of the group."

"Virgin?" I said, unbelieving.

Max shrugged. "Well, he doesn't fuck around too much." Again, the sadness. "Not with me, anyway."

"You never made it with him?"

"Now, that's a question," Max answered, and seemed to fold into himself. I think he was losing the mood. Our mood. Max must have felt the same warning signal. He quickly changed tone and changed the subject. "Have you ever been to the firehouse?"

"No. I've been meaning to get down there, but I haven't had the time."

"You should make the time," Max said strongly.

Whether he meant it or not, Max was shoveling guilt in my direction. I wanted to have sex with this handsome stranger in his leather vest, not discuss the booming gay revolution.

I justified myself. "I only recently started my own business. It takes up all my time." I smiled at him, I hoped with allure. "Except midnight at the trucks," I added. "I do find time for that."

Max smiled back. And definitely with allure. We were stopped at West Street, waiting for a hole in the late-night traffic. Bouncing headlights at regulated speed zoomed by quickly or cruised by slowly. The zooming cars were going home in a hurry, the cruising ones were not going home at all, not yet anyway. Some stopped and parked. They peered out of the darkness of their cars at the available wares, me and Max and any other wandering and waiting males.

"Well, I'm glad you found the time for the trucks, anyway," Max said, "if not gay liberation. What do you do?"

When I gave him my silent, sly, and all-sexual stare, Max appended his question with a small laugh. "I mean, what kind of work do you do?"

I hesitated, but only for a bare second. We rushed across the street before the next surge of headlights began. "I'm a private investigator."

When we were on the other side of the street, Max stated, "A detective." His eyes were wide.

"Starting today," I added. We walked toward the entrance to the docks. We weren't the only men heading in that direction. Others with dungarees on their hips, swaggers in their walk, and lust in their hearts and minds and bodies also gravitated toward the tiny opening that would propel us all into another world. A timeless nighttime world of sex and grime and unseen faces.

"I received my license today and I'm open for business. And I applied for a gun permit." I don't know why I told him about the gun. Hoping to impress him, I suppose. My ego has not exactly survived undamaged during the last six months. But I was hoping Max wouldn't ask me where my office was. I didn't have one yet. I was working out of my home on Perry Street. But I did have business cards printed. Simple, just my name, occupation, and phone number. I took one from my pocket and handed it to Max.

I was about to hop atop the waist-high cement barrier when Max stopped me. "Wait." I stopped in midstride. He looked at the card. "You're really a detective?" he asked. Surprise was gone from his voice, replaced by interest.

"Is that so difficult to believe?"

"I thought detectives were rugged masculine men who wear fedoras and spit nails."

"Thanks," I said, not thanking him. "I like to think I'm rugged and masculine, anyway."

"I didn't mean that," Max quickly apologized. "But . . ."

"You've been reading too much Mickey Spillane," I said. "I'm not muscular, I don't wear a fedora, and the only nails I spit are the nails I bite from my fingers. We're Travis McGee now. Bums at heart." I laughed. Max didn't. He slipped the card into his back pocket.

"How much do you charge?" he asked.

A tiny figure whizzed by so fast I thought it was a cat. He looked liked a cat—small, wiry, wearing black dungarees, a long-sleeved sweatshirt, and a motorcycle cap. A bit over-dressed for this overheated night, I thought. He hopped the cement barrier in one graceful sweep, slipped under the wire and into the darkness of the pier. No doubt, joining the others on his knees, I thought, in silent but sloppy prayer to the god of raunchy sex.

"That's a matter of debate," I said. "I mean, a debate only with myself."

"You don't have a set fee?"

Price is an issue that I've been batting back and forth.

7

"Generally, a hundred and twenty-five dollars a day, plus expenses," I finally answered.

Max whistled. "That's a lot of money."

"It's all relative. Most cases can be disposed of in a day."

"How do you know, if you just hung out your shingle?"

I gave Max a secretive smile. "I've been practicing." For almost five years, I thought.

"Without a license?"

"Of course not," I said. I didn't want to talk business tonight. That wasn't what I came to the docks for. "Come on," I said, setting both hands on the concrete barrier, flinging a leg and then my whole body up and atop it. Max jumped up after me.

I held the ripped fence that was supposed to keep intruders out of the abandoned pier. Max bent low and under and skedaddled between the broken boards. Before he disappeared inside, he glanced back toward the street. My eyes followed his. Two men dressed as women were standing on the far corner, singing, or some fascimilie thereof, a song of the Supremes. And Johnny hadn't stayed at the trucks. He was waiting to cross the street. A car passed slowly, stopped and parked. The driver was working up the courage to exit his automated closet. Max ducked under the board. I followed carefully.

The pier was dark but not deserted. Through the cracks in the sides of the wooden structure, or through the holes in the crumbling ceiling, or through the gaps in the rotting floor, enough moonlight and reflection shone through to give direction. The polluted water of the Hudson could be heard slapping against the cement pilings underneath our feet. Muddy and sloppy sounds. Unknown shadows mingled in the darkest corners. Braver shadows stood stock-still against the wall, the moonlight advertising their availability. Single shadows floated toward other single shadows.

Max took me in hand and walked to the busy corner on the side. We could hear the rasping sounds of stilted breathing, the verbal and hushed sounds of raunchy encouragement, the sounds of sucking. We could smell the decaying wood, the

8

musty air, the sex. Each joined to create a charged atmosphere of hungry male animal coupling. Max and I joined the pack. But only briefly. Max led me past them.

We walked a few steps. Max held my hand firmly. Shadows and sounds of men in orgy mingled with the darkness and disintegrated until there was nothing to be seen or heard except black night. But Max had mental directions. He and I disappeared into the blackness and onto a stairway. Without losing our grip, I walked behind Max. My other hand slid along the wall, guiding me upward. I had been at the docks a number of times but never in daylight. I had never even known there was an upstairs. My usual destination was the other end of the pier, almost into the river, where three hollow rooms were better lit because of the lack of a ceiling. There, at least you could see who you were sucking.

A body wending its way down the stairs clumsily pushed us from the wall. "Damn it," I heard Max mutter over my "Son of a bitch." After the body passed, we returned to the safety and guidance of the wall and continued our climb. A loud groan came from behind us. One of the group in the darkened orgy had reached his loud climactic moment of the evening. His instant gratification echoed in the dark, then faded out into contented heavy sighing.

We continued our slow, careful climb. The stairs creaked under our feet. I could hear quiet footsteps coming up the stairs behind me and louder footsteps coming down the stairs in front of me, but I could not see an eye, let alone an outline. The figure coming down didn't shove me and Max from the wall. His hands touched our bodies and he politely bypassed and walked around us, his fingers gliding over us for guidance, not for groping. The figure behind us stayed behind us.

Finally, we set our feet on flat boards that crunched and moaned from our weight. We had reached the top. But I still couldn't see a thing. The darkness could only be penetrated by feel. And I didn't even feel a wall. With my hand still in his, Max turned one corner, then another. He obviously knew his way around. He stopped, I pushed into him. He drew me into his arms.

This time the kiss wasn't playful. It was passionate, intended to arouse. It quickly achieved its intention. Magnets met in full force. When my hands were under Max's vest, caressing his bare back, when Max had unbuttoned my shirt, and his hands were sliding over my chest and onto my back, he spoke softly. "I should hire you as a bodyguard." The sweat from our bodies was steaming. I inhaled the aroma, a healthy aroma, an erotic aroma.

"Why?" I asked, whispering in his ear. I pulled my face from his but still held him around the waist, my palms pressing against his back, then lowering to his waist, molding into the flesh, the sweat. I could barely see the whites of his eyes. I didn't have to.

Soft sounds of the nighttime pier invaded our private haven—purring from the unseen couple nearby, footsteps tiptoeing lightly so as not to disturb the sexual secrets of the dark spaces, groanings from the wood of the dilapidated pier, the sounds of water splashing against the pilings. I felt a hand sweep over the back of Max's vest. I pushed the intrusion off.

"Why should you need a bodyguard?" I whispered again.

Max fell into my arms with force, his arms moving under and all the way up my shirt and sliding over my back, his fingers winding around my neck, gripping me tightly, his face neatly cuddled in the cleavage of my collarbone. No more talk. It was action time. I held him tightly, my hands sliding down his back and into the waist of his Levi's. His mouth was smothered into my neck. "Help me," he cried softly, trying to catch his breath. He sounded more sorrowful than loving. I kissed the top of his head. The aroma of the sweat we captured between us became too powerful to ignore. I rubbed my bare chest against his leather vest, slipping, squishing. My fingers dipped into the waistband at the back of his Levi's, sweeping over the edge of the elastic of his shorts. Max became heavy against me. Too heavy. I lifted my hands out of his Levi's, tracing my fingers over the wet that was accumulating in the small of his back.

10

The acrid smell of two men in heat, of two steaming bodies, mingled with a familiar caustic and unpleasant odor. I couldn't immediately place it, but it aggravated an agreeable and expanding sexual experience. It disturbed the thrill.

The arms around my neck slackened. I hoped Max's passion hadn't died so soon. His arms dropped from my neck and down my back. His entire body began falling. I held him, but his body was weighted. He slid down, his face moving over my chest, though not in passion. In dead weight. "Max?" I said, slightly louder than the surroundings permitted. He slid lower, his body becoming even heavier. As he fell, my hands moved up his back and under his arms, enfolding his vest, and became flooded and wet. Not with sweat. It was too thick. "Max," I said again, louder. There was no answer.

I struggled to keep him upright, then knelt down to let his body slide over and onto my shoulder. I pushed my knees to lift the weight, straining, caught my balance, and had him in the air and on my back. I grasped him around the thighs and walked toward where I thought the steps might be, around a corner, then around another corner, the way we came, I hoped.

Sounds of delicate laughter approached me. A hand reached out and groped me. I pushed past it. The voice again giggled to another. Finally, in front of me, there was the slight light at the end of the tunnel, the light being the bottom of the stairway. The weight on my back began to slip. I adjusted it but still felt unsure. I started down the stairs.

I took the first step cautiously, feeling its length. I stepped onto the second just as cautiously, again measuring its length, the burden of Max balanced on my back. The wooden stairs groaned loudly, or maybe I just thought they did. I held on firmly and began to move down the stairs more confidently but slowly. I counted the steps. There were twenty-six before I landed on the rotting wooden beams of the floor of the pier, catching my breath.

The shadows in the dark and busy corner were not disturbed by my appearance. I was only another shadow. With a burden.

11

The sounds continued unabated—the breathing, the moaning, the encouraging.

I saw the entrance. Within the decaying building, it was the only lighted area. It faced the street, a small triangular mist of natural moonlight and manmade streetlights. The vague lights and the passing headlights of the cars gave me direction. I had to lower Max from my back before I was able to carry him through the threshold of wire mesh and broken boards.

Once again onto the outside loading dock, I eased Max down to the cement surface onto his back. His eyes were open, but they were dead and mostly white. I felt for a pulse anyway. It wasn't there. My hands were red with blood. I pulled Max up to a sitting position. The back of his vest was covered with the same red, pulsating out of a slit in his vest. I laid him down gently.

A young man approached. "Looks like your buddy had too many poppers," the guy said, small laughter in his voice.

I looked up. My gaze swept the humor from his face. "Call the cops," I said.

The boy stared, recognizing blood. He snapped his head around, looking in every direction. He backed off, walking rapidly to the highway, finally racing off between the traffic and across the street and then turning the corner. I looked around me. Two men were approaching from the north. They were half a football field away. A bedraggled man exited from the doorway of the midnight sexland behind me. He barely gave me and Max a stoned glance before he sloppily propped himself up and eased himself off the dock, then walked away, swaying. A car passed, slowing down, two cruising eyes glaring out of the open window. When the eyes spotted me and bloody Max, the car picked up speed and disappeared into the distance.

I hopped off the pier and pulled Max toward me. I didn't toss him over my shoulder. I let him fall into my arms and carried him across the street, his legs hanging down and useless, his head dangling stiffly. The passing cars either ignored me or quickened their drive.

I sat Max on the sidewalk, leaning him against the telephone booth. I found a dime and called the police. It wasn't long before the sound of sirens drew near and penetrated the playland across the street. The men inside scurried out and scattered like hungry roaches interrupted by an unexpected and glaring light.

Chapter
2

"Okay, Cain, what happened?" Carney asked.

I had been sitting alone in the small room for almost a half hour, trying to sort out exactly what did happen. I was horny. I went to the trucks. I met Max. We went to the docks. We climbed the stairs. We held each other closely. Then Max was dead. I carried him out and phoned the police. That's exactly what I told Carney.

"You fags will never learn," Carney said with disgust. "Christ, that pier is a disaster area. Why the hell do you go there? What the hell are you trying to do, commit suicide?"

How could I tell Carney about the erotic pleasure of seeking anonymous sex in a dangerous and raunchy environment? He wouldn't understand. I'm not sure I do. I let him browbeat me.

"You of all people, Cain. You should know better."

"Maybe I should," I finally said.

Carney had won a round. He was placated. His tone turned softer. "How well did you know this guy?" he asked. He wasn't lecturing now, he was working.

"I told you, I just met him. He told me that—"

Carney interrupted. "He had your card in his pocket."

"I gave it to him. He told me he was vice president of G.A.A., the Gay Activist Alliance."

"That's the group down in SoHo that rents the old firehouse, isn't it?"

"Yes."

"Are they a large organization?"

"I don't know. I've never been to any of their meetings."

"Really! I would have thought you'd be the first person to join one of those so-called gay liberation groups." The word *gay* stuck in his throat.

"I'm only liberating myself," I said. "I'm a lousy team player. As you well know."

Carney shook his head. "I don't know about you, Cain." He waited, as if expecting me to respond. When I didn't, he added, "I don't know about any of you fags. Shit, we pull off a raid on one of your goddamn bars, and you work yourself up into a worldwide sweat. And that was more than two fucking years ago."

"A sign of the times," I said. "Stonewall was our Fort Sumter. The sixties are over, Carney. The women burned their bras. It's 1971. Time for us to burn our jockstraps."

Carney ignored the remark. "Shit, and it was a goddamn Mafia bar at that," he said. Again he waited for me to speak.

I did, but I brought the subject back to murder. "Max was vice president of G.A.A. That's about all I know about him. Oh, yeah, he wanted to hire me as a bodyguard."

"You?" The overtone of disbelief in his voice irked me.

"I am in business," I said.

"No, you *were* in business," Carney countered. "When you quit the force, you went out of business. Cain, private cops are a dime a dozen in this city, and they're all worth about as much." When I didn't say anything to that either, he asked, "Did you get your license yet?"

"Yesterday," I said, reaching inside my wallet and producing my laminated authority. Carney didn't even glance at it.

"You know, under different circumstances, you could very well lose that goddamn license as fast as you got it. If we caught you in one of our raids at the docks, you'd be up the river without a license." Carney laughed at his small attempt at humor.

It wasn't too many months ago when I was working under Carney. I was only one of many men in city blue who patrolled his precinct. Only I didn't patrol, I was chained to a desk for four fucking months. But I had been a good cop on the beat, for close to five years, in Brooklyn. I was transferred to Carney's command in the Village when I kicked open my closet door. The desk was Carney's idea. He didn't, as he said, "want you out there on the street with all the other fairies. You might get your wings clipped."

But Carney also told me that I was a good cop. "In Brooklyn," he specified. And he wouldn't let me be a good cop in the Village. He sat me at a typewriter. He wouldn't let me be a gay cop on the streets. And he treated me exactly the same as the rest of the men treated me when I told them I was gay. Well, maybe he treated me a little better than some. He didn't try to beat my brains in.

But since I'd quit the force, Carney's attitude had changed. On my last day on the job, he told me why. "You did the right thing, Cain, getting out. I don't have anything against you personally. To each his own, I guess. But we can't have the public knowing that the city allows fags to serve in the department. Christ, the city would be in chaos."

I didn't laugh when he said it, although it was an absurd statement. Instead, I asked him if he thought that there weren't any other homosexuals besides myself in the New York Police Department.

"If there are, they're in the goddamn closet, where they belong," he said. On my last day in city blue, he put an arm around my shoulder and walked me to the door that led me to the street beat, without my uniform. "Good luck, Cain. I hope you make it okay."

Carney brought me back to the present. "Why should your friend need a bodyguard?" he asked.

15

"We didn't get that far," I said. "And he wasn't my friend. I didn't even know him."

Carney gave me a look of disgust. Vinegar in his coffee. I returned the same look. It was a brief standoff. When he wiped the vinegar off his face, I wiped off mine.

"And you don't know anything else about him?"

"Only what I told you," I reiterated.

Carney shook his head, leaned back comfortably behind the gray metal desk, his brow as creviced as Death Valley in July. "Then we don't have much. Harmony was stabbed. Tidy. A lucky strike, or a knowledgeable one. A thin blade through the back that pierced his heart. The weapon wasn't found. Probably in the river."

The clinical description chilled me.

"You didn't see anybody," he said, maybe to himself.

"It was too dark," I told him again.

Carney sat studying me, finally making a decision. "After you sign the statement, you can go home. I'll take care of it." He dismissed me by rising out of his chair.

I followed suit, but I didn't cross to the door. "How will you take care of it?" I didn't want to sound belligerent, but I think I did.

Carney caught it. "Listen, Cain, we don't hate fags here." I didn't believe him, and I guess it showed. "No matter what you think," he quickly added. "And I'll prove it. I'll get your killer for you."

"Not for me, Carney. For Max. And we're not fags. And we're not queers. And we're not sissies. We're not pansies, either. We're homosexuals, Carney. We're gay. Period."

I couldn't sleep that night. The cracked ceiling in my tiny bedroom and the inquisitive corners of my mind conversed together until well past dawn. A mixture of Max Harmony plus worry over making a go of it as a private investigator prevented easy rest. When I finally did fall out, it was almost ten in the morning and the sun was struggling to shine through the torn shade on my window. Let it shine. I slept.

My phone rang. I opened an eye. Almost two o'clock. I closed the eye. It rang again. But the sound wasn't rattling from the instrument next to the bed; it was faint and far away. After the third ring, I remembered and jumped out of bed and staggered to the office.

I picked up the phone on the fifth ring. But my mind was still sleepy and confused. I had practiced answering my new business telephone countless numbers of times. "Archie Cain," I repeated in rehearsal. "Archie Cain." "Archie Cain." When I picked up the phone, I barely muttered a "Yeah."

"Are you the guy who was with Max when he died?" The voice was male but didn't reach baritone.

"Yes. Who is this?"

"I wanna talk to you."

"Who is this?"

"David Hardin."

"Should I know you?"

"Max and I were lovers. Can I come to your office?"

"No," I said. The harsh sound of my own voice forced my brain into some kind of life. "I'll come over to your place."

He gave me the address. I wrote it on the small white pad that rested on the well-organized but virtually empty desk.

I wasn't surprised at the call. And I would have preferred to have met David Hardin at my office. But I couldn't afford an office. I had arranged the spare bedroom, a bedroom as tiny as my own, into an office. A large used file cabinet, which I had spraypainted a navy blue, was the centerpiece. I stored my business material in the small metal desk, a Gimbel's special six years ago. That is, I kept my business cards there, and some unmarked stationery and envelopes. I couldn't even afford letterhead stationery yet. Not much else filled the desk: empty file folders, blank yellow legal pads, ballpoint pens, sharpened pencils, paper clips. My framed license hung on the wall behind the desk. My electric typewriter rested on a stand beside the desk.

After a cup of coffee that nudged my brain awake and a shower that did the same for my body, I dressed, hit the street, walked east, and took the IRT to the Upper East Side. I had been surprised when Hardin told me the address. I hadn't expected Max to have lived in the ritzy, expensive side of town. It wasn't even convenient to the subway. It took me fifteen minutes to walk from Lexington Avenue to 85th Street between York and East End. Another block and I could have walked into the East River, or the Mayor's house.

Hardin didn't live in an attractive building. The outside was clean but nondescript. A flat colorless front, a small doorway molded into it. There were nine mailboxes, painted gold and cheap-looking, in the tiny hallway. A button was under each box, with eight names typed neatly and set behind clear plastic. I pressed the button under the card that was printed in ink, HARDIN/HARMONY.

The response was quick. "Who is it?" crackled a voice over the speaker. The words were distinguishable but tinny. Unlike the mailboxes, which were undistinguishable and tinny.

"Archie Cain." I was buzzed inside.

I climbed the stairs to the top floor without difficulty and without becoming winded. My karate classes helped not only the mind but also the body.

David Hardin was holding his apartment door open, or maybe the apartment door was holding him up. His eyes were half open and half red. His skin was smooth and clear, and there were no dark circles under his eyes, but no hint of life shone through the glassy fog, either. Too stoned or too tired, I thought. Probably too stoned. His hair was long and thin, blond with dark roots, and uncombed. His height didn't reach mine. He wore Levi's that sagged and no shirt or shoes.

Hardin led me inside and offered me a cup of coffee. We sat in the small dining room around a large round oak table with a thick carved pedestal. Above us was a loft constructed of two-by-fours and thick plywood. There was a wooden ladder at the side. There was more than a hint of burned marijuana in the air.

When Hardin saw me inspecting the wooden structure, he said, "It saves space. Bedroom upstairs, dining room downstairs. And living room," he added, pointing through the archway to a large room that was decorated with numerous antiques. Hardin laughed insecurely as he described the arrangements. A large brown wicker couch that resembled an Egyptian barge dominated the living room, and a colorful Oriental rug lit up the floor.

A full pot of coffee, steam easing out of the glass top, was on the table, along with two cups and saucers. The table was covered with a colorful but faded braided and fringed fabric. I waited for Hardin to tell me why I was there. He filled the cups and fiddled with a jar of honey while he spooned two heaps into his coffee. "You were with Max, weren't you?" he asked.

"Last night?"

He nodded. "That's what the police told me. Me and Max are lovers," he added quietly.

I remembered someone at the trucks the night before asking how Davie was.

Davie wasn't in mourning. Not on the outside, anyway. Although he did look like he had had a rough night. The only outward sign of agitation was the constant stirring of his coffee. His shoulders were rigid. I plopped a bit of milk in my coffee and sipped, my eyes on Hardin.

"Did you and Max have sex?" he asked. When I didn't immediately answer his question, he assured me, "We didn't have a monogamous relationship." The word *monogamous* was slurred and almost indecipherable.

"No, Mr. Hardin, we didn't have sex," I told him.

"Call me Davie," he said. He forced a small smile.

His attitude was friendly and open. As friendly and as open as any pothead I've known, and I've known too many. But he puzzled me because he stayed silent. Most potheads talk incessantly, about nothing and everything. It was obvious that he was on more than pot. Since Hardin wasn't going to push the conversation, I finally asked, "When is Max going to be buried?"

"I don't know," Hardin said. "His family took him home to

New Jersey. They didn't even call me about the funeral. And I don't expect them to."

"I'm sorry," I said.

"It wasn't entirely unexpected. Max took me home with him one weekend after we first met. His family treated me with courtesy, but they only tolerated me. They didn't like me. That was the only time I saw them. Max went home for Christmas and Easter, that's all. He invited me to go with him, but I never went."

"How long were you and Max lovers?"

"About four years."

"You don't seem to be too upset by his family's attitude."

"Should I be?" His eyes were defiant if glazed.

When I didn't reply to his question, he continued. "I don't have a choice. Max and I only lived together, fucked together, and were lovers for four years," he said, an ironic tinge unconcealed in his words. "His family knew him all his life."

If Hardin was trying not to sound bitter, he didn't succeed.

"Why did you want to see me?" I asked, finishing my coffee. It was home brewed, not instant. Hardin offered to refill my cup, but I didn't let him.

"I wanted to see what you looked like. The last man Max went to bed with."

"We never went to bed," I told him again.

"The last man Max had sex with," Hardin elaborated. The tone in his voice was friendly and not at all accusatory. But his words were.

"We didn't have sex. We never got that far."

"You weren't at the docks to see the boats off," Hardin slurred, bringing his cup to his lips with both hands, another smile forming on his face before he sipped.

"No, we weren't."

Hardin rested the cup on the saucer. His smile was gone. "Do you know who killed him?" he asked.

"No."

"Are you going to find out?"

"No," I said. "The police are."

20

"But you're a private detective. That's what Captain Carney told me."

"I am," I said, "but I have to make a living. Nobody hired me to find out who killed Max." I had half expected that was the reason I was there now. But Hardin didn't make an offer. I said again, "The police will find the killer."

Hardin nodded his head a bit, gave off a slight huff. "Yeah." He continued staring at me. That is, his eyes were on mine. I'm not sure he was seeing me. I met his gaze, neither one of us speaking. After too many minutes the situation became uncomfortable and finally pointless.

I broke the silence. "Is there anything else you wanted? Besides finding out what I looked like?"

"No," Hardin answered.

I pushed the chair back from the table and walked the two steps to the door.

"Can you lend me some money?" Davie suddenly asked. I turned around. "The rent is due and I just got the electric bill today." He paused. When I didn't reply, he asked again, "Can you?"

I didn't even know the guy and he was asking me for money. "Don't you work?"

"Of course," Hardin said, trying to sound offended. The offense rang false. He dropped his head. "Sometimes." He lifted his head. "But I need some money today."

"What do you do?"

"I sell antiques," he said. He quickly added, pleaded, "Business is kind of slow. And I'm too upset. And . . ."

I waited for the conclusion to his "and." It never came. Instead, he specified, "Just a couple of hundred dollars. Please."

"I haven't got it, kid," I said. And even if I did have some spare cash, it's not likely I'd pour it down the sink. Or up a nose, on in a joint, or in a bottle of pills. Which, from where I stood, seemed to be exactly where it would go.

I turned back to the door. Hardin didn't stop me or even speak when I reached for the knob. But before I left, I again faced him. He was refilling his coffee cup. "You're not very upset over Max's death," I noted.

Hardin looked at me with eyes propped open and no smile. "I'm stoned. To the gills."

No shit.

As I closed the door, I heard him call out, "Wanna buy the Cleopatra couch?" I didn't.

Forty-five minutes later, after trekking from the no-man's-land of the Upper East Side, I was back in my apartment, in my office. I called my answering service. There were three messages, and before the day was over, I had two clients.

I had placed ads in *The Village Voice*, the *Daily News*, and the *Post*. A small ad stating the same information as my business card: "Archie Cain, Private Investigator," and my business telephone number. I had hesitated before placing the ad in the *Voice*, mainly because I was concerned about attracting weirdos who couldn't pay for my services. But all three responses were in answer to my ad in the *Voice*.

And only one of the three was weird. Well, not exactly weird, but I didn't accept him as a client. The YMCA in Chelsea wanted me to dig up information on a resident who was living in one of their rooms. When I went down to the Y office and asked why they wanted this information, I was told that the resident was a promiscuous homosexual who was giving the Y a bad name. I turned them down flat. When I stomped out of the manager's office, I was left with the impression that I was not the first investigator who was offered the job. And I wasn't the first who turned it down.

A client I did accept was an antiques shop owner who felt she was being shortchanged by her partner. She was a beautiful middle-aged woman, but her middle years were about over. She'd soon be old. Her partner, and her lover, was a young stud who I soon discovered was robbing her blind. To find this out, it had taken me four days of discreet and persistent inquiries at a bank in Brooklyn, where the partner kept a separate account. The partner was charged with grand theft, the partnership terminated, the relationship ended.

The third business call I had received on that first full day of business was the most interesting. Andy Warhol hired me. It was a simple one-day job. Warhol wanted to buy some Art Deco jewelry from a new supplier. The supplier carried his wares around in a silver tackle box usually used by fishermen. Warhol liked the wares but was suspicious of the supplier. It took less than four hours to discover that the supplier was legitimate but poor, starting a business on a shoestring, so to speak. Just like me. Warhol thanked me and paid me in cash.

Since the ad in the *Voice* had been successful, and since I was now making money, I replaced the ad for four consecutive weeks, at a substantial discount. I didn't repeat the ad in the *Daily News*, but I reran the one in the *Post*.

After a week, the file cabinet in the spare bedroom/office wasn't exactly bulging, but it wasn't empty now, either. I finished typing up the final report on the antiques shop business and relaxed over a large glass of orange juice and the *Voice*, reading a gossip column on page 22 by someone or something named Glo Glitterati.

You all remember that killing at the docks last week? You might have read it here. You certainly didn't read it in *The New York Times*, or even the *Daily News*. "Gay militant stabbed in trick's arms." The trick was Archie C., a private dick (pun intended). The gaylibber was Max H. The police are so quick to respond, darlings that they are. They love their homosexual neighbors. Yeah, they love 'em. About as much as Baby Jane loved her sister Blanche. The dandy little district attorney downtown has accused David H. of killing his lover Max H. in cold blood. Or hot blood, as this case may be. Is jealousy the motive? The D.A. with his darling blue eyes and his stunning pinstripe suit doesn't say, and his office wouldn't give us any useful lip. That's okay. We wouldn't believe them anyway. Neither would the Gay Activist Alliance, that odd SoHo mixture of gays and dykes and drags. They've begun a defense fund to "Save Dave." G.A.A. is a downright queer benefactor for the supposed killer of its vice president.

It was not the first time I'd seen my name mentioned in the newspaper in connection with a crime. It used to happen all the time in Brooklyn, when I was still able to be a cop on the beat and not a jockey behind a desk. But I was surprised that Captain Carney hadn't called me before the grand jury as a witness.

I telephoned Larry to see if he wanted to go to the G.A.A. meeting at the firehouse. He said he'd meet me at my place at seven.

Around four o'clock, I walked to the precinct. It wasn't a long-distance stroll. Ostensibly I went there to find out about my application for a gun permit. It was kind of ironic, considering that as a policeman I, of course, had been permitted to carry a gun. But once I had left the force, I was required to apply for a permit just like any other citizen. It pissed me off.

I ambled over to the front desk and spoke to the desk sergeant. He was a former working buddy, but he treated me like a stranger. A queer stranger. He sent me to a clerk, who called the office downtown. The clerk gave me a small smile. She was a working buddy, too. Before. While she was on the telephone and being shuttled from nameless person to nameless person, I spotted Captain Carney. I indicated to the clerk that I'd be right back.

"Carney," I said, stopping him before he went into his office.

He didn't seem unhappy to see me. "I told you we'd catch him," he said, a gleam of pride bursting his chest. He walked into the office. I followed.

"Congratulations," I said, deadpan.

Carney dropped some papers in a basket on his desk.

24

"Thanks," he said. "But it was really no big deal, Cain. The kid had no alibi and, hell, he's about ready to confess." The chuckle in his voice made it sound like a big deal.

"You didn't need me as a witness for the grand jury?" I said. I didn't mean for my words to be a question, but they came out that way.

"We haven't indicted yet. We might not even need a grand jury. Not if he confesses. You didn't see anything, anyway."

"I was there."

"Doesn't matter," Carney said. "We've got him. You'll get your chance to tell your tale at the trial. If there is one."

"You got a motive?"

"Yep. He was tired of Harmony screwing around behind his back."

"That easy?" I asked.

"That easy," Carney stated flatly. When I showed no signs of leaving, he asked, "Anything I can do for you, Cain?"

"Yeah, I'd like to see Hardin."

Carney shook his head. He almost laughed. "No. No. What for?"

"I was there when Harmony was stabbed," I pointed out.

"Hardin's heading for Attica," Carney said. "What's the point?"

"I assume Attica will be after the trial," I said. "If there is one."

"Facetious bastard, aren't you?"

Yeah, I am. "I'd like to see him."

Carney thought it over. Finally, "Sure, go on. Why not?" He checked his watch. "Tomorrow. Visiting hours are over for today."

I thanked him and went back to the clerk. She handed me my application form. "Your permit is ready. You have to go downtown and pick it up."

"Thanks." I turned to leave.

"Archie." I turned back to her. "You shouldn't have quit," she said quietly. Her eyes stayed on mine a bare second. Then she turned and walked away.

Thanks, I thought, as I hit the street. You're on my side now. But where were you six months ago when I was getting my head bashed in and nobody knew a fucking thing about it?

Chapter
3

It was after eight, closer to nine, when Larry knocked on my door.

"Thanks, guy," I said. I didn't invite him inside. I double-locked my door and joined him at the elevator. "The meeting starts at eight."

"I'm never on time for anything," Larry said with an exaggerated flair. "That's my trademark."

I well knew it. That's why I didn't count on getting to the firehouse in time for the start of the meeting.

There was no rain in the air as Larry and I walked south, but the night was still humid. And still warm. Indian summer was hanging on for all it was worth. But I was tired of the warm, and eager for the nip of fall. And I longed to wear my brown leather jacket again. But not tonight. Tonight it was just a sweatshirt and 501's. And my dark blue cap for style. My cigarettes were tucked in the sock, just above ankle-length shit-kicking boots. Larry wore shorts, a T-shirt, sneakers, and a headband used by joggers. The weather was warm but not that warm. But Larry was all style. I would bet that he never ran for his health a day in his life.

Larry and I make an odd couple. He's about a foot taller than I am. Maybe more. He swaggers when he walks. He's naturally muscular and radiates strength and charisma. I have to work for my muscles, and nobody can pick me out of a crowd. His curly black hair is trimmed short and his face is clean of hair. My curly blond hair now reaches my neck and my mustache droops down my cheeks. He's a semisuccessful and struggling actor waiting for the brass ring. I'm a struggling detective just looking to make a living. Larry has a loud personality. I'm quiet. He's obnoxiously handsome. I'm Mr. Average. Larry is black. I'm white.

"I've never gone to any of the meetings," Larry said. "I've been wanting to go to one of those Saturday-night dances, but I just never get the chance. From what I hear, they're pretty hot." As Larry talked, he cruised every attractive stranger who passed by, man or woman. Some were even unattractive. To me, anyway.

"I never made it to any of their meetings, either. But I understand that every Saturday night the firehouse is packed. The discos are getting stiff competition."

"Competition? Honey, the manager of Drones is livid. He says if it was up to him, he'd shove all us faggots back in the closet and lock away the key. He'd only let us out to dance—at Drones, of course." Larry is masculine, but he can put on a very funny verbal drag at the drop of a hat. Preferably a large straw hat with a wide brim and a billowing red ribbon. Sidney Poitier imitating Lena Horne imitating Butterfly McQueen.

The only time Larry mentioned my involvement in the death at the docks was the day after it happened. For twenty-four hours, he treated me like a celebrity. After that, nothing. Larry's ego is too large to share a spotlight, even with a friend. Sometimes I wonder why our friendship has continued over the years. Maybe it's because Larry's mind never strays beyond disco dancing or sex. He never takes life too seriously. I'm the opposite. And sometimes I need a reminder that life is only a game.

Larry stopped before we crossed Houston Street. He had been cruising this approaching number from a block away, making hushed comments: "I'm in love." "Ahhhh." "Look at his basket." "Be still, my bleeding heart." I laughed as usual, but halfheartedly, as usual.

As the number approached, Larry began chatting to me about absolutely nothing and in tones as loud as his manner and with exaggerated masculinity. His words were meant to be heard by the approaching number, not by me. When the number was almost upon us, Larry stopped and stared. "I know you," he said, much too loudly.

The number grinned and before long they were in deep conversation. Well, the conversation wasn't deep, but the attitude was. Sparked. The number was short, dark, and handsome in a raunchy sort of way; he spoke with an accent and was excessively and sexily macho. Larry ignored me, didn't introduce me, and showed no indication of cutting the conversation short. He was giving another performance. I'd seen it before. And the stud was responding in kind, giving Larry every opportunity to strut his stuff. Larry's straight man (so to speak).

"I'll meet you at the firehouse," I said. I didn't wait for a reply. I knew Larry heard me. But to acknowledge me would have been an interruption in his familiar performance. And at the moment I wasn't even on the same stage. I crossed the street, dodging cars that were turning down the thoroughfare. An urban bullfighter without a cape.

When I reached the other side, I stopped and turned when Larry shouted out, "Why, you bitch!" He had an exaggerated pout on his lips and his hands on his hips.

"Fuck off, queen," I yelled and laughed.

Larry laughed, too, louder and with more animation. One up on me. "I'll see you down there," he shouted and turned back to his number.

I doubted I'd see him. Typical Larry. I continued the walk alone.

Larry and I had a hot and heavy affair one summer about six years earlier, when Larry was much more subdued, less of a posing queen, and I was much younger. Larry also had a lover at the time. But I was naive then. I thought the guy he lived with was a straight roommate.

I was aware that I wasn't alone on my journey to the firehouse. The closer I got to my destination, the more company

I had. Men, most lone stragglers like myself, were headed in that direction. We could recognize one another as gay. Most of us were wearing Levi's with keys strapped to one side or the other and work boots, or bell-bottoms and sweatshirts and sneakers. We offered one another side-sweeping and evaluating glances. But we didn't do any serious cruising.

And all our feet led to the doors of the G.A.A.'s firehouse. Each of us stepped through the small door to enter the welcoming world of gay liberation.

I didn't expect it. The crowd. An untold number of folding chairs were set up in front of two large tables in the street-level garage that at one time held firetrucks. And all the chairs were filled with men. Some women were scattered throughout the large room that filled the first floor of the firehouse, but by and large the gathering was male. Surrounding the folding chairs, it was standing room only, and each space was filled with sweating bodies. There was no air-conditioning.

I squeezed myself behind the last row and found a space for one more small body near a radiator. On the radiator stood a small stocky man in a dark suit and necktie. One of the few who were formally dressed. He was hanging on to a pipe, observing and listening to the proceedings. Most of the other standees were hippies, many with headbands. And if you judged by hair length, I was one of them, without the headband. I tilted my cap back on my head.

A motion was made by one of the people at the table. I assumed he was an officer. The motion was seconded, then voted upon. A man seated behind the table strode to the microphone set up at the side. He was young, maybe twenty years old. His body was slim, his hair dark, Beatles-long, and neatly trimmed. He wore blue jeans, as did most every man in the room. His were bells. His T-shirt read, SAY IT LOUD, GAY IS PROUD.

"Before we close the meeting, I would like to introduce Helen Shaker. As you all know, she's been secretary of G.A.A. since we began." There was slight applause. "By authority of our constitution, last Friday the executive committee met and voted Helen to replace Max Harmony as vice president until the next election." The applause was larger but not overwhelming.

The man with the neatly trimmed shoulder-length hair and militant T-shirt held up his hand to close the applause, then continued. "Tonight's regular meeting will be cut short because the executive committee will be having an emergency session." He checked his watch. "Right now, upstairs."

A small number of hands around the room flew up. The man at the microphone recognized a hand from the front row. The hand moved to adjourn. His motion was quickly seconded. A vote was taken. The meeting was adjourned. Groans sounded throughout the room but soon died out.

The procedure was professionally handled. Chairs crunched and slid against the cement floor as members made their way through the aisles. Most of the people made a beeline toward the door. The drone of the crowd grew to a chattering din. Small groups mingled together, laughing, talking, in cliques: the hippies, the denim bunch, the drags, the "straights." The officers at the table began conferring among themselves. I made my way through the disarranged chairs to the head of the class. It was then that I noticed Johnny talking with the man who had adjourned the group. Cute Johnny, of the crew-cut head, who had spoken to Max outside the trucks that fateful night.

I walked up to them and interrupted. "Are you the president?" I asked. I didn't ask the question of Johnny.

"Yes" was the answer, with barely an acknowledgment. The leader with the Beatles-cut head pulled Johnny off to the side, out of hearing range. I don't like being ignored. I moved back into hearing range and stood in front of the two.

"My name is Archie Cain," I said.

I was noticed. Both men stopped talking and looked at me.

"You were with Max," the Beatles-head said. "My name is Ron. This is Johnny."

I shook Ron's hand. When I took Johnny's hand, no recognition showed in his eyes.

"I understand you started a defense fund for David Hardin,"
I said.

"Yes," Ron said.

A swishy form who was looking down from above and leaning over the iron circular stairway called out, "Ron, let's go."

Ron hurriedly shuffled his papers from the table into a neat pile and folded them into a battered briefcase.

I interrupted his packing. "Why is G.A.A. defending Hardin?" I asked. I also pointed out the obvious. "He's accused of killing your vice president."

My words stopped Ron. "We don't believe he did it. You were there when Max was killed. Do you think Davie did it?"

"I didn't see who did it," I said.

"Ron . . ." The too-effeminate voice from the staircase was persistent.

"Don't go away," the president said to me as he moved to the stairway. "I want to talk to you." It was an order. I don't like to take orders. Ron disappeared up to the next floor.

I looked around. Johnny was standing behind me. "They shouldn't be too long," he said, planting a smile on his lips but not in his eyes. "Let me buy you a soda." He walked toward a Coke machine. I followed, annoyed at the president's abrupt departure and his domineering attitude.

Johnny wore dungarees, but he didn't wear them well. They seemed a size too large and they weren't Levi's or even bell-bottoms. They looked like they had just come back from the cleaner's. Too neat. And his shirt was no better. Rather formless and colorless and very crisp and clean. Somewhat like Johnny himself, which is not to say he was unattractive. Quite the contrary. He was boyishly cute, and I sensed a muscular body under those ill-fitting clothes. His crew-cut hair was certainly trimmed too short for the style of the times. But I guess the haircut suited him. He wasn't a stylish person.

"I recognized your name," Johnny said. "You were with Max when he bought it."

"Yeah."

"You're a detective, right? That's what the papers said."

"Private."

"Are you a member of G.A.A.?"

"No."

"From what I read in the papers, you didn't even know Max until that night," Johnny said. I had no answer to that. "I saw you that night," he added.

So, he had recognized me. "I remember. Did you know Max well?" I asked.

"Well enough."

"Do you think his lover killed him?"

Johnny shrugged. "Maybe. But I seriously doubt it. Still, he was a jealous bastard."

"Is that the voice of experience?" I asked.

Johnny reddened. "No," he quickly answered. Then just as quickly recovered. "Are you going to help G.A.A.?"

"Help G.A.A. do what?"

"Never mind," he said and slid coins into the soda machine. "Ron'll tell you." Another well-placed but forced smile.

Johnny was making an attempt to be friendly, but it wasn't a good attempt. I changed the subject. "What's happening up there?" I asked, nodding to the staircase. Johnny handed me a Coke and I thanked him. He opened one for himself.

"They're planning a zap," Johnny said.

"A zap?"

"Yeah. City Hall. The equal rights bill is bottled up in committee. I think they're planning a sit-in in Councilman Cuite's office."

I didn't know who Cuite was and I didn't care. I sipped the Coke and scanned the firehouse. With the room almost empty, it looked old and tired. "So Davie was a jealous bastard," I said. "Jealous enough to kill?" I turned back to Johnny.

"Not likely," he answered. "But it is a motive, I suppose." He strained his neck back and took a healthy slug of soda. "But, like I said, I seriously doubt it." He rested his butt on the front table and watched the few men who still mingled near the exit door.

"How well did you know Max?" I asked him.

32

Johnny turned his attention back to me. "He was a friend."

"A good friend?"

"I guess."

"You don't seem broken up by his death," I pointed out.

"He's dead. There's work to do. He'd want us to carry on."

"Liberation work," I stated. Johnny didn't respond. "And you don't think Hardin killed Max."

"Do you know Davie Hardin?" Johnny asked.

"I've met him."

"Davie is a lazy bastard who's strung out on downers. He's a leech, he's a wimp, and he's a phony. But a killer? No, not likely."

"If he's all that, why did Max stay with him?"

"They were together a long time," Johnny said, which didn't say anything.

Johnny turned his attention to the people climbing down the iron staircase. Ron was there, along with Helen Shaker, the newly announced VP who had taken Max's place. Seven others followed, only one of whom was a woman. I recognized them all, but only by their faces. They either had been sitting at the front table at the meeting or in the front row. Johnny walked over to Ron.

I waited at the head table alone, sipping my Coke. It was five minutes before the special executive group completed their good-byes. Some of them gave a nod and smile to me before they left. All of them looked at me. I felt like I was in Macy's window. Johnny left by himself, after also offering me a long glance. I was wondering if he was cruising me. It's sometimes difficult for me to tell if I'm being cruised. But I hoped I was.

"Gay liberation is going to be the death of me yet," Ron said, inserting a coin in the soda machine. "It's never-ending work. Want a soda?"

I held up my Coke. It was almost empty, but I didn't want another. Ron made his selection. "It certainly was the death of Max," I said.

"Gay liberation wasn't the reason Max was killed," Ron said.

"And neither was jealousy, according to Johnny. Why do you think he was killed?"

"New York City," Ron said simply and bitterly. He sat on a folding chair facing me. "Homophobic New York City. We're out of the closet now. It's open season. If we won't go back in, kill us."

"Random faggot death? The luck of the draw?"

"That's pretty much it," Ron said. "It's not the first faggot death we've had in the Village."

"You're not broken up about Max's death, either," I said. "Didn't anybody really give a shit about him?"

Ron didn't look at me. "I loved Max. He was my best friend," he said. "Not only that. He was a well-liked guy by just about everybody here." Ron's swinging arm encompassed the entire empty room. "When my term expires, he might have been elected president, easily. Whether that's good or bad is beside the point. Max was popular."

"And now because of some crazy killer, he's history," I pointed out. "A stab in the dark."

Ron seemed startled by my statement and looked up at me. "You're a cold-blooded bastard, aren't you?" he said. He wasn't asking. He shook his head. "Let's get the hell out of here."

I followed him to the door. He flicked some switches to shut the lights except for a small bare bulb that shone above a tiny barred window in the rear. I walked outside. Ron followed and locked the last door.

"No, Archie, on the contrary . . . Can I call you Archie?"

He sounded like a politician. "Cain'll do," I said. We walked north. The crowd that had been at the meeting had long dissipated. The street was pretty near empty, of both people and cars. Warehouses lined the blocks, some tenements. But all was quiet. A silent sleep after a night of liberation.

"When I heard that Max was dead, I didn't go out of the house for two days," Ron said. "I didn't see anybody. I disconnected my phone. His death hit me hard. It hit us all hard. But . . ." He sighed. "We have to go on. There was one important focal point in Max's life. Gay lib. And we're carrying on for him. No, Archie—Cain—to say that I'm not broken up about his death is unfair. Max's death is tearing me apart."

His voice confirmed his feeling. So did the unshed tears in his eyes.

The traffic on Houston Street was light. A man with a beard as matted as the hair on his scalp, and wearing rags for clothes, asked for some spare change. Ron dug into his denims and handed him some coins. We continued our walk toward Sixth Avenue. We could see the lights of the Waverly. A small group was lined up outside the theater.

"That executive committee meeting we just had . . ." Ron paused. I looked at him. He continued. "We were planning our next demonstration." Another pause, then, "But we also talked about you."

I stopped. "Me?"

Ron stopped with me. "We want to hire you to find out who killed Max."

"G.A.A. wants to hire me to find a random killer?"

"Yes."

"Then you don't believe his lover killed Max, either?"

"Of course not," he said, as if that was the silliest idea in the world. "Nobody does. That's why we set up the defense fund for Davie."

"Why are you so sure he didn't kill Max?"

Ron began walking again. I joined in step. "How much do you charge for your services?" he asked.

"Why are you so sure Davie didn't kill Max?" I repeated.

"Will you take the case?"

"You might say I have a direct interest in it," I said. "A hundred dollars a day plus expenses." I'd knock off twenty-five bucks for liberation, I thought.

"That's more than I counted on," Ron said, more to himself than to me. "I'm going to have to take it back to the committee. We don't have a helluva lot of money to spend."

"You rent an entire firehouse," I told him.

"And our dances on Saturday night pay for that. It doesn't

leave much for anything else." He thought for a moment in silence. "No," he finally continued. "They won't go for it. That's too much money."

"What about your 'Save Dave' fund?"

"Which has exactly sixty-four dollars and twenty-two cents." Ron gave off a hollow laugh.

"It doesn't look like many of your members want to save Dave."

"You mean many of our poor members." He emphasized *poor*. "Moneymen don't want to be liberated, Cain. They can't afford to be."

I silently agreed. Not if they're safe and snug in their moneyed closet, I thought. "Why are you so sure that Dave didn't kill Max?" I was getting tired of repeating the question.

We turned the corner into a small side street. A litter-ridden oasis within the Village of gay dreams.

"Come on up," Ron said. He pulled open a dilapidated door stuck between a bakery on one side and a fading gin mill on the other.

I climbed with Ron to the sixth floor of the narrow building and into a stifling one-room apartment with one small window. A waist-high bathtub was next to the kitchen sink. At the moment the tub had a small counter top on it. Atop the counter was a two-burner tabletop stove. A single mattress was on the floor, the bed unmade. The furniture consisted of a card table set near the window, two chairs, and wooden crates topped with ashtrays, candles, books, and stacks of papers and magazines. Neatly packed clothes were inside the boxes in plain sight. Large liberation/protest signs and psychedelic posters graced one wall, Janis Joplin graced another. A small fan was sitting on the windowsill. Mercifully, the window was open. There was no fire escape.

I sat in one of the chairs as Ron poured water into a pot, turned a burner on, and set two mugs on the table. I wiped the sweat from my forehead. Ron switched the fan on. It didn't help to cool the cramped quarters; it merely circulated the stagnant air. Ron plucked a small wooden box from behind the mattress, opened it, and produced a joint. He lit it.

"Max was worried," Ron said, sitting across from me, dragging on the joint.

"About what?"

Ron shrugged his shoulders. "He didn't tell me." He passed the joint my way. Ash sprinkled on the table. I begged off.

"You said he was your best friend," I reminded him.

"He was," Ron assured me and inhaled deeply. He held his breath. "But I don't know." Ron, between his clenched teeth, sounded confused. "In the last couple of weeks, Max changed." He exhaled. A thin line of smoke filtered through his lips.

"Changed how?"

"Not in what he said, or what he did, but . . ." Ron searched for words. He toked again and held the smoke in his lungs. "I guess in attitude," he said. "He always used to be the most radical of the group, wanting to zap this, zap that, chain ourselves to the fence at the Mayor's house, have a lay-in at Times Square. Of course, in most of these the executive committee voted him down. His ideas were usually just too far out. But not all the time. Max did come up with some good ideas. The candlelight march, that was his idea. We just had to cut through all his radical bullshit to get to the meat."

Ron toked again. I prompted, "But he changed."

"Yeah, it got to the point where he was barely offering any suggestions at all. Crazy or otherwise. In fact, he tried to scuttle a couple of our good zaps. When we were about to invade that radio station that made those homophobic remarks about queens taking over Manhattan in their twenty-four-dollar beads, Max wanted to call it off. That was unlike him. I mean, a demonstration like that was right up his alley."

"I read about that one in the *Voice*," I said. "You were arrested before you ever made it into the studio, weren't you?"

"Yeah. And Max was there with us. Once a decision was made, he was with us all the way. But that's beside the point. The thing is, in the beginning, he was against the idea of the zap. And that just wasn't Max. I don't know. In some ways, he was so naive."

"In what ways?"

"Well, in the beginning, when we first started G.A.A. right after Stonewall and when the Gay Liberation Front went kaput, Max wanted to make an appointment with the Mayor and ask him to sign an equal rights bill for homosexuals. Max thought that by just asking and the Mayor signing, it would become law. That was naive. He didn't know anything about politicians or the law. Hell, the Mayor doesn't just sign a bill and end discrimination. There are committees, debates. Max had to learn all about the workings of city government, how the law worked. And he did learn. Max wasn't dumb. Naive isn't the same as being stupid. Well, I guess maybe sometimes it is."

"What else? How else did he change?"

"He used to stay here with me at least three nights a week," Ron said, dragging on the joint until it burned his fingers. He placed the roach carefully on the outer rim of the ashtray, then pushed himself up and poured boiling water into two mugs. He set a small jar of instant coffee on the table.

I glanced at the single unmade mattress. Before I asked, Ron answered. "No, me and Max weren't carrying on." He went to a small closet that was covered by an old bedspread on a curtain rod. He pushed the spread aside and pointed to a sleeping bag. "Max slept on the floor. He stayed here because we always had so much work to do. It's endless." He gestured at reams of paperwork piled neatly on crates made into book-cases. "But the last week or so Max didn't stay over at all."

I walked over to the boxes, sat on my haunches, and leafed through the material. Fliers announcing demonstrations, dances, meetings. Bundles of small stick-on posters: VOTE GAY. Everything very well organized. Various newsletters. Maga-zines. Some porno. I flipped through those, after giving Ron's crotch an automatic glance. He returned it to my crotch, auto-matically.

"What kind of work did Max do?" I asked.

"In G.A.A.?"

"In real life," I specified.

"Real life." Ron smiled. "He was a copy editor for *Current Social Thought,* a social policy magazine on the Upper West Side."

"Is that why he and his lover could afford that apartment on the Upper East Side?"

Ron laughed. "No. Davie had that apartment even before he knew Max. And it's rent-controlled. Hell, they pay pretty near the same rent for that apartment uptown as I do for this shithole."

"Were Max and Davie happy together?"

"Maybe, at one time."

"Not recently?"

"They'd been together about four years, maybe five, long before G.A.A. came into existence. They met in Keller's at the end of Christopher Street. In 1967, I think. And Max is a one-man man. Sure, he fucked around. Don't we all?" A quick seductive smile that quickly vanished. "But his lover was his lover, not a trick. When Max met Davie, Davie was a successful antiques dealer, a wholesaler, and making a fair wage. That is, until Davie discovered dope. Over the last two years, he barely worked at all. He sponged off Max."

"And Max let him?"

"Max loved him."

"Do you think that's why he changed? Davie was on his mind?"

"No," Ron said firmly. "The problems between them have been ongoing. That was nothing new."

"How about jealousy?"

"Max wasn't jealous of Davie. Hell, Davie hardly ever left the house."

"Was Davie jealous of Max?"

"Yeah," Ron said. "But not seriously. Davie's was a bitchy jealousy. And Max never took it serious. Neither did Davie. Deep down, Davie knew Max loved him. Jealousy wasn't really the problem between them."

"What was the problem?"

"Dope," Ron said simply. "Davie was drowning."

Ron ruffled through a pile of magazines on the floor. He plucked out a copy of *Current Social Thought* and handed it to me. I thumbed the thin magazine. Max Harmony was listed on the masthead as Copy Editor. The magazine was all words, no photographs. There were a few scattered illustrations, some graphs. I rolled up the magazine and kept it in hand.

"Did you ask Max what was wrong?"

"More than once," Ron assured me, blowing over the rim of his cup, then sipping carefully. "He told me that he and Davie were going through a rough period. But it wasn't any rougher than usual. No, that wasn't it."

"Davie," I thought to myself, and I must have said the name out loud.

"Davie didn't kill Max. I don't even think he loved him. Maybe in the beginning, but not anymore. He lived off Max. Max paid the rent, bought the food, the dope. He became Davie's meal ticket. Davie never had it so good."

"It doesn't sound as if you like Davie very much. How come G.A.A. is going all out to help him?"

"Who else will help? Davie is innocent. He hasn't got any money. He's gay. That's what we're here for, to help the gay community. Will you take the case?" He added quickly and with hope, "Gratis."

I looked him in the eye. The stoned eye. "No. Not unless I get paid. I have a living to make." I moved from the table to the mattress, sat down, and leaned against the wall. A brief flash of Ron in the nude blinked through my mind. An automatic blink. Ron was too fastidious for my taste, both in attitude and dress, but he was still a man, an available man.

"We can't afford you," Ron said. "Sorry." He didn't sound sorry. He suddenly said, almost angrily, "Don't you want to be part of the gay movement?" He emphasized his point by laying his hand on the table, too hard. The contents of his mug splashed onto the crackled plastic surface of the card table.

"I've done my share," I said, without explaining. I could have told him about my coming out in the department. But that was past history. Personal history. I flipped through the pages of *Current Social Thought*, though my mind wasn't on the magazine. I wanted to help, but I couldn't commit my time to the endeavor, not unless I got paid for it. I couldn't very well begin a new business by not charging my customers a fee. And yet I wasn't feeling good about turning Ron down.

"There are other detectives," I said. "Maybe they charge less."

Ron placed a paper napkin under his coffee mug and moved to the mattress, sitting next to me. "They're probably not like you," he said, a tiny, playful, and not entirely unalluring smile on his lips.

"In what way?"

"They're not openly gay," he said, his smile now broad.

I smiled, too.

Ron's personality changed when he smiled. Without the smile, he was all business, almost dour, and emphatic about gay liberation. The smile made him warm and almost sexy. I leaned over to kiss him. It wasn't a large lean. The mattress was small. Ron returned the kiss, and we fumbled for about fifteen minutes on the mattress, even going so far as to unzip—in my case, unbutton—each other's jeans. His fingers stroked through my hair, quickly moving to my chest. I tried stroking his hair, but the feeling wasn't there. Our playful romp never reached passionate proportions. We ended up embarrassed. Neither of us felt a strong attraction to the other, but the situation seemed to demand we try.

As I rebuttoned my jeans, I asked, "What about Johnny?"

"What about Johnny?"

"How does he figure in Max's life?"

Ron didn't bother to zip up. He slipped his sneakers off his feet and pulled his jeans off. He sat at the table and sipped his cooled coffee. His briefs were black and hugged his slim body neatly. But they weren't sexy. These newfangled colored underwear for men were not my style. I tucked my shirt in next to my white Fruit of the Looms.

"Johnny and Max were friends," Ron said.

"Good friends?"

"Max didn't talk about him." He gulped his coffee. "Not too much, anyway."

"When he did talk about him, what did he say?"

"Listen, Cain, I'd rather not talk about Johnny, okay? I have my own problems with him." Ron became lost in his own thoughts, but he quickly returned. "But that's another story." Did I detect a familiar small sign of unrequited love? A sign I could easily recognize, having ridden that same road myself a few times, usually with guys who were married or straight or just plain not interested in me.

"Don't ask about Johnny," Ron said. It wasn't a request, it was an order. Another order. Ron was used to giving them. I wasn't used to taking them. "Not now."

I rarely take orders. Even when I was a cop it was difficult. Maybe that's one of the reasons I came out at the precinct. Knowing I'd end up quitting and knowing I wouldn't have to take orders anymore.

"You asked for help," I said. "Yet you won't answer questions."

"What the hell has Johnny got to do with this?" He didn't wait for an answer. "Besides, we can't afford you." The look he gave me was as cold as the city in February. But he still held out a small flicker of hope. "Can we?"

I washed the hope away, reluctantly. "No, you can't. And I can't afford to work for nothing."

I left Ron's apartment feeling lousy. Okay, I had to make a living. And so far, I'd been doing it. But did I have to turn G.A.A. down flat, just because they couldn't afford my price? Yes, I told myself. Yes. I had to keep my business on a business level, or I'd never make a go of it. Maybe if I was already established it would be a different story. Just maybe. But not now. Not when I was just starting. I won the debate with myself, but I still didn't feel good about it.

Back at the office—my spare bedroom—I opened a new file,

labeling it G.A.A. No, I wouldn't be on hire to G.A.A. But my spare time is my own. I felt a little better.

I was stretched out in bed, mulling over the next day's moves, when the telephone rang. My nonbusiness line. Before I had the chance to say hello, Larry's falsetto voice cried out. "You bitch!" he said. "You left without me. And I still haven't seen the firehouse."

"Did you get fucked?"

"Wasn't he gorgeous?" Larry exclaimed, his falsetto gone now, his voice all sexual and all serious. "And he had the biggest dick. You know the kind. It stays hard forever."

"All your numbers have big dicks. Don't you ever meet anybody with a small dick?"

"You mean like yours?" Larry crowed.

"Your mother," I told him and laughed.

"You're jealous, queen. So how was the meeting?" Larry changes subjects as quickly as he changes his mind.

"There was a crowd there," I said. "Probably about a couple hundred guys."

"Really? Let's go to the dance on Saturday night."

"I planned on doing exactly that," I said.

"Without me?"

"No, with you. Wanna go?" I didn't wait for an answer. "I'll call you before then," I said. "I'm tired. I'll let you go now." I didn't stifle a yawn. "It's been a long night."

"Well, I hope it was worth it," Larry said suggestively, a leer sneaking over the wires. I laughed. "Okay, sweetheart," he said. "Sleep tight. Love ya."

" 'Night."

Before I went to sleep, I read *Current Social Thought*. That is, I tried to read it. It was dry rot. "Shaft's Black Blues" was the most interesting title of all the articles, but the title proved to be the only interesting thing about the damn piece. It cited statistics about the number of unwed mothers in the inner cities. It quoted a professor on the need for new food stamp programs. It berated Richard Nixon for slashing government grants to social programs. The article didn't mention a thing about Isaac Hayes's mind twisting and mesmerizing movie score.

Chapter
4

Current Social Thought had its office on West 77th Street between Broadway and West End Avenue—a family neighborhood. A kid was walking his dog, an old woman wearing a babushka was struggling with a fold-up cart full of groceries, a wino was puking in the gutter.

The office was housed in a small brownstone storefront with a large stoop. Through the window, I could see magazines and papers piled high and a woman talking on the telephone. I walked up the one flight of the outside stoop, went into a tiny outer lobby, and pressed the buzzer next to the glass door. The woman looked up, gave me an evaluating glance, said something into the phone, laid the receiver down, then walked over and opened the locked door.

"Are you here about the job?" she asked. She was thin, neatly dressed in green denim bell-bottom pants, a floppy blouse, and sandals. She sounded like Glenda Jackson and resembled Joan Baez. Her straight dark hair was pinned back into a ponytail.

"No," I answered.

"Shit," she said, then turned back into the office and picked up the phone. Joan Baez with Janis Joplin's mouth. I followed.

"Listen, Harry, I have to have that article by three o'clock, or else it won't make it into this month's issue. . . . I don't give a fuck. Get it to me. I don't have anybody to pick it up.

. . . Okay, by three." She hung up the phone and began shuffling through a disorganized mound of papers on her disorganized desk. "Damn."

She seemed to have forgotten about me.

"Are you Maureen Meredith? Managing editor?"

She stopped shuffling, looked up from her papers, and offered a friendly glance. "Yes." There was a pasted smile on her face. "And you are?" she asked, her voice finely tuned British.

"A friend of Max Harmony."

The smile disappeared. "Oh, Max. Dear Max. He was a son of a bitch as an employee but a helluva guy."

"He wasn't a good employee?"

"Who are you?"

"Archie Cain," I said, and held out a hand. She shook it but seemed to be waiting for me to say more. "I was with Max when he died."

Her eyes widened perceptibly. "You're the private detective. I read about you in the *Voice.*"

"Yes."

"What do you want here?" It was less an accusation than curiosity.

"How long did Max work for you?"

"Why do you want to know?" More curiosity.

After placing some magazines on the floor, I sat down in a chair without being invited. "I'd like to find out more about Max," I said. "Call it the guilts, call it frustration. I only met him that night, but . . ." I trailed off.

"Who hired you?" she asked. Now the tone was accusatory.

"No one," I said.

"Then what are you doing here?" she asked. She stood up to challenge me. If I were standing, she wouldn't tower over me. She was trying to create that impression. But she wasn't tall enough. Her presence wasn't even very commanding, merely phony and superior.

The door behind me opened. Maureen Meredith looked up and I turned around. A small, handsome blond man entered. In addition to handsome, he was gregarious. He smiled at me and held out a hand. "I'm Sidney Meredith," he said. "Maureen's husband."

I recognized the name from the masthead of *Current Social Thought*. His accent was as British as his wife's, his eyes were darling blue. I took his hand, a strong grip. Before I could speak, Maureen said, "This is Archie Cain, Sidney. He's asking questions about Max."

Sidney's hand went limp in mine. I released it.

"You must be the editor," I said.

"That's right," Sidney said, forcing a weak smile back onto his face.

"How long did Max work for you?"

Maureen quickly stepped in. "He's the private investigator who was with Max the night he was killed."

Sidney looked from her back to me. "What do you want to know?" he asked.

"Sidney," Maureen said, softly but with casual authority. She may not have been a commanding presence to me, but it was obvious that she commanded her husband.

The look Sidney gave Maureen cut her short. A look that told her "Fuck off." He had more spunk than I thought. To me, he said, "Would you like to go for some coffee, Mr. Cain." He wasn't asking. He moved to the door. I followed. If I had had a hat I would have tipped it to Maureen. But I didn't have one, so I merely nodded and said, "Nice to meet you." She didn't return the salutation.

When we stepped outside, Sidney said, "Wait here. I'll be right with you." He had an Albert Finney accent that curled my socks.

He went back inside the office. I could see them talking behind the glass, and I wished I could read lips. I couldn't, but I watched anyway.

They made a handsome couple. Sidney's ash-blond hair framed his small face in a neat cut. He was no taller than his wife, which is to say they were both small, but he had it all over her in the sex-appeal department. From my gay eyes, Maureen wasn't sexy. Her body was too tightly controlled, her hair too taut, her eyes hard, her movements those of a nervous cat. I don't like cats. I lit a cigarette. Sidney, on the other hand, had a nicely proportioned body. His small round buttocks fit snugly into his tan chino slacks, though the pants legs themselves were baggy. The two top buttons of his striped shirt were open, and dark hair, in contrast to the blond hair on his head, sprouted sensuously from the neck of his shirt. Yeah, he was the hot number of the family, not her. But then again, for a female, maybe Maureen was sexy, who knows? I wouldn't. But I doubted it.

Before I finished my cigarette, Sidney joined me on the sidewalk.

"Maureen's a little paranoid," he explained as we walked to the corner. "Christ, she think's the Nixon Administration is sending his spies from the FBI after us." Sidney smiled at me, though his lips barely parted. The smile was in his eyes.

"Why would he do that?"

"Some of the articles we print are considered too leftist for some people." A hint of a smile from the lips this time.

The articles I read may have been left leaning, but in my opinion they were hardly radical. And they were so damn intellectual—almost unintelligibly so—I doubt if the magazine had a strong following among street radicals. Or among anyone, for that matter. I would guess that it had a following among intellectuals who merely discuss the problems of the world with one another and no one else. But FBI material? Sounded to me like Maureen Meredith had an overblown sense of her own importance.

We turned the corner onto Broadway, and Sidney ushered me into a small coffee shop. It wasn't lunchtime yet, and we had our choice of tables. We chose a small one against the wall. "So what can I tell you about Max?" Sidney asked, his eyes eager.

"How long did he work for you?"

A waiter looked down at us and took our order for two coffees.

"Probably close to two years," he answered and seemed to wait for the next question.

"Did you know he was gay?"

Sidney gave off a small laugh. It was a shallow laugh. "Of course. Max didn't hide his preference from anybody. And that damn G.A.A. took up most of his life."

"Did it interfere with his job?"

The waiter set the coffee before us. Sidney didn't let the man's appearance stop him from talking. He looked deep into my eyes while he spoke. "Without a doubt. Maureen even wanted to fire him. Well, not seriously. Maureen gets upset easily. If Max ever cut out during the day to go to a demonstration or something, he would make up the lost hours on his own time. Maureen doesn't like to work that way. But Max was a good proofreader and a damn good copy editor. And he didn't mind doing anything else around the office. Whether typing or delivering manuscripts. Whatever. He was a good worker." Again, Sidney offered a wonderful smile, and again, with his eyes only.

"Did you ever meet Davie, his lover?"

Sidney shook his head. "No," he said. His eyes strayed to the coffee cup in front of him and rested there. He plopped a little milk along with a spoonful of sugar into his cup. His eyes lifted to me again, then dropped quickly, as if embarrassed.

I poured some milk into my cup. Sidney had been offering me sly side-glances ever since we left his office. And sensuous eye-smiles, which were mighty tempting. But I've been around gay life long enough to know those glances could have meant only a curiosity, or a warm friendliness, and that's all. But then again, Sidney didn't seem curious, and we didn't know each other well enough to be warm friends. He seemed interested in what I was inquiring. I wondered if he was interested in anything else I might offer. I asked, "Did you and Max ever go to bed together?"

Sidney didn't lift his eyes from his cup, and he didn't answer my question. His hand held the spoon inside his cup but didn't stir it. He was staring at his cup intently and through long thin eyelashes shielding eyes that weren't smiling this time. I re-phrased the question. "Did you and Max ever make it to-gether?"

He couldn't sit there forever, not stirring his coffee and mesmerizing his cup. He dropped his spoon, looked up, and stated almost proudly, "I'm married. No, I never went to bed with Max." His denial was too loud. "Not really," he added quietly, his eyes returning to his cup, then slyly up at me again. "What did Max tell you?"

"I didn't even know Max."

"They why do you think we were carrying on?"

"I didn't think you were. I asked a question."

"Well, we never went to bed together," Sidney said firmly.

It was an evasive answer, I thought. He was playing with semantics. It figured. He was a writer. "But you did carry on," I said, "but not in a bed." Sidney didn't say a word, but his eyes, now probing mine, didn't deny my accusation. I probed back. "In the office? Is that where you had sex?"

"Don't say that," he said. His words were soft, but the fear in them couldn't be missed. He peered around, assuring himself that we weren't overheard. His smile was long gone, maybe never to return. Not today, anyway. "That sounds so grubby." He paused, but I didn't cut in, and my gaze never left his face. "Once," Sidney finally said, barely audible. "Maybe twice," less audibly.

"Are you bisexual?" I asked. My words were audible and not even whispered.

Sidney shrugged. "I don't know," he muttered.

"Was Max in love with you?"

Sidney's eyes widened. "No," he said, more than a whisper, less than a shout.

"Were you in love with him?"

Sidney pushed back his chair from the table. I feared I had lost his smile forever. "Maureen was right. I shouldn't have answered any of your questions." He arose and walked out the door, leaving behind a full cup of coffee and an unpaid check.

I also left a full coffee and stopped at the front of the restaurant, paged the waiter, and paid the check. I followed Sidney back to his office. I didn't try to hide my presence. Sidney kept turning around to see if I was there. When he neared the office, he turned around again and walked toward me. I stopped and waited. He looked me in the eye but didn't slow his pace and passed me by. What was this, some fucking game?

I debated briefly whether to return to the office and see his wife or to follow Sidney. Maureen could wait, I decided. I caught up with Sidney.

He stopped, glancing down the street to the office, expecting his wife to come out and thrash him, I expect. "What do you want?" he asked, his voice on edge.

"Relax, Sidney. I won't tell a soul."

The look in his eyes was pleading but distrustful. He seemed afraid or unable to speak.

"Cross my heart and hope to die," I added, a tentative smile forming on my lips, as I crossed my heart and hoped to die.

He gave a long furtive look at the storefront up the street, but he offered no matching smile. Then he turned and walked toward Riverside Drive. I trotted along beside him.

"I don't know what's happening," he said. He was as sorrowful as a kid who had just broken a window with a baseball and was afraid to go home. He turned his face toward me. "What did you say your name was?" he asked.

"Cain. Archie Cain."

"Cain, I don't know what to do. I don't know what to do," he whimpered. My attraction to him was weakening.

We waited for the light to change. "You don't know what to do about what, Sidney?"

"About me," he said. This time almost a shout. There was panic in his eyes. Yes, unquestionably, there was fear. I was prying open his closet door. Gay liberation has a long way to go, I thought. It hasn't yet reached the Upper West Side.

"Have long have you and Maureen been married?"

"Six years. A little over." The light turned green and we crossed the street.

The park was almost deserted. There was a chill in the air,

a pleasant autumn chill. No children played in the grass, no joggers ran the paths, no Frisbee players were leaping for their flying saucers. Only a few afternoon strollers, alone or in couples, rambled by. No men were even cruising the park. Not surprising. The nightlight in this park brought the men out, not the daylight. I know, it used to be one of my cruising grounds. Still is, on occasion.

"Was Max the first man you ever made it with?" I asked.

"The only man," Sidney quickly assured me.

"Did Max seduce you?"

"No. Yes." Then quickly, "But I wanted him to." Every word was a cry for help.

I recognized Sidney's confusion. Not unlike the kind I'd gone though some ten years ago. Was it that long ago? The confusion of the sexes. Women? Men? One? The other? Both? I couldn't help him decide. And in the final analysis, it isn't a choice at all. But Sidney would have to figure it out for himself. With me, way back when, my decision was quickly reached. Men, all the way. As I said, not really a choice. It's the way I'm built.

I veered away from the subject of Sidney's confused sexuality but didn't entirely lock his closet door.

"How long have you and Maureen been in this country?"

"Going on three years now," Sidney answered, almost with a sigh of relief. "Maybe four, five," he quickly added, and eyed me as I if had asked the forbidden question.

"Are you going to become U.S. citizens?"

"Maureen already is." A slight fear came into his voice. "I have a green card. But if they find out about Max and me. If they find out . . . my God. If they . . ." He let it lie.

We reached the iron railing that separated the park from the Hudson River. A small ocean liner far away, closer to the Jersey shore, was sailing toward the ocean on calm waters. I leaned on the rail and lit a cigarette, offering Sidney one. He refused.

My voice was as calm as the river. "If who finds out about what?"

Sidney's face was pointed toward the small ship. "About Max, of course." He said it like the fact was inevitable. It seemed to me that it was more than sex and Max that he was worried about.

I felt an excitement build up inside me. My voice stayed on an even keel. "What about Max?"

Sidney turned his back on the ship and leaned his elbows against the railing. A small breeze waved a strand of hair over his eye. He pushed it back in place. He looked at me. "Immigration. They'll never let me become a citizen when they find out about me and Max . . ." He paused. "Having sex." The last words were a conspiratorial whisper.

False alarm. My excitement melted. Sidney wasn't worried about murder. He was worried about his unacknowledged homosexual feelings and the immigration laws.

"Who's to tell?" I said to assure him. "Max is dead." Immediately after the words left my mouth, I realized what I had inadvertently implied.

"My God," Sidney said, aghast. "I wouldn't kill him. I . . . I . . ."

I waited for the words to finish. They came as if pulled by a chain. "He meant more to me than . . ." Sidney said softly. His eyes gleamed with tears he was barely able to keep in check.

I felt the need to physically comfort him. But if I put my arms around him, I knew he would cringe at such a public display of affection between two men. But still, the man needed comfort, longed for it.

As if sensing my wish to help, Sidney stepped away. He stared at me for about ten long seconds. Then he walked back toward the path, straightening his shoulders, tossing his head back and siphoning tears into his eyes. I caught up with him quickly and was at his side, silent.

When we neared the street, Sidney said, "Don't tell anyone, Cain. Please." His voice was in control, but he didn't look at me. "I could be in big trouble." He was like a groundhog, afraid to come out of his hole and see his shadow. Or afraid someone else would see it.

"Your sex life is none of my business," I assured him.

Sidney began to cross the street.

"Wait," I said and stopped him. "Not yet." I nodded to the bench under the trees that lined the street. He didn't need much much convincing. Sidney followed and sat next to me. The breeze starting up again. Sidney's long thin hair fluttered.

"Were the problems Max had at work serious? Was he going to lose his job?"

"No," Sidney said. He seemed to relax at the change of subject, from Max and sex, to Max and business. "He was good at what he did, I told you that. And I doubt if we could find anyone else who could put up with our bullshit. You know, deadlines, deliveries. Everything. No, Max's hours were erratic, but he had a permanent job. I wouldn't have fired him. Neither would Maureen."

But Sidney couldn't allow his own confusion about Max to be buried completely in business. An unforced frown appeared on his forehead. "Max and I . . . ." He searched for the correct words. "We had sex," he completed with relief. "But I didn't force myself on him. And I certainly wouldn't fire him. I . . . ." His thoughts drifted off, then returned quickly. "Yes, the truth is, Max seduced me. But it was a two-way street." He seemed to be finding it easier to talk about his relationship with Max. He wanted to talk, needed to talk. I was there and willing to listen. "God, I wanted him to, so badly." He leaned back, his mind wandering to a fond memory. "And he did. And it was wonderful." He brought himself back to reality, and his body stiffened. Maybe it was the sharp gust of wind that suddenly whipped up.

"Was Max blackmailing you?" I asked.

Sidney looked at me like I had slapped him in the face. "Are you crazy? Max? Never!"

No, I didn't think Max would stoop that low, either. But then again, I hadn't known him at all. And being blackmailed would be a motivation for murder.

Sidney disappeared into his own thoughts again, his arms folded against his chest, hiding the little bush of hair that lured

53

itself out of the top of his shirt. I lit another cigarette. "Why do you think Max was killed?" I asked quietly.

"I don't know. People get killed every day in New York."

Tears were again beginning to form in his voice. A man on the edge of a jag, I thought. I arose. "Come on," I said. "I'll walk you back to the office." I was dragging too many warm memories out of Sidney's mind. It was time for him to stop thinking about Max and start thinking about his wife. A minor cure and a temporary cure for a lost and probably unrequited male love.

"No. Please." He arose but pushed an arm at me to stay put. I stayed, Sidney walked.

He crossed the street. He needed time alone to pull himself together before he faced a mate who was the wrong sex.

Chapter 5

A taxi took me to Riker's Island. I had no problem gaining entrance to see Hardin. Carney was as good as his word. Hardin was escorted to the seat on the other side of the long table. An armed and uniformed guard stood behind him, a discreet distance away but within hearing distance.

Davie didn't seem surprised to see me. On second glance, I wasn't sure he saw me at all. His eyes were as glazed and as dead as a misty crystal ball. And his blond hair was blonder than it had been. The dark roots were barely visible now.

"Got a hairdresser in there?" I asked.

Davie flattened his hands over his head. "Doesn't it look great?" He tried to act shy and be the blushing virgin, but he didn't succeed. Odd, to say the least.

No, I didn't think the hair looked great. "You've changed,"
I said.

"Yeah, well," he said, his hands still fluttering over his head.

"Not your hair," I said. "What happened?"

"What do you mean?"

"You're sitting in this cage because you're accused of killing
your lover," I said.

"Yeah, I know." He giggled groggily.

"Did you?"

"Somebody had to do it." This time he sounded like his
mouth was full of cotton.

"Did you kill Max?" I think I was almost angry, and I didn't
know why.

"They think so," he answered without hesitation.

"Who?"

"The cops."

"Did you kill Max?"

Davie didn't answer. He turned his head, his eyes wandering
over the guard and around the room with no specific purpose.

"Were you jealous?"

The wandering eyes rested on me. "Sure, sometimes."

"Who were you jealous of?"

"You."

"You didn't even know me."

"It doesn't matter."

"Were you jealous of Sidney?"

"Who?" he asked, then his mind seemed to remember. "You
mean that closet case at Max's office?" He laughed. An empty
laugh, like his mind. "No, I wasn't jealous of Sidney."

"Johnny?"

Davie laughed again, a little louder. The laugh was as hollow
as a jail cell. "At one time," he said. "But, no, I wasn't really
jealous of Johnny. Hell, Johnny and Max never even made it
together."

"How do you know that?"

"If they did, they would have become lovers," Davie said
simply. His eyes seemed to get lost again, gliding over the other

inmates, the other visitors, the guard behind us, who stared back.

"Davie." I snapped his attention back to me. His eyes fell on me again. Unseeing. "Do you have a lawyer?" I asked.

"They gave me one."

"Who?"

"The cops."

"Who's your lawyer?"

"Some public defender." He grinned. "A hunk." He grinned wider.

"You don't sound unhappy," I said. In fact, he didn't sound anything. His mind seemed as blank as his eyes. He was answering my questions by rote, without any thought or emotion.

Davie leaned onto the table. "You wouldn't give me any money," he said. He grinned again. A wide Rootie Kazootie grin. "I had a tag sale. I sold some things in the apartment. And I made some money. That was okay for a while. But not for long." Rootie Kazootie was gone.

"What are you talking about?"

"Money. I'm talking about money. Life." He laughed at a secret only he shared.

"Are you stoned?"

"I love it," he said. "It's not all that bad in here." Hardin's eyes again gave the room a complete sweep. He circled in his chair to see the guard behind him staring him down. He turned back to me with a sly, stoned mask on his face and said very quietly and very secretively, "It's easier to get dope inside this place than it is on the street." His emotionless attitude and tone hadn't changed, but I could sense triumph behind his words.

"Are you that rich?" I asked. "Or that stupid?"

"What do you mean?" The question was clear, even though his voice was slurred. For the first time, he seemed to be slapped out of his daze.

"Whether on the street or behind bars, dope costs money," I elaborated. "Did Max leave you a million bucks in his will?"

"Max didn't leave me shit," he said. His fog was temporarily lifted. And he couldn't and didn't hide his disappointment, maybe even bitterness. A sign of life under all that stoned covering. "And I sold everything before his family could get their fucking hands on it. All the furniture, the pottery."

"And you spent the money," I said. "On dope."

"No, Cain," he said childishly. "I paid the rent, too."

"And you have nothing left."

"Zero." He made a circle with his forefinger and thumb.

"Then how do you get your dope in this place?"

"There are ways," Davie said, an almost diabolical gleam in his eye. Frightening on the surface.

"What ways?"

"Easy ways," he said. His neck again twisted around at the other visitors, at the guard. I was losing him, his concentration was almost gone. The fog had returned.

I tried to bring back his attention to me. "And you didn't kill Max."

"Maybe. Maybe not."

"What the hell kind of answer is that?"

"I haven't decided yet," he said, very serious and very stoned. "I think I like it here." Hardin looked puzzled at his own words. "Did I say that?" he asked himself. He seemed to be searching his mind. "I must be stoned."

"You are," I pointed out with more than a slight note of annoyance and frustration in my voice.

Hardin didn't catch it, or didn't care. "Yeah, I am. I asked you for money, didn't I? Last week? Last month?"

"Yeah."

"And you didn't give it to me."

"No."

"Neither would anybody else."

"And you sold all your furniture."

"Yeah."

"For dope and to pay the rent."

"Uh-huh."

"And you have no money left?"

"Zilcho."

"You could work for a living."

"I could, but why bother?" He said it almost gleefully. "In here, I don't have to work." He laughed. Another of his private jokes. But his quiet laughter stopped as quickly as it started. "Yeah," he said thoughtfully. "Maybe I did kill Max."

I let that lie for about ten seconds, then said, "No, you didn't."

Hardin shrugged his shoulders.

I tried to look into his soul, but I couldn't even get past the blanket in his eyes. Hardin waited. His body did, anyway. His eyes were all over the room again. And who knew where his mind was?

Davie shrugged his shoulders again and pushed back his chair with a screech. He stood up, looking down at me. The guard came over, took his arm, and escorted him back to his hell.

Puzzling son of a bitch, I thought. And crazy. As I walked out of my half of the cage, I wondered why I didn't feel sorry for him.

When I returned to my office, I called my answering service. Five messages. Every one of them a job. Three from the ad in the *Voice*, two from the *Post*. It was going to be a busy day tomorrow. Before I nodded off to sleep for the night, muddled thoughts of Davie strained my mind. I didn't think Hardin had killed his lover. I didn't think he had the guts, and he certainly didn't have the energy. Staying constantly stoned was a full-time and exhausting job. Why is he trying to convince himself he did?

I awoke early, dressed slowly, had some coffee and toast, and walked to 14th Street. Sinbad Associates wanted to see me. Mr. Sinbad had seen my ad in the *Post*.

At first glance, Mr. Sinbad appeared to be in his early thirties. At second glance, he was probably closer to forty. He had a crew cut and tiny wrinkles around his eyes. The bits of graying hair skimming out of the block of his head and around his ears gave his age away. But whether thirty or forty, he was handsome in an old-fashioned sort of way. The kind of man you would expect to see in a British military drama on Broadway. But he wasn't British, although he did have an accent. It was thick and reminded me of my Polish grandfather.

"Ve import hand-carved statuettes," he said. "Each and every von of dem is stamped 'Made in Spain.' " He handed me one of his imports. It was a small elephant, heavy in weight and creamy white. I assumed it to be carved out of ivory.

"No," Mr. Sinbad said. "It is pure marble. I become avare dat imitations are coming into da market. Dis . . ." He opened his desk and produced a carved tiger, handing it to me. "Dis is an imitation," he said with disdain.

The work of both carvings seemed identical. But the weight of the imitation was much less than the original.

"Plastic," Sinbad said. "I vant you to find out who is importing dese things."

"Where did you get this?" I asked, handling the fake.

"A dealer sells dem at de Ole Times, da flea market on Canal Street. A cheap dealer," he said with a scorn a businessman saves for a competitor.

"Is that illegal?" I asked. "Competitive, yes, but illegal?"

"Yes. Dey are illegal if dey are misrepresented," Mr. Sinbad said. He pointed to the small printing on the labels stuck to the bottom of each of the carvings. Both said the same: ORIGINAL MAHANA.

"Mahana is de artist," Sinbad explained. "Dis is original." He held up the elephant. "Dis is not." He pointed at the tiger. "Vill you find out for me who is doing dis? Where dat dealer is getting dese?" Sinbad asked.

I quoted my price. Sinbad agreed to it. "I'll find out," I told him. We shook on it. Sinbad had a firm grasp. He seemed satisfied with my services, even though I hadn't given him any yet.

I also took on the other four clients who had called yesterday. One was a man who suspected his wife of having an affair. When I first decided to become a private investigator, I made

59

a vow not to get bogged down in cheating wives and cheating husbands. But vows, like rules, are made to be broken. I took the case. I needed the money. I wanted an office that wasn't a spare bedroom.

The third job I took was a gentleman client who wanted me to find out who bought a painting at an auction uptown. The gentleman didn't sound desperate. That job could wait until next week. The schedule was all right with him.

I also decided to spend four hours a day, two days a week, as an undercover guard in a Midtown thrift shop. I adjusted my rate accordingly. But it still paid well and wouldn't disturb my other pursuits.

The fifth client was a lawyer looking for a missing beneficiary. The missing heir was presumed to be in Los Angeles, and I could work on that one long distance, utilizing Ma Bell and the U.S. Postal Service. The lawyer sounded like a sleazebag. And he was in no particular hurry, either.

I heaved a sigh of relief. It looked like I just might be able to make a living.

I gave my mind free rein to travel back to Max without feeling guilty about taking time away from my paying work.

Aside from his involvement with G.A.A., Max seemed to have spent all of his extra time at the office. With Sidney, a married man with a heated crush, and with Maureen, who had delusions of grandeur and a fear of the FBI. I laughed at that one. But I couldn't laugh off Sidney. His feelings were too deep, his involvement with Max too emotional. On Sidney's side, anyway. How emotional was Max toward Sidney? Davie said he wasn't jealous of Sidney, so that presumed a flimsy involvement between Sidney and Max. But then again, Davie was dope crazy.

It was only after finishing a late leftover supper of fried chicken, which hadn't turned out right the first time I cooked it, that I decided to make a nighttime call to the office of *Current Social Thought*.

I dressed in dungarees and a heavy long-sleeved denim shirt. Autumn was with us now, but not viciously so. I slipped my special penknife in my back pocket. I would have liked to have slipped my holster on my shoulder with my .38 inside it, but I hadn't had the opportunity to pick up my permit.

My business phone rang.

"It's Ron," the voice at the other end said. "I have to talk to you. Can you meet me at the Stud?"

"Now?" I asked.

"Yes."

The Stud was a denim/leather back-room bar down the street from my apartment. I told him I'd be there in a jiffy. I pushed my arms into my denim jacket.

Since it was still early evening, only a handful of men were corralled around the bar. Ron was sitting alone and at the far end. He waved me over and ordered me a beer. I declined. He ordered me a soft drink. He paid.

"That son of a bitch," he said harshly and loudly. Even the leather-vested hunky hirsute sexy friendly bartender heard him. But after he realized the words were not meant as a criticism of his service, he returned to the other end of the bar. My loss. I think Ron had had one beer too many.

"Which one is a son of a bitch?"

"Johnny."

"What about him?"

"Fucking goddamn hypocrite," Ron said, again too loud. The bartender didn't even turn around this time.

"The last time I saw you, you didn't want to talk about Johnny," I reminded him.

"I think he killed Max," Ron said. This time I was the only person to hear him. His mouth was almost in my ear. When he leaned away from me, I could see an odd and excited fear in his eyes. Or was it despair?

"Why do you say that?"

"Because the son of a bitch is trying to tear G.A.A. apart."

"In what way?"

Ron listed. "He won't come to zaps. He won't picket. He says Max would have made a better president than me." Ron seemed to run out of words. Or breath. Or both.

61

"Hence he killed Max."

There was hurt reflected in Ron's eyes when he looked up at me, but he didn't speak.

"Sounds like a lovers' quarrel," I said, half in jest. I still believed Ron harbored an unrelieved passion for Johnny.

"Are you crazy?" Ron exclaimed.

All right, maybe I was on the wrong track. "Okay, Ron, why the change of heart?"

"What do you mean, change of heart?"

"Why didn't you tell me this last week?"

"I didn't know it last week," he said, almost a plea. "All of a sudden, Johnny turned on me. He changed."

"In what way?"

"Never mind. He changed."

"Just like Max changed," I said.

Ron gave me a look that could have made me slide off my stool. But I sat firm. Ron steeled himself and said, "Johnny was at the docks the night Max was killed."

"So was I. And I didn't kill him."

"Johnny was following Max."

"Why would he follow him?"

"You find out, you're the detective." There was a note of derision in his voice.

"Yeah. The detective who's not under hire to G.A.A."

"We couldn't afford you," he justified.

"If you're so convinced that Johnny killed Max, why don't you go to the police?"

Ron gave off a short snort of contempt. The police, in the eyes of militants, were the pigs. In answer to my question, he said, "Find out why Johnny was following Max." Ron upended his beer and slipped off his stool. And *slipped* is the right word. He almost fell on his ass. He quickly pulled himself together, standing tall and straight. Too tall.

"But you won't tell me why you think he was following Max," I said.

Ron stood there, on the verge of leaving, yet not saying a

word. I asked, "Why do you think I'd be interested in finding out who killed Max?"

"Because you know Davie didn't do it," he said.

"Do I?"

"Find out why Johnny was following Max and you'll find out who killed Max," Ron said. He slammed his beer can on the bar, leaving a splash, and walked out of the bar, too controlled.

A muscular middle-aged stud with a graying beard on his chin and a leather vest on his chest sauntered into the back room. But not before offering me an inviting and lingering look. I reluctantly declined and left a half can of soda on the bar.

Chapter
6

I walked up Christopher Street to the subway station, wondering why Ron had suddenly turned against Johnny. Or why Ron had decided to talk about him at all. Had Ron made a pass at him and been rebuffed that badly? I made a mental note to find out where Johnny lived.

I waited for the train on the uncrowded platform. Two men were cruising each other in front of the doorway to the john, and a man nearby was talking into the telephone. Otherwise the station was empty. I walked over to the telephone booth. When the man finished his call, I opened the door and went inside. I plucked a dime out of my pocket and, since there was no sign of an uptown train in the distant tunnel, I called Larry.

"Hello," he said, subdued. When I announced myself, his tone changed, loud and boisterous. "What you say, bitch? What you up to?"

"Have to go uptown. Busy day," I said. "Just wanted to check on Saturday."

"Saturday? The dance! My God, that only gives me two days to prepare," Larry said in exaggerated panic. "Oh, I can't do it! I have to get my hair done. And I must go to Bloomie's for a new gown. And my makeup! My makeup will take hours. Are you kidding, honey? I need at least two weeks' notice before appearing in public, you know that."

"I'd say closer to a year," I said. I heard the train careening down the tunnel. One of the cruisers plopped a dime in the men's room door. He and his newfound friend entered.

"Prick," Larry said. "Go catch your train, bitch."

"I'll be over to your place at eleven on Saturday."

"That should give me just enough time. But, my dear, can you make yourself beautiful before then?"

"Your mother," I said and hung up on Larry's outraged laughter.

I departed the subway hole at 79th Street and walked cautiously down to 77th Street. The air was chilled; autumn was definitely here. The storefront office of *Current Social Thought* was dark, except for a small night-light in the rear. I strolled past the building. When I heard footsteps behind me, I turned. An old man was walking his dog. I continued on to the end of the block, counting individual buildings as I passed.

I turned the corner and made my way up 78th Street. When I passed an alley, I paused. A car's taillight was disappearing up the street. People were passing on Broadway. No one was heading down the street. I scurried into the alley. I was about to break and enter. If I was caught, my P.I. license wouldn't be worth the plastic it was laminated with. But I didn't plan on being caught.

The alley not only led to the side entrance of a large apartment building, but it curved around into the backyards of the other buildings on 78th Street. As I had hoped, the alley also backed up into the yards of the buildings on 77th. I counted down.

I climbed the four cement steps cautiously and silently. The back door was locked, as expected. I slipped my penknife out of my back pocket and drew out the special thinly tapered awl with its curved nose, inserting it into the keyhole, slowly turning until I felt it catch. I probed carefully. The lock clicked. I opened the door.

The hallway was dark. I closed the door and paused. The only sounds were the sparse nighttime traffic on the street in front and the creaks of an aging building. The door to the office was also locked. Although the window was grimy, I could see a tiny night-light in the back of the room. I took a thin sheet of hard plastic I had cut from a venetian blind and inserted it between the door and the frame. The lock slipped open easily. Didn't anyone believe in a dead bolt? I thought. And if Maureen Meredith was so worried about the FBI, her worry didn't extend to security for her office. I gently closed the door behind me.

The floor on one side of the office was littered with past issues of the magazine in cardboard boxes. Shelves held scores of shadowed books. The two filing cabinets were unlocked and as disorganized as the rest of the office. I flicked out my penlight. After scanning through file folders, I came up with nothing but old and uninteresting manuscripts or new and uninteresting manuscripts.

I sat at the desk next to the typewriter and opened the middle drawer. There were numerous paper clips, some typewriter ribbons, pencils, pens, napkins, blank envelopes. The top side drawer held letterhead paper, blank bond paper, carbon paper, and large manila envelopes. The bottom drawer was personal. There were a pair of brown gloves and some used, small, empty, and folded brown paper bags. Fliers from past G.A.A. demonstrations were crushed inside the drawer. There was a small address book that could fit in the palm of my hand. On the inside cover printed in pen was: MAX HARMONY, 523-A EAST 85TH ST., NYC. I shoved it into my back pocket and moved to the next desk.

The chair at Maureen Meredith's desk was padded much more comfortably than the chair at Max's desk. The drawers were locked tight, but the center one was easy to pick, and it opened the side ones. I pulled out a file folder from the middle drawer. Letters on important-looking stationery. A senator, two congressmen, and one from the office of Housing and Urban Development. The congressmen congratulated her and *Current Social Thought* for helping spearhead the drive for a proposed day-care bill. HUD was asking her to come to Washington to testify about the effects of illegal drugs on pregnant women.

I slipped the letter file back into her desk drawer and locked it. Obviously, I had been wrong. People did read her magazine. Important people. And maybe she had cause to be worried about government spies.

I wondered why I thought of it as *her* magazine, and not *his*. Sidney was the editor, not Maureen. But I didn't wonder for long. I knew why. Pecking is a hen's favorite pastime.

I moved over to what must have been Sidney's desk. It was uncluttered, the drawers were full of manuscripts and neat. But I didn't even find a pen in the drawer. Sidney may be the editor, but Maureen was the dominant partner of the masthead, as well as the marriage. Not for long, I thought. Not for the marriage, anyway. Sidney's newly discovered feelings weren't going to go away, that's for sure. But I sensed that Sidney was. Going to go away, that is. His way. A man finally becoming true to his own feelings. I wondered if Maureen knew that her marriage was heading for troubled waters. Or was she too busily involved with the magazine to realize she no longer had a husband?

I hopped back to Maureen Meredith's desk and thumbed through her Rolodex file. Each card held a name and a telephone number, and I scanned them, becoming fatigued in the process. It was a large card file. Congressmen and senators and other federal, state, and city officials were listed. Interesting but not something I had the need to know about. Max was also listed. His home address and phone number. G.A.A. was marked in parentheses, along with DAVIE.

I went out the way I had entered, taking care to lock the

doors behind me. A nagging thought sifted through my mind. Could Maureen Meredith know about Sidney's so-called affair with Max? Was she the jealous type? She didn't seem so to me. But I understand women about as much as I understand what makes an airplane fly. In either case, not much.

The crosstown bus took me to 86th Street and York Avenue. The Hardin/Harmony apartment building was on the next street over. At an elegant apartment house on the corner, a doorman appeared to be sleeping on a stool in the lobby. Otherwise, the street was deserted. Deserted of people anyway. Cars were shoehorned onto both sides of the street. The streets were too clean, just like the entire neighborhood. The Upper East Side was not the Village, I thought. I was glad I hadn't moved here when I left Brooklyn. The Upper East Side was an entity of its own. A sterile entity.

There was a dim light over the doorway of 523-A East 85th Street. I walked into the tiny outer lobby and pressed a random button. An aged crackling female voice quickly asked who was there. I didn't answer. She didn't buzz me in. I pressed another button and received the same response. And another, until someone buzzed me in without inquiry.

I waited outside the small inner lobby for five minutes, not making a sound. No one came in or out, no door from above opened, no one called down. Some stairs squeaked when I climbed to the fifth floor, but I couldn't avoid the noise, and no one responded. I listened against the apartment door of Hardin/Harmony. No sound. Not very likely, what with Max dead and Davie jailed.

The door didn't have a dead bolt either, and was as easy to snap open as the office I had just left. Was this New York City or Nebraska? I wondered. Was I the only person with an apartment that had a dead bolt for security?

I didn't hesitate to switch on the light. Roaches scattered as if from an atomic bomb.

There were dirty dishes in the sink, a half pot of coffee on the stove. And that was about it for the kitchen. The living room looked as if scavengers had been well fed. Gone were the Cleopatra couch, the rug, the chairs, the coffee tables, the knick-knacks. A broken pottery jar lay on the floor among scattered fliers from G.A.A. demonstrations and dances. A bookcase was still there but looked about to fall apart. Some books were on the shelves, but not many, and none worth noting—mostly books about antiques.

Even the large dresser that had stood in the corner near the window was gone. Supermarket cardboard boxes replaced it, filled with underwear and socks and T-shirts and sweatshirts and pants. Some of the clothes looked newly washed, but most of them didn't. The one large closet in the hallway near the bathroom was stuffed with pants and shirts and winter jackets. Two suitcases were full of more clothes. Boots and shoes and slippers were scattered on the closet floor, along with a mound of more dirty clothes.

The only useful piece of furniture still in the apartment was the round oak table under the loft. I wondered why it hadn't sold. I wouldn't have minded having it in my own apartment. When I looked at the thick base, I saw why it was still there. A side crack was about to expand the single base into two. On top of the table, a small ripped piece of masking tape said $450.00. A stiff price, I thought. No wonder he hadn't sold it, especially with a cracked pedestal. I stepped onto the wooden ladder that led to the upper loft, popping my head up into the bed area. The space was as large, or larger, than a double bed. The mattress was covered with a grimy sheet and a thin blanket. I climbed halfway up the ladder to see the shelf that stretched the length of the back wall. Porno magazines were scattered over the shelf, along with numerous bottles of poppers, both empty and half full, and an almost empty jar of Vaseline. There was an ashtray with three cigarette butts and too many marijuana roaches.

I lifted myself all the way up into the loft, then flipped a switch next to the ladder. The dim overhead light came on. I sat back, fingering through the fuck&suck books. I propped a pillow against my back and thought about jacking off. But the pictures wouldn't do the job. Too posed, too artificial. And the

68

loft was too dark. I looked up at the light fixture. It was sunk into the ceiling and only one fading bulb worked. One of the screws was missing, and the other three were barely screwed in. The fixture was as sloppy as the loft itself, I thought.

I spotted near the corner of the shelf a small book with a locked metal snap. It looked like the diary my sister used to have as a teenager. MAX was crudely carved into the imitation black leather cover. I slipped the book into the front of my dungarees and inside the elastic of my briefs, then eased myself back down the ladder.

The hallway was as quiet as I when I had entered. The lock snapped into place when I closed the door.

I fixed myself a cup of instant coffee and made myself comfortable in my twin-size bed. I lit a cigarette and thumbed through Max's address book. Most listings were by first name only, no addresses, only phone numbers: Pete, Marc, Marty, Arthur, Arthur B, Jim, Arnie. Ron was listed, Johnny was listed. Various city agencies, state agencies, the Columbia Law School.

I had to use a screwdriver to pry open the damn diary, not without damage to the vinyl and the metal lock.

Each entry was dated, starting about a week before Max's death. Much of what Max had written was rambling train-of-thought, with little connection—thoughts about life, love, death, and liberation. Chaotic and poetic. And dull. But it did indicate that Max was not a happy man.

When his words did become everyday coherent, it seemed his main preoccupation was his ambivalent feelings toward his lover. "I wish Davie would get a job. I can't keep supporting us both. The love we had together is changing. I'm going to have to give him a choice—get a job or get out. The only trouble is, the apartment is in his name. But I don't know how else to spark him. He's not interested in G.A.A. He won't get a job. He doesn't even leave the house anymore. He's too dependent on me. And on those damn pills."

I wondered why Max would leave the book around for Davie

to read. Probably because he wanted Davie to read it, I thought. I wondered if Davie had read it.

Another coherent entry, two days later. "Davie said he'll get a job. I know better. He's said it before. When I told him I'd throw him out if he didn't find work, he reminded me that the apartment was in his name. I wonder if Ron wants a roommate?"

The next day. "I could never live with Ron. He's too fucking organized and his place is too small. I wish Johnny wasn't so damn evasive. If he was more open with me, I could fall in love with that man. Though, Lord knows, we're opposites. But that doesn't matter. I DO LOVE HIM. There, I said it! Fool!" Another paragraph, very short. "Sidney is becoming a pain in the ass. I wonder if Maureen told him?"

More ramblings, streams of unhappy consciousness.

The last coherent entry was puzzling and frightening. "I can't see Johnny anymore. I can't go back to work. I'll be going to jail for a long, long time."

I buried thoughts of Max and Sidney and Johnny and Ron, worked up a playful image of a hot-assed marine in the barracks, whacked off, and went to sleep.

Chapter 7

Johnny's telephone number but no address was listed in Max's address book. I hoped it was the Johnny I wanted. Probably. It was the only Johnny listed, but there was also a John.

It was going to be a busy day. I wanted to track Johnny down. I also wanted to return to Riker's Island to find out if

Hardin knew about the diary. I also wanted to see Maureen Meredith. But, most important, I also had a living to make.

I called the Los Angeles Police Department. They were helpful only after I dropped Captain Carney's name. The missing beneficiary I was seeking had been given a traffic ticket for an illegal turn on a one-way street two weeks earlier. The LAPD gave me his address. I called Information, but he had no phone listing. I typed a letter informing the beneficiary of his good luck, asking him to telephone me collect as soon as he received the letter. I enclosed my card in the envelope.

I didn't have to start my two-day-a-week guard duty at the thrift store until next Thursday. And I received a call from my client who had wanted me to find proof of his wife's infidelity. He told me that his wife had packed a bag and left. He offered to pay me for a day's work, but I hadn't done any work at all on the case, so I refused. When he offered me a half day's pay, I accepted. I put off my other clients, Mr. Sinbad and the guy who wanted to find out who bought a painting at the auction uptown.

I called the number listed for Johnny. It was the correct Johnny. He was surprised to hear from me and asked how I got his unlisted number. I lied and told him Davie gave it to me.

"When did you see Davie?"

I didn't answer the question. "I'd like to come over and talk to you," I said.

"About what?"

"Guess."

There was silence at the other end. He wasn't going to guess, so I added, "I want to talk to you about Max."

"What about him?"

"Can I come over?"

"No," Johnny answered quickly. "I have to go to work."

"Where do you work?"

No answer. I offered a suggestion. "How about if I come over to your place tonight?"

Another silence. This time I waited for Johnny to break it.

"I'll meet you at a bar," he finally said, reluctantly, I thought.

"The Stud at eight," I suggested.

"Make it nine," Johnny told me.

I called the office of *Current Social Thought*. There was no answer. There was a listing in the Manhattan telephone directory for MEREDITH, M & S at an address on West End Avenue. I subwayed uptown.

It was a large, old, well-cared-for apartment building, only four blocks from the Merediths' office. No doorman graced the entrance, although with the bench in the anteroom, it seemed at one time there might have been a man who watched the door, carried grocery bags for tenants, had an always-handy umbrella. The days of old glory. The building had a large entrance lobby. I searched the list of tenants. MEREDITH lived in 13-C. I pressed the button, but there was no answer. I decided not to go to their office. I wanted to see Maureen Meredith alone.

I walked back to the subway and trained down to Canal Street. The flea market that according to Sinbad sold the fake carvings was in an aged and massive building on the busy thoroughfare. An antique-looking sign hanging over the entrance read OLE TIMES.

There was some activity inside, with browsers glancing through booths that offered everything from cheap jewelry to posters from the 1939 and 1964 World's Fairs, to very expensive and very old oak furniture. The booth I was looking for was on the lower level. Three small tables were displayed with carvings and statuettes. Most had the look of antique, but some were obviously new reproductions. I picked up a white tiger. Its weight didn't match its size: plastic, not marble. The proprietor was friendly.

"That's by the original artist," he said, his long brown tangled hair straying over his brow.

"What's it made of?"

"Plastic," the man admitted.

"I understand Mahana only worked in marble," I countered. The proprietor stared, asked, "Do you know his work?"

"Somewhat," I said.

"Well, when I say these are originals," he said, amending his previous statement and taking the statuette from me, "I mean they're original copies of the original work."

He turned the tiger over. The label was there. MADE IN SPAIN. And underneath in tiny letters were the words ORIGINAL COPY OF MAHANA.

I asked him the price and said I'd think about it. Before I left, he made a play for me, promising to deliver the merchandise to my apartment and at my convenience. "I'm Glenn," he said, too friendly. His eyes were bright and almost warm, his smile infectious, his body small and compact. Overall, a tempting proposition.

"Archie," I said. But I passed. He was too interested, too eager. Half of the fun of the game is the chase.

There didn't seem anything illegal about the carvings. They were copies, all right, but clearly marked copies. I tried to telephone Mr. Sinbad but received no answer.

I walked back to the Village up through SoHo. When I passed the G.A.A. firehouse, the door was open. I stepped inside. The large meeting room was empty. Folding chairs were stacked neatly against one wall. Oddly enough, the place looked musty but smelled clean. I heard sounds upstairs. I climbed the circular iron stairway, and before I reached the top, a female voice sounded out, "Is that you, William?"

"No," I answered, reaching the top.

"Can I help you?" the woman asked, looking down at me, a long-handled push broom in her hand. She was a small woman with long thin blond hair tied into a ponytail. She wore dungarees, a sweatshirt cut off at the sleeves, a shoelace headband, and a friendly if cautious smile. I recognized her as Helen Shaker, the woman who had taken Max's place as vice president.

I reached the top and held out a hand. "My name is Archie Cain."

She shook my hand, but the smile disappeared.

"How come you charge so much for your services, Cain?" she asked. Before I could answer, she added, "Ron told me what you charge. Don't you give a damn about gay liberation?" She didn't try to conceal the annoyance in her voice.

"I have to make a living," I said. "And yes, I care about gay liberation. My own."

"A bit selfish, aren't you?"

"Yes. Aren't you?"

"No," she answered. "Not where liberation is concerned. What do you want?"

"Do you think Davie killed Max?"

"Of course not."

She didn't move away from the top of the stairway. I spotted some comfortable-looking stuffed chairs behind her. I tried to ease my way in, but she wouldn't budge. "Excuse me," I said, and walked around her. Our shoulders touched.

She turned and followed me. "Why should Davie kill Max?" she asked rhetorically. "Max was his bread and butter. Davie didn't have to work. He didn't have to do anything. Max supported him."

I flopped down into a chair. "Then Max was a sucker."

"You could say that," she said. Her face didn't soften, but I sensed that her annoyance with me was easing.

"Have you raised much money for Davie's defense?"

"Some. More than I thought we would. But sure the fuck not enough to pay some shyster private eye."

"I don't do charity work. I told you, I have a living to make."

"Then go make it. Don't bother me." Her movements didn't match her words. She sat across from me in another chair. The stuffing was falling out of both chairs, but hers was neatly patched. "All the money we raise will go for Davie's defense, not for some—"

"I get the feeling you don't have much use for Davie. Why bother defending him?" Before she answered, I held up a hand.

"I know, I know. He's gay. You have to help your brothers in trouble." But I said it with a small smile.

A slight smile also broke through on Shaker's face. "What are you doing here, Cain?"

"Asking questions," I said.

"But we can't afford to pay you."

"I didn't ask you to," I stated. She looked me over like I was a bug and she a scientist. It was a cautious, if friendly, look. I think I won one. Her smile stayed put, maybe even grew.

"Who is this Johnny?" I asked, lighting a cigarette.

"You mean Johnny Grabowski? The guy who was carrying on with Max?"

"Were they carrying on?"

"So it seems." A secret grin widened the corners of her mouth but quickly disappeared. "Max had about had it with Davie. If Johnny had a place, Max would have moved in with him."

"Johnny doesn't have a place?"

"Yeah, but not a home. But even if Johnny had a pad on Fifth Avenue, he would have been a fool to share it."

"Who?"

"Max."

"You don't like Johnny, either, do you?"

"Either?"

It was a question, but I didn't answer it.

"At one time, I thought Johnny was okay," she continued.

"But you don't anymore."

"Johnny's out," she stated flatly.

"Out of what?"

She displayed a snide expression. "Out of his fucking mind."

"Explain," I said.

"You'll see," she said, sharing a secret—but only with herself, not with me. "You a member here?"

I passed that one by. "Ron doesn't like Johnny either, does he?" I said. "Not anymore, anyway. You people change as fast as a diaper on a newborn."

"Are you a member of G.A.A.?" she asked again.

"No."

"Come to the meeting next Wednesday, Cain. You'll see."

"See what?"

"What Johnny's made of," she said, offering that secretive smile again.

"What's Johnny made of?"

"Sticks and snails and puppy-dog tails," she said. "Or some such shit."

It was my turn to smile. "Where is Johnny's place that is not a home? Where does he live?"

"At the Y on Twenty-third."

"Did Davie know about Johnny?"

"You mean that Johnny and Max were making it together?" she asked. "*Supposedly* making it," she amended when I gave her an unbelieving glance. I nodded. "Not unless Max told him. And I doubt that. You got an extra one?" she asked when I crushed out my cigarette in the large metal ashtray on the crate serving as a coffee table. I gave her one and lit it for her.

"Thanks." She inhaled, relaxed back into the chair, tossing a leg on the box. "No, Davie didn't kill Max. Certainly not because of Johnny."

"How about Sidney?"

"Who the fuck is Sidney?"

"Never mind. Were you a good friend of Max's?" I asked.

A pause. "I'm not a good friend of any man. I hate all men." Her manner belied her words. She elaborated. "I hate all men as a group, but I like individual men."

"Well, I'm glad I'm an individual and not a group," I said, smiling. She smiled back.

I looked around the room. Compared to the meeting room on the ground floor, it was small, but I could see doors leading to individual compartments. The plywood walls looked newly constructed. I pushed myself out of the chair and opened a door. Inside was a tiny room with a scarred desk and four folding chairs. "Did G.A.A. build all these rooms?"

Helen followed me. "We worked our ass off to make this place livable. You should have seen it when we moved in."

When I turned around, she had crushed out the cigarette and was lighting a joint. She inhaled and offered it to me, but I waved it off. She didn't speak while she was smoking. I walked the room, peering through doors, though some were locked. Helen didn't stop me. I ended up back at the dilapidated but comfortable chair. When she took her last toke, she carefully dabbed out the lit end and placed the roach in her pocket.

"Max could have been president of G.A.A.," she said. She flopped back onto the chair, resting her arms behind her head.

"That isn't what I heard. I understand his views were too radical."

"Who says?" she asked. I didn't answer. I didn't have to. She continued. "Well, to tell you the truth, he *was* too radical. I know that. So does Ron. But the membership liked him. He was a popular guy. They would have voted him in in a second. But I wouldn't have voted for him and I would have fought him all the way. He would have made a lousy president. And Ron would never resign, not if Max was going to take over."

"Was Ron planning to resign?"

"He will now. He's going to run for city council."

"And you'll become president of G.A.A.," I pointed out.

She shook her head up and down slowly and grinned, but the grin soon vanished. "I guess I'll become president," she said, then bummed another cigarette. "You might as well know it, Cain. That is, if you don't already. Three weeks ago I made a motion to have Max impeached."

"Why?"

"He was a spy," she said simply. But she quickly added, "Of course, nobody believed me. Ron thought I was crazy. He doesn't anymore."

"A spy for who?"

"Who knows?" Again, a knowing smile.

I wanted to pounce through that secretive wall. "That's a bit much, isn't it? Spies in G.A.A.? Is the organization that important?"

"Somebody thinks we are," she answered.

77

I didn't think they were, but I asked, "Do you know who he was spying for? If he was spying."

She nodded. That smile stayed put, not opening up.

"Who?" I asked. She wasn't going to answer. "That's a crock of shit," I said. "Maybe I didn't know Max that long, but he was a gay militant, not a traitor."

Helen swung her feet off the crate, leaned forward, and clasped her hands together. "We planned zaps in executive session," she said, as if inviting me into a conspiracy. "Do you know why?"

"Because you were afraid of spies. Johnny told me. Sounds a bit paranoid."

"Not really," she said seriously. "Why do you think so many of our zaps went wrong?"

"I didn't know they did."

"Well, they did."

"How many of you are on the executive committee?"

"President, vice president, secretary, treasurer, sergeant at arms, and all the committee heads."

"Which makes a nice handful. What? Eight? Ten? Why was Max the stoolie?"

She leaned farther into the space that separated us. Her words became hushed. "I set him up."

I waited for her to continue. She scanned her eyes around the room as if the walls were bugged. I thought she was being overly dramatic.

"After the exec meeting where we planned the marriage license bureau zap," she elaborated, again peering around, "I took Ron and Max aside. I laid out a plan that only the three of us knew about. We three would hide out in the stairwell near the office until all the demonstrators were in line at the bureau. One of them was carrying a box, too, a wedding cake. We were going to hold a gay wedding party." She laughed. "Anyway, after everyone else was in line, we three would sneak out into the hall, rush into the office, and handcuff ourselves to a desk or a typewriter or something." She leaned back. "We were evicted even before we got the chance."

"Why?"

"Loitering in a public building or stairwell or some such shit."

"What does that prove?"

"At the exec meeting, it had been planned otherwise. Ron, Max, and I were to have gone in first, cuffed ourselves to the desk, then the group would come in with the cake. But I changed it, and only Ron and Max knew about the change," she emphasized. "And we were the only ones who knew about our hiding place. The pigs pounced before we got a chance to get in. They seemed to know right where we'd be waiting. We were the only three tossed out of the building. The others got inside and cut the cake, but they couldn't cuff themselves to the desk because we had the cuffs. They were laughed at. The zap flopped."

"Hence, one of you stooled to the cops," I said.

"You got it." She leaned back and folded her arms behind her head. A winner's pose. A stoned winner's pose.

"Did you tell Ron that?"

"Bet your ass," she said. "He said he'd take care of it."

As soon as the words were out of her mouth, realization filled her eyes. She quickly sputtered, "Ron didn't kill Max."

A voice from down below yelled, "Hey, anybody up there?"

Helen jumped up, tripped over the broom, and regained her balance. She called down the stairway, "Yeah, I'm up here." The someone from downstairs climbed the metal steps. Helen Shaker looked at me, her face flushed.

" 'Bout time you got here, William. I thought I'd have to sweep this fucking place up by myself."

William was a short, stringy-haired young man in bright elephant bells, swishy, loud, and flamboyantly dressed in an orange sweatshirt three sizes too big. He spotted me. "Well, hello," he said, extending a limp hand and trying to sound provocative. His attempt was wasted. Not anywhere near my type. I shook his hand, said hi, and walked around him to the stairwell. Helen followed.

Before I descended and when William was out of hearing range, I asked her, "Why did you tell me all this?"

Her flush had disappeared. "You're helping G.A.A., aren't you? We can't afford your services, but you're one of us." A small smile crossed her lips. This one was quite warm. She leaned in and whispered to me. "Ron didn't kill him."

"But you won't tell me about Johnny?"

"Be here at the next meeting," she said, turned, and walked away.

I climbed down the stairs. I liked Helen Shaker, but she smiled too much, and for the most part, too insincerely.

Two guys dressed in standard Levi's came in the door as I was leaving. They gave me a hearty greeting, a soft cruise, and went upstairs. Outside, the street was busy with daytime workers hauling boxes, wheeling crated furniture, yelling at one another in Spanish, a language that was music to my ears but which I could never understand, even after having had a course in high school. I walked north. When I passed through Washington Square Park, I stopped at a vendor for lunch, a hot dog with sauerkraut and a Coke.

Sated for the moment, I headed west toward Perry Street.

When I got home, I dragged out the box at the bottom of my closet, unwrapped my .38, and loaded it. Cursing myself for not stopping downtown to pick up my permit, I checked the clock on the kitchen wall. There was still time.

Before leaving for the land of government bureaus and customhouses, I had a telephone call to make. Mr. Sinbad answered after the first ring.

"You're right. They're selling those statuettes down on Canal Street. They're copies, all right, but they're clearly labeled as such."

"Are you sure?" Sinbad asked, incredulous. "Vhen I vas down dere, dey vere marked as originals."

"Not anymore."

"Did you find out vhere he vas getting dem?"

"There didn't seem any point," I told him. "There's nothing illegitimate about the wares."

"Damn it!" Sinbad shouted. "I'm paying you to do vhat I tell you. Find out vhere he's getting dose pieces. Vhat the hell do you think I'm paying you for?"

His attitude and his accent pissed me off. "You haven't paid me a fucking thing yet and the—"

"Because you haven't done a thing yet! And don't swear at me."

My voice rose above his. "The man isn't doing anything illegal. My job is over."

My words mollified him, or at least outshouted him. His tone softened. "I'm sorry, Mr. Cain, but I vant to find out vhere he's getting dose statues."

"Then go ask him. My job is done." I wasn't placated enough to feel sorry for him.

"Vhat kind of attitude is dat?" Sinbad asked. I could sense that he was holding his temper in check. "You're in de business, aren't you?"

"Yeah," I told him. "I'm in the business. And I pick and choose my cases. The man isn't doing anything wrong."

"Come on, Mr. Cain, I'll pay you. Vhen the job is complete, I'll send you a check." He was pleading in a coyish manner that I found nauseating.

"As far as I'm concerned, the job is complete. I did a day's work for a day's pay."

There was a brief silence at the other end. Finally, subdued, Sinbad said, "All right, Mr. Cain. I'll send you a check."

"Thank you."

"Vill you be available for future jobs?" he asked.

"Of course."

Sinbad offered me a less than cheerful good-bye and a promise of a check in the mail.

After he hung up, I fretted and debated. Should I have continued the investigation of the statues even though there was nothing illegal about them? It would have meant more bucks. But, still, I didn't see anything illegal or even unethical about them. Finally, I decided I had been right. I had to run my own business my own way.

Before locking my apartment door, I hesitated at leaving my .38 behind. I would have liked to have had it tucked in my holster, but I couldn't very well pick up my gun permit with a gun under my arm. I slipped the empty holster on, just to get used to the feel.

I trained downtown and was back in my apartment within an hour and a half, a permit in my pocket. My holster was no longer empty.

Ron was surprised to hear my voice. He was more surprised when I began asking questions about Max. "I thought you had a business to run," he interrupted, not without a bit of sarcasm. "We can't afford you, remember? Why bother?"

"Do you want to help Davie or not?" I asked him.

"Of course," he answered. "But I told you what I thought."

"About Johnny?"

"Yes."

"You told me nothing." Before he could react to that, I added, "Can you meet me at the Stud tonight?"

"I have a city government committee meeting this evening at the firehouse," he said.

"What time will you be through?"

"Before eight."

"I'll be at the Stud," I told him.

Ron said he'd try to get there after the meeting. I told him to be there, no ifs, ands, or buts.

After a shower, I stepped into a clean pair of shorts and my 501's. I slipped my denim jacket on over a checkered Western shirt. The jacket hid the holster under my arm. Unseen except to knowledgeable eyes.

I cabbed over to the precinct. Carney was on his way out the door. I stopped him before he hopped into his car.

He smiled when he saw me. "You saw Hardin, Cain. Satisfied now?"

"No," I said. "He was stoned out of his mind, Carney. Christ, you have more dope dealing going on in your jails than you have on the streets."

"So what else is new?" he said, leaning an arm on the top of his car.

"Why don't you do something about it?" I asked him, straying off the subject.

Carney waved his hand at me, brushing me off. "Shit, Cain, you're worse now than when you were a cop. You try to change the system, I can't."

He wasn't my boss anymore. I could say anything I wanted. And I did. "You don't even try, Carney."

He gave me a look to melt steel, pulled open his door, and lowered himself into the car. Before he slammed the door, he turned to me. I expected a lecture. I received a confession. "I was young once myself, you know. Maybe even idealistic. You'll learn. Don't come here browbeating me, Cain, about the corrupt system. I know it's there. My job is to jail the bastards. Once I do that, I go home for the night and forget about it. I sleep like a baby." He closed the door and opened the window. "We can't even clean the scum off the streets, and you want us to clean up the jails, too?" He started his engine. "You do it, Cain. I don't have the energy or the time," he concluded.

"Wait a minute, Carney," I said. "I know it's there, in jail or out. And there isn't a fucking thing any of us can do about it. Except, like you say, just do our job. I didn't mean to get you started." It was almost an apology.

Carney smiled again, a slow meaningful smile. "Maybe you're learning, kid." He moved to put the car in gear.

I rested an arm on the top of the door. "Did Harmony have a record?" I asked him.

"A record? Hell, within the last year, the punk was pulled in four times. Disorderly conduct, resisting arrest, trespassing."

"From the demonstrations of G.A.A.?"

"Yeah."

"That's it? Nothing else?"

Carney shook his head. "Nothing. He never spent any jail time, either. Not to speak of, anyway. He was out on bond on all those charges. Two were finally dismissed, and he had to pay a fine on the others."

"Otherwise, clean?"

"Yeah." Carney looked up at me. "Why?"

"I don't know anything about the guy," I said. "I'm trying to figure out why he was killed." And I was trying to find out why Max thought he was heading for a long jail term.

"Harmony was killed because of faggot jealousy," Carney said. "Hardin's the one." He put the car in gear.

I let his bigoted remark slide down my back. "Hardin didn't do it."

"Bullshit." Carney looked over his shoulder and waited for another car to pass before he pulled out.

Chapter
8

After a hearty meal at an Italian restaurant around the corner, I headed for the Stud, that dark alcoholic haven for the ever horny. It was only a little after eight on a Thursday night, but the place was hopping. The weekend was approaching, the men were anxious, the music was loud, the pool table busy. I bought a beer and sidled my way to the back room. The darkness there was starting to heat up as well. By two, anyway. The duo of indistinguishable men was standing or kneeling in a shadowed corner feeding each other. I sipped my beer and left them to their evening meal, returning to the front of the bar.

I recognized a few numbers who were standing around and I chatted briefly. I wasn't exactly unknown in the bar, but I wasn't a devotee of the place, either. It was convenient for a quick beer after work and out of uniform. That is, when I had a steady job and a blue uniform. Now that I was working on my own and without a uniform, I hadn't found much time for a happy-hour beer.

I watched two guys playing pool. They were both lousy players and I probably could have beaten either one. But they were also ultramasculine with that animal attraction. When a shadow at the back room pushed itself out, I recognized Ron. He spotted me immediately and came over. His hair was disheveled, his knees dusty.

I smiled and said, "I didn't recognize you on your knees. You got here early."

Ron patted his long hair to neatness, brushed his knees. "The meeting wasn't as long as I expected," he said. He smiled at his friend, who emerged from the back room. The man smiled back, a smile of satisfaction, and moved on. "Had to release some frustrations—any way I could," Ron said. After a quick arrangement of his clothes, the friend left the bar from the back door, obviously contented with Ron's lip service.

"Are you that frustrated?"

"I'm going to resign from the presidency of G.A.A. next Wednesday," he said simply.

"Why?"

"I have to. I can't be president of G.A.A. and run for city office at the same time."

"What are you running for?"

"City councilman. First openly gay candidate," he said proudly.

"Why can't you run for office and still be president?"

"Our constitution prohibits it," he said.

"Who's going to become president now?"

"Helen. Acting president." He didn't sound happy. "First we lose a vice president. Now the president. But I don't have any choice," he said. "Next Thursday is the last day for filing." There was a small plea in his voice, but he brushed it off as quickly as he brushed the dust off his knees. "Well, I guess G.A.A. will survive."

"You don't have to justify your actions to me," I told him.

"I'm not justifying, I'm explaining. Max knew I was leaving to run for city council. The whole executive committee did."

"I understand there was a move to impeach Max."

Ron laughed. "Yeah. You been talking to Helen?" He didn't wait for an answer. "At one time or another every other officer in G.A.A. was going to be impeached. When Helen doesn't agree with what's being proposed, she suggests impeachment. Her solution," he said, disdainfully. "If she had her way, there'd be only one person running G.A.A. Her. That's no way to run an airline."

"But you didn't think Max would make a good president, either, did you?"

"Hell, no."

"But he was popular with the members," I said.

"So what?" Ron said. A defensive tone appeared in his voice.

"If you resigned, Max was next in line. An incumbent could easily be voted in come election time." I paused, then added, "An incumbent who was a spy?"

Ron looked at me warily. "You have been talking to Helen."

I didn't deny it. "You don't think Max was working under-cover?" I asked.

"No, I don't," he said emphatically and with a forced laugh. "Another of Helen's hallucinations."

"But still you didn't want Max to become president."

Ron didn't try to hide his annoyance or surprise. "What the hell are you saying?"

"What does it sound like I'm saying?"

"It sounds to me like you're saying I'm glad Max is dead." His stance dared me to disagree.

"No, I'm not. But I would guess you're glad he's not there to be the acting president."

Shock and disbelief crossed his face. Ron was an open book. "Are you hinting that I killed Max?"

"No, I'm not," I said again. I hadn't meant to, anyway. But that's all I said. I waited for Ron to continue.

"Well, I didn't kill him," he said. "Johnny. Look at Johnny," he almost shouted.

"What is this hang-up you have about Johnny? Just because he won't drop his pants for you?" I was surprised at my own defense of Johnny.

Ron almost laughed, but it came out as a snort. "That's stupid, Cain. And I don't have a hang-up on Johnny."

"He's certainly not just one of the boys," I said. "Not to you."

"He sure the fuck ain't." He voice was loud, too loud. He meant more than he said.

When a couple near us turned around, Ron shuffled his feet, reached in his shirt pocket, and took out a joint. He nodded for me to follow him into the back room. I did. He lit the joint and smoked feverishly, not offering me a toke.

I let him smoke. I waited. As the cannabis cluttered his brain, Ron gave a deep sigh. A horny stud covered from head to toe in black leather walked into the darkened room and wandered around, eyeing us. When he saw that neither of us was interested in action, he ambled off and out the door.

Ron bent over, stubbed the burning end of the joint on his boot heel, and pocketed the roach. "I'm sorry, Cain," he said. "Everything is getting to me. All at once. No, I didn't want Max to be president, but he wasn't a goddamn spy. He wouldn't be any good at it. I don't even think he wanted to be president. And I didn't kill him," he added strongly.

"And you think Johnny did," I said.

"I didn't say that," he said quickly and lit a cigarette.

"Didn't you?"

Two young numbers joined us in the dark. Both Ron and I grew silent. The two eyed us, but they weren't looking for company. They had already found it in each other, and we were inhibiting their action. I suggested to Ron we return up front.

When we exited the back room, Ron said, "I'm tired, Cain."

He looked tired. "Why are you so positive Johnny was involved in Max's death?"

"I don't know, Cain. I don't know." He shook his head wearily as if he hadn't even heard me. "I don't know what's going to happen to G.A.A. now, once I leave." His mind was occupied with G.A.A.; mine was occupied with murder.

"Are you that indispensable?"

There was hurt in Ron's eyes. "No, but I don't know who's going to take over."

"Helen," I said.

"She'll make a lousy president, too," he said, almost bitterly. "I'm not sure G.A.A. can survive her." His voice tried to build upon an energy his body was lacking.

"Is she a spy, too?" I asked facetiously.

Ron didn't smile, but his eyes were clear when he said, "I'd like to forget my troubles for a few hours. What did you want to see me about?"

"Was Max in any trouble with the law?"

"Every officer in G.A.A. is in trouble with the law. Or has been, anyway. We've all been arrested."

"No, I mean anything more serious."

Ron's brows furrowed into very thin, even, young lines. "Not that I know of."

"Did you know Max wanted to hire me as a bodyguard?"

"No," Ron answered. "Why would he do that?"

"I was hoping you'd tell me."

"I have no idea."

"Was he going to quit his job?"

"I doubt it. He wanted to get away from Davie, to get his own place. He couldn't afford to be out of work."

I tossed in a curve. "Were Max and Johnny going to bed together?"

Ron fielded it deftly. "That's a laugh. Well, at one time I thought they were making it together." He took a deep drag on his cigarette. "Maybe I was naive." He said those last words more to himself than to me. When he looked back to me again, he said, "Johnny was so hung up about sex that if he made it with anybody at G.A.A., I didn't hear about it. He kept his sex life quiet, if he had one at all. With Max? Never. He was friendly with Johnny, but that's all. And even that cooled. Sex between them? No. Johnny probably doesn't have sex with anybody, for that matter. Certainly not with me, damn it."

So, Ron did harbor a tiny flicker of unsatisfied flame for Johnny. "Max and Johnny couldn't have been carrying on without your knowing about it?"

"No," Ron answered. "Max would have told me. We had no secrets."

According to the diary, Max thought he was going to jail for a long time. If that was true, then he was going to leave his job. Yes, he did keep some secrets from Ron. And according to the diary, Max loved Johnny. No, Ron didn't know him at all.

"Did you ever make it with Johnny?" I asked him.

A small fury burned in Ron's eyes. It was a frustrated moment before he spoke. "No."

"But you wanted to," I said. "Crew cut and all."

Ron flattened his hands over his head, combing his locks. He straightened his shoulders, as if to stand at attention. "As much as you want to make it with him."

I blushed, but only on the inside. Was my attraction to Johnny that obvious? I didn't reply to Ron's unveiled accusation. "You won't tell me why you thought Johnny was following Max that night?" Looking over Ron's shoulder, I could see Johnny coming through the swinging doors and heading toward the bar. Ron didn't see him.

"Ask Johnny yourself," Ron said. "You might be surprised what you'll find out."

"That's exactly what I intend to do," I said, nodding in Johnny's direction.

Ron turned in time to see Johnny moving away from the crowd at the bar. Ron's face dropped and he laid his beer can on the shelf. "Thanks a fucking lot," he said contemptuously before scrambling out the back door.

Johnny approached, carrying three beer cans. He offered me one and I took it. He was wearing a blue and gold high school jacket. Out of place in a denim/leather dive, yet oddly alluring. "Where'd Ron cut out to?" he asked. He set one full can on the shelf and brought the other to his lips.

"I don't think he likes you very much," I said, sipping my beer.

"I have the same impression. I don't know why, either," he said. He wasn't very decisive when he said it. "He's changed."

"It seems everybody's changing."

"Including the times," Johnny said. "So Bob Dylan says."

"And you don't know why Ron has changed."

"Well, maybe," he said and turned around. "Let's sit down."

Johnny headed toward two recently vacated stools near the wall and at the entrance to the back room. I followed. We sat within viewing distance of the blackened sex cave. Traffic was steady now, bodies going in slowly, coming out quickly. The room was in the warming-up stage of a busy night. Johnny rested one hand on his knee and watched the shadowy figures in erotic engagement.

"I don't know how they do it," he said. "Having sex in public like that."

"It's no different than the trucks."

"That's for sure."

"You don't indulge?" I asked.

Johnny turned to face me. "Not in public."

"You were at the trucks the night Max was killed," I pointed out.

Did I detect a slight reddening of Johnny's face? If I did, it was very slight. Or maybe it was even the glow from the warm light atop the door. He sipped his beer.

"Did you follow Max that night?"

"I didn't."

"Listen, Johnny, I was there. And . . ." I paused, expecting an interruption. When I didn't get one, I continued. "I'm not the only one who knows you were hot for Max."

"Ron." Johnny laughed. An empty laugh. By way of explanation, he said, "I guess he doesn't like me because Max did."

"Max did what?"

Although our private little corner was dark, a blue neon light from a beer sign revealed Johnny's face, which flushed. Definitely, this time. And his eyes shone a dark blue. "Max liked me," he said.

"Did you like Max?"

"Yes," he said quietly and turned away. "Why did you want to see me?"

"I like you, too," I said. I hadn't planned to confess that, but there it was. Johnny looked at me. There was also a sly sexy tone in my voice, and it wasn't artificial. I'd been deliberately burying my attraction to him. But his naive, almost innocent reaction to the back room and the trucks was provocative.

Johnny didn't return my gaze. Not in the manner I would have liked, anyway. I felt him tense. "But that isn't why I asked you to meet me here." He sipped his beer, maybe even relaxed. "I want to know about Max."

"What about him?"

"How well did you know him?"

"I've been going to G.A.A. for only about three months."

"But you spent a lot of time with him," I said. I could have also added, "You followed him." But this time I swallowed the words.

"I didn't spend all that much time with him," he said. I sensed his defenses building up, like a slow, unseen, but very deliberate Berlin Wall. "I spend as much time with Ron or Helen."

I chugged some beer. "Max wanted to hire me as a body-guard."

Johnny chugged, too. "Did he?"

"You're not surprised?"

"Yes, I am." No, he wasn't.

By now the traffic toward the back room was boot to boot. Our stools were becoming a barrier to the parade of denim and leather. We left them and moved to a back wall where we had a full view of the pool table.

"You're not very active in G.A.A., are you?" I noted.

"I haven't missed a meeting yet," Johnny countered.

"How many demonstrations have you been in? Or zaps?"

"I work during the day. I have to make a living."

"Where do you work?"

"Why do you want to know?"

A crowd of five streamed through the back door, loud and boisterous and eager for another playful night in the city. Johnny and I again became an unwelcome barrier. We wormed our way into a far corner.

"Why are you so defensive?" I asked Johnny.

"Shit," he said, suddenly jumping forward and shouldering his way to the back of the bar. He picked up the can of beer that he had bought for Ron. The crowd thinned out briefly as the group of newcomers made a beeline to the back room without even buying a beer. I moved toward the pool table. When Johnny rejoined me, he said, "I thought you weren't working for G.A.A." The bartender must have turned his hidden knob. The music became annoyingly loud.

"I'm not working for G.A.A.," I told him, leaning into his ear. "I'm working for myself."

We were asked to move by a player who was trying to sink the nine ball in the side pocket. When I stepped back, another obnoxiously boisterous group came in through the back door. Johnny was shoved almost into my lap. And I was standing. I held him up, my chest against his back, my crotch against his ass. For a moment neither of us moved. I deliberately pressed myself closer to Johnny. For one brief second, he returned my awkward and backward caress by pressing his back into me. But he just as quickly stepped forward out of my reach. He didn't turn around. His back and shoulders became another Berlin Wall—trespass at your own risk.

I placed a hand on his shoulder and talked into his ear. Shouted. "Let's get the fuck out of here. It's too noisy."

We laid our beer cans on the shelf at the window and Johnny followed me through the back door. We stood outside the entrance, watching the early-evening parade of men in leather, of men in sneakers, of men and more men. Neither of us had a particular destination in mind. My apartment was only around the corner, but I didn't think Johnny would accept the invitation. I nodded toward the river.

"Is it wise to wear your gun in the bar?" Johnny asked as we slowly walked west. The cool autumn air was taking its toll on street cruising. The streets weren't empty, but you could see that the time for warm-weather cruising had passed. Winter cruising was upon us, bundled up, but only from waist to neck. Let no man, nor rain, nor snow, stop these men from wearing Levi's and showing them.

"The gun is part of my job," I said.

"What is your job?"

"Finding out who killed Max."

"I didn't kill him," Johnny said quickly, even though I didn't ask. He gave me a careful glance and we continued our walk toward the Hudson River in silence.

"You have a sensitive touch," I said after the silence became too uncomfortable.

"What do you mean?" Another shield thrown up between us.

"I wasn't giving it a sexual connotation. But you did feel the gun butt in my holster. And I thought I had it pretty well hidden." When Johnny didn't say anything to that, I continued. "Well, maybe it did have a sexual connotation, at that."

Johnny didn't say anything to that, either. I don't know why, but I was embarrassed by my attraction to him. And irked with him for ignoring that attraction. I cursed myself and tried to dismiss erotic thoughts from my mind. It wasn't easy. Johnny was probably a couple of years younger than I was. His hair was as closely cropped as a Green Beret's, totally out of date, yet not unfitting. His dungarees weren't Levi's, he wore sneakers and not boots, his jacket was suburban drab and boyish, and he didn't have a mustache. All in all, not someone I would be attracted to. Not my type, as they say. But yet I found the son of a bitch sexy. And no matter how I tried to dismiss the thought, my mind kept wandering into the bedroom with Johnny.

He broke my silent and frustrating reverie when he said, "I never had sex in the trucks."

93

An opening. "Then what were you doing there the night Max was killed?"

"Working up the courage," he said simply and, I thought, sadly.

"Do you have sex at all?" I asked.

He answered with a question. "What do you think?"

"I don't know," I said, perhaps too seriously.

We were approaching West Street. We could see the trucks. They weren't midnight busy yet, but early stragglers were checking them out. The cool autumn weather would not keep them out of the backs of the trucks. Neither would the snow. I know. I'd been there when white covered the ground and no cars could move.

"The trucks are a convenient place to get your rocks off," I said. I realized after I said it that Johnny might construe my words as an invitation. I didn't mean them that way. I wanted Johnny, but not at the trucks. I quickly veered the subject into another direction, a somewhat nostalgic direction. "My God, I remember coming down here before the bars really got started on Christopher Street. Must have been six, seven years ago when I used to come over here from Brooklyn."

"You used to live in Brooklyn?"

"And work."

"What kind of work did you do?"

I smiled at him, a careful, playful smile. "You wouldn't tell me where you worked," I said. But I realized how childish I was becoming and quickly added, "I was a cop."

"A city cop?" Johnny asked. He could have also asked, "What happened?" The tone was there.

"When I was in Brooklyn, I came out of the closet."

Johnny was astounded. "Why?"

"Why?" I said to myself and Johnny. "For over ten years I'd been . . . been fooling around with men. Just trade at first. Like everybody else. They could touch me all they wanted. But I'd never touch them. Then I became an active partner. I just got tired of hiding my life. There's no doubt that the gay liberation movement, that Stonewall, spurred me along," I

94

said, waving a hand, encompassing the entire Village. "Naive as I was, I didn't think my coming out would make a damn bit of difference in the department, to anyone but me." I laughed, remembering, cynical. "I was wrong. Before you could say Cock Robin, I was pushed out of Brooklyn and into the Village. As my former commanding officer in Brooklyn said when he told me about the new assignment, 'Since you're a fag, you might as well work where all the fags are. It might be a smart move on your part.' I think he actually believed that he was doing me a favor by transferring me to the Village."

I hadn't planned on telling Johnny my life story. In fact, I hadn't talked to anyone about the entire episode. Not even Larry. My words came too easy.

"It didn't work out?" Johnny asked.

"No," I said, capping my blubbering mouth. But I opened it again. "I was on the streets on patrol for one night. One lousy fucking night. And I was attacked. Not by muggers, by men in blue."

"Your own men?"

"Not mine. But, yes, cops. The next day the captain put me behind a desk, a woman on one side of me, another on the other. I was expected to stay there for the rest of my uniformed life."

"Do you know who jumped you?"

"Yes, but it didn't matter. They all jumped me, if not with fists, with their eyes, with their silent words." My own words were tasting bitter and I didn't like remembering. "I quit," I said, fumbling for a cigarette. I lit it after three tries.

Johnny didn't pursue the subject. His own mind seemed to be lost in his own thoughts.

"I never had a lover." I was surprised the words came out of my mouth.

"Why not?"

Johnny was easy to talk to. "I don't know. Never had the chance, I guess. Too busy hopping from one trick to another, having too much fun." Fun, I thought. I can't even remember their faces. Or their bodies, for that matter. I didn't want to think about it.

"There used to be pony rides over there," I said, and pointed to an empty sand lot near some parked trucks.

"Really?" Johnny said, snapping himself out of his own thoughts, and me out of mine.

"Really," I said, smiling. It seemed a lifetime ago when a trailer was camped in that empty lot, the Gypsies, or whoever, selling pony rides for the kids. "I guess I began coming here when the trucks first started heating up."

"Why the trucks?" Johnny asked. "You're a good-looking guy. You shouldn't have any trouble finding somebody to go home with."

"There's no emotional involvement at the trucks," I said. I scared myself when I said it. I never even realized I thought it. Was I afraid to get seriously involved with another man? I quickly tossed that thought in the trash. I was feeling too comfortable with Johnny, opening up too much. A bad trait for a cop, even a private one. I changed the subject. "What kind of work do you do, Johnny?"

"Assistant manager," he said.

I thought he'd continue. When he didn't, I asked, "Of what?"

"A flea market on Canal Street."

I almost stopped in my tracks. "Ole Times?" I asked.

Johnny did stop. He stared at me. "How'd you know that?"

I tossed my cigarette butt, lit another, and offered Johnny one. He refused and lit his own. "I didn't know it. But it's the only flea market I know of that's on Canal Street," I said. "I had a job down there."

"What kind of job?"

"Confidential," I told him.

We continued our walk. Johnny in silence, me in thought. We stopped at West Street. Across the street was the pier where Max was killed. Neither of us wanted to revisit the scene. We headed north, skirting the docks.

After two more long blocks of silence, I broke it. "You know, Max was in love with you."

Johnny turned his head to look at me. "I know."

96

"Did he tell you?"

"No," Johnny said.

"Then how do you know?"

"Come on. When someone is in love with you, you can tell."

"Yeah," I said.

"And," Johnny continued, "Davie came to see me."

It was my turn to eye him.

"He told me I was breaking up a happy home," Johnny said.

"Were you?"

"No. The home wasn't happy. And," he added, "I wasn't breaking it up. I told Davie that. I didn't set out to steal Max from him. I told Davie that, too. That's all he wanted to hear. It was a quick conversation."

"You didn't love Max." It wasn't a question.

Johnny shook his head and said quietly, "No, I didn't."

"And you weren't the jealous type," I said, again not a question.

"Jealous of what?"

"Of who," I corrected. "Why were you following Max and me that night?"

We were at 14th Street. We turned the corner and headed east.

"I wasn't following you, Archie," he stated.

It was the first time Johnny had used my first name. "Then why were you at the trucks?"

"Why were you?"

"To get a blowjob," I said.

"Well?"

"You just said anonymous sex wasn't your style."

"When you gotta, you gotta." He tried a small laugh, but it didn't ring true.

"You're full of shit," I said.

"What do you want, Cain?"

It was Cain now, not Archie. We headed north again, up Eighth Avenue.

"You never even went to bed with Max, did you?"

"Yes, I did," he said quickly.

97

"Where? At the trucks?"

"No."

"Certainly not at Max's place. Not with Davie there twenty-four hours a day." I didn't give him a chance to answer, quickly adding, "And not at the YMCA."

"How'd you know I live at the Y?"

"I'm a private eye, remember," I said with a smile, which I think Johnny accepted. "I didn't know the rooms at the Y had private phones."

"They do if you pay to have them installed," he said, then asked again, "How'd you know I lived there?"

Another smile, from my side of the street.

"And why are you carrying that gun?" Johnny asked. "And in a bar."

We turned the corner onto 23rd Street and could see the lights that led to Seventh Avenue. Large, bright red lights graced both sides of the street. One side blared, CHELSEA HOTEL. The other challenged with YMCA.

When I didn't answer his question, Johnny said, "When you pressed against me at the bar, I felt it, you know that. Why were you wearing the gun at the bar?"

He seemed to enjoy the memory of my pressing up against him. Or maybe I just wanted him to. "I hoped that wasn't the only hard thing you felt."

Johnny shook his head. "You son of a bitch. Is that all you think about?" From someone else, those words might have revealed a come-on. With Johnny, they revealed annoyance.

"What do you think about?" I asked.

Johnny had stopped. We were in front of the Y. I put one foot on a step, hoping to be invited inside. "I'm thinking about why you're asking all these questions," Johnny said, not moving to join me on the stairs. His voice had changed. And while it wasn't exactly friendly again, it wasn't defensive, either.

"Somebody has to ask," I said. "Davie didn't kill Max."

"No, huh?"

"No. And G.A.A. is trying to raise money to free him," I pointed out. "You're G.A.A."

"Not everybody at G.A.A. agrees on everything the organization does," he said, closing the issue.

There were two bicycles parked alongside the building. I waited for Johnny to climb the stairs. He didn't, and he didn't avert his eyes from mine either.

"I can't invite you inside," he said quietly, but I thought he wanted to. I hoped he wanted to. He nodded to the door. "They have rules."

"Do you want to?" I asked, a smile forming on my lips. Not an eager smile but, I hoped, a warm one.

A warm one was returned. "Yes, but . . ." He turned his face away from mine.

"We can go to my place," I offered.

Johnny's smile vanished, but his changeable mellow mood didn't. "I can't," he said. "Listen, Archie, I . . ."

It was Archie again. I was pleased. "But you do want to," I said. It was a challenge.

Johnny hesitated but finally said. "Yes, I do." Again, quietly.

"You wanted to with Max, too, didn't you?"

His jaw became firm. I could almost see his teeth crunch together. "Yes," he said, not opening his mouth.

"But you didn't, did you?"

It was only a slight nod of his head, but the meaning was clear. "No," he said. He walked up the stairs and I waited until the glass door closed behind him. Inside, safe, behind the glass, Johnny briefly turned to look at me. We stared at each other, maybe even with longing. He turned away first.

As I walked toward Seventh Avenue, I smiled inside. Johnny was a confused virgin. And I was just confused.

I reached the corner and headed north. I found an empty phone booth at 31st Street. Sidney's voice was sweet and oh so British when he answered the phone.

"Hello, Sidney. This is Cain."

The sweetness turned sour and, almost in a whisper, Sidney asked, "What do you want?"

"I'd like to speak to Maureen."

His voice was sharp. "About what?"

I heard a background voice. Female. Maureen. "Who is it, Sidney?"

I realized what Sidney was afraid of. "Relax, Sidney. What was said between you and me will stay between you and me. What I want to talk to Maureen about has nothing to do with you and Max."

"It's for you, Maureen," I heard Sidney say. "Archie Cain." It was an unsteady voice that said it.

Maureen's voice came on the line. Again, very British, and also very loud. "Yes, Cain. What do you want? It's ten-thirty, you know."

Her attitude irked me. "It's also New York City."

"What do you want?"

"Max quit his job, didn't he?" I said. "Just before he was killed. Why?"

The words were barely out of my mouth when the click sounded in my ear. I didn't bother to call back. I walked uptown.

The movie houses on 42nd Street were well lit, but the films they displayed on their marquees were showing their age, or the changing demeanor of the street. Too many kung-fu movies I'd never heard of, and too many straight fuck movies.

A contented sense of nostalgia ran through my mind as I walked up the deuce and past the movie houses. It seems this was my night for remembering. First the trucks, now the deuce. This was the street where I discovered gay sex. Could ten years have passed already? Yes, they surely could. My family lived in Jersey then, but we often visited the big city. Mom and Dad went shopping after they dropped me off on the strip to see a movie. They'd pick me up five hours later in front of the Port Authority Bus Terminal. On the way home, I'd tell them about the movie I saw but not about the friendly men who sat next to me, rubbing my knee.

This is the street where I met Larry, too. Small world. I don't even remember which movie house it was.

For old times' sake, I went to the Empire Theatre and paid

my admission. For old times' sake, yeah sure. And a frustration with Johnny that I couldn't define. An old lousy Roman Empire movie was playing. It didn't matter. I didn't go there to see the movie.

I was disappointed in the prospects standing around the darkened balcony. There weren't many, and no one I would approach. Not like the old days.

I climbed to the second balcony, with little hope. But all I needed was a little. One was enough. And he was there. A young man, a horny man, a daring man. He tasted delicious. I was home by midnight.

Chapter
9

On Saturday morning, I lounged in bed for an extra hour. There was no need to hurry. I already had my schedule planned. Even if I didn't get out of bed until nine, I'd still have plenty of time. I dozed on and off for another hour and was up by eight-thirty.

The eggs in the refrigerator had been standing too long, but I fried a couple anyway, along with four slices of bacon and a couple pieces of toast. I washed the dirty dishes, left them to dry, then slapped my holster under my brown leather jacket and subwayed uptown.

It was a little after ten o'clock when I stood on West End Avenue in front of the Merediths' apartment house. An old woman came out with a small dachshund on a leash. She held the door for me and smiled. A friendly smile. Trusting soul. Poor soul. I smiled back. The door slammed shut and locked behind me.

The elevator took me to the thirteenth floor, nonstop. Sidney answered the door after I pressed the buzzer. He was naked except for a pair of very wrinkled and very sexy light blue boxer shorts. He stared with bulging eyes for a good two seconds before reacting. "I thought you were the delivery man. What do you want?" Again, that uneasy, almost panicked trepidation.

"Sidney, I'm not going to expose you," I said. "I just want to talk—"

"Expose me as what? There's nothing to expose. Please, Cain." The last two words were a plea from the top of his blond head to his bare toes, and blue boxers in between.

I stepped past him into the living room. A fairly large room with simple wooden furniture, a large couch, and no rug. Sidney closed the door behind me.

"Maureen isn't here. She went to the office," Sidney said rapidly.

He looked down at himself, suddenly realizing that I was dressed and he wasn't. He took a step toward another room, but it was only a small step. He stopped himself and decided to remain half naked, I guess.

"Sidney, I told you that conversation we had about your sex life was just between you and me. What I want to see Maureen about has nothing to do with sex."

Doubting eyes. "You sure?"

"If I wanted to talk about sex, I wouldn't do it with a woman," I said and smiled.

Sidney gave off a slight laugh and an insecure shrug of his entire body. "She won't be back until tonight. She's working." He seemed undecided, but finally he made a friendly offer. "Want some coffee?"

"I'd love it," I said, and followed him to the kitchen.

The coffee was on the stove in an old metal pot. Very homey. Sidney reached into the cabinet for two mugs. He was tempting in his wrinkled shorts, the splattering of dark hair on his chest, the warm-looking hair under his armpits, his morning-tossed straw head of hair. When Sidney set the mugs on the table, he noticed me staring at him with admiring eyes. I probably would have blushed if I had remembered how. That's okay, Sidney turned red enough for both of us. His movements were stiff when he reached inside the refrigerator for a carton of milk. He knew he was being appraised. But he didn't make a move to go get dressed. "Sugar?" he asked.

"No," I said. Sidney sat across from me at a small metal table like one my grandmother used to have in her kitchen.

For a business couple who corresponded with senators and congressmen, these two people live pretty shabbily, I thought. Oh, no doubt the apartment cost a pretty penny per month. But they had a thing or two to learn about decorating. Yeah, the kitchen reminded me of my grandmother's. It had the warmth. It was old-fashioned and careless. It seemed that *Current Social Thought* was not a money-making enterprise.

"Take off your jacket," Sidney said.

"No, that's okay." I kept it on.

Sidney sat across from the table, sipping his coffee, naked from the waist up. His eyes tried to avoid mine but didn't succeed. I sat opposite, my heavy jacket covering my chest and my gun.

"Have you ever been to G.A.A.?" I asked him.

He shook his head and said, "No."

"They can help you."

"Help me? In what way?"

His English accent lent him an aura of casual, if affected, comfort. "To find your way in the gay world," I told him.

"There is no gay world for me, Cain." He almost laughed. He was starting to relax. "I couldn't do that. I told you, I'm an alien. The feds wouldn't let me stay in this country for one second if they knew I was gay. And I'm not," he emphasized. I thought he was finished, but he said more, barely audible. "It's not that easy."

"Nothing in life ever is," I said.

"I'm not homosexual," Sidney insisted. "I'm bisexual."

He didn't sound very convincing. "Yeah, sure."

Sidney didn't debate me. There was nothing to debate. He knew the truth as well as I.

"Was Max the only man you ever went to bed with?" I asked, enjoying the good coffee. I corrected myself. "That you ever had sex with."

"I never went down on him," Sidney told me sharply.

A familiar attitude. I had it once. I could have sex with more men than I could count, but if I remained passive, I wasn't queer, I was only getting my rocks off. "Your time will come," I said, my eyes smiling at Sidney over the rim of the cup.

"I never went down on any man," Sidney was quick to assure me.

"Then you have had sex with other guys besides Max?"

"No," he snapped. "Max. I loved him. I . . ." He stopped. He couldn't believe his own words.

"Max didn't love you," I pointed out.

Sidney shook his head. Tears in his eyes were ready to spill over. This man is too sensitive, I realized, for someone who lives in the big city. "But . . . but . . ." He never finished. Those unshed tears were sponged back into his head to be replaced by bitter words. "But he wouldn't . . . he wouldn't . . ." He stopped again, then abruptly added another "he wouldn't," adamantly closing the subject.

I opened it again. "No matter how hard you persisted."

When Sidney looked at me again, his eyes were rock hard. "He told me, no more. We weren't going to do . . . it . . . again. Ever."

"And did he mean it?"

"Yes. It was that Johnny," Sidney blurted out. "That son of a bitch. Max said he and Johnny were . . ." I thought Sidney was going to bawl. "Johnny is the one," he continued. "Max wouldn't even let me . . . he and Johnny . . . just him and Johnny . . . all the time."

"He stopped having sex with you because of Johnny?"

Sidney almost screamed. "But it didn't matter, anyway." On the verge of hysteria, he drew in a deep breath, his chest expanded fully. He held it, then exhaled, deflated. He caught the outburst before it escaped. His voice was calm, controlled, too controlled. "I was only stringing Max along," he said.

Sidney was convincing himself his lies were real.

"I wanted to see how far the bastard would lower himself," he continued. "I'm glad he quit. I didn't love him. I'd never love any man."

"Then Max did quit his job."

"I didn't say that."

"Somebody did. And it wasn't me."

"I meant I'm glad Maureen was going to fire him. I hated Max." He seemed ashamed that he said the words. I heard the faraway sounds of traffic on the street. Quietly, he added, "Yeah, Max told me he was going to quit. And I told Maureen."

"Did he tell you why?"

"No. I didn't ask. Max meant nothing to me."

The wall Sidney was erecting around himself was becoming too strong. I wondered if he'd ever let it down, to see his own truth, to face himself. Denial, denial. But only to himself. I hated to see him go that route. I hated to see any man go that route. But now was not the time to rebuild. The hysteria that peeped through was still simmering. I tried gentle persuasion.

"Sidney, I've been there. I know what it's like. Believe me. With me it was in the movies on Forty-second Street. A blow-job from a man was as easy to get as a candy bar. And all that time, I told myself I was straight and could stop anytime I wanted. But the thing is, I never wanted to. For two years." Another sip, then I tried another smile. "Until I became the blower."

Sidney's entire body reddened. At least the part of it that was above the table. Even the shiny hairs on his chest seemed to become a sharp rust. "In the movies!" he exclaimed. "I don't believe it." His innocence was compelling.

"The trucks aren't the only place to go for quick sex," I said.

"What trucks?"

"The trucks where Max was killed."

Sidney's face was pained at the reminder.

"What does Maureen think of your double life?" I asked him.

He sat up straight. "What do you mean?" I didn't answer. "What life? She doesn't know." A mass of converging contradictions.

"If you believe that, you're only kidding yourself," I told him.

"She doesn't know. And it doesn't matter. We never have sex anymore, anyway."

He looked at me with guilty eyes. He was telling tales out of school.

I finished my coffee and stood up. "A helluva marriage," I said and walked out of the kitchen to the living room. Before I opened the door, Sidney asked, "Where are you going?" He was right behind me.

I turned to him. "I have business to take care of. I didn't come to see you, I came to see your wife."

"We have a good marriage, Cain. Sex isn't the only reason to get married. We love each other. We need each other."

He was talking to himself. And he was reciting a litany. A familiar litany. I cut him off. "If you loved her so much, why were you pestering Max? Is that why he was going to quit?" I didn't expect an answer and wasn't disappointed when none was forthcoming. "Who are you trying to convince, Sidney, me or yourself? If you're trying to convince me, I don't believe you. If you're trying to convince yourself, you won't."

"But Maureen and I do need each other," he insisted. He insisted too strongly. "You don't understand," he said, disgusted.

"Then why do you hang out at the trucks after hours?"

His eyes went into shock. He brushed his hair out of his eyes. "I don't. I would never go down there. It's dangerous." Again, not very convincing.

Before I closed the door, I looked back at Sidney. He was slightly green. Blond hair, blue eyes, flushed body, blue shorts. A rainbow of a man.

Chapter
10

I walked the short distance to 77th Street. My mind was crowded with thoughts of Sidney. Confused Sidney. Frightened Sidney. Sidney, who can't come to grips with his homosexual feelings. "Pain in the ass" Sidney, as Max had written in his diary. Sidney, the closet case. Max, the liberationist. Two extremes in the same gay world.

I was sure Sidney knew about the trucks. They would be the perfect shadow for protecting his identity. He couldn't see or know who did him, they couldn't see or know him.

Even before I climbed the stone steps, I could see that the room was occupied by more than one person. Maureen was sitting behind the desk on the receiving end of a lecture. A man was leaning into the desk. When Maureen made a move to interrupt him, she was cut off with loud words that I couldn't hear and an angry gesture that I could see. A hand swept through the air, dismissing any interruption.

The man sweeping the arm and doing the talking wore a dark brown suit with an overcoat flung over his arm. His back was to me. His hair was crew-cut short and almost gray. I climbed the steps and walked into the hallway. I was about to interrupt the one-way conference with a loud rap on the glass, but I stopped. I saw the profile of the man who was browbeating Maureen. The shock of recognition pulled my hand down in midair, and I quickly stepped out of view. The man in the brown suit was Mr. Sinbad, my former client.

My mind took a U-turn and landed in a corner. Was this a coincidence? What the hell was going on here? I didn't stand

107

around to figure it out. I quickly stepped pass the glass door and skipped two at a time down the stairs to the sidewalk, walking toward Broadway, rather confused.

I stopped at the corner, lit a cigarette, and waited. But not for long. Sinbad came bounding down the steps of the brownstone, buttoning his topcoat. He turned and walked in my direction. I turned toward an empty phone booth, pulled open the paneled door, stepped inside, and closed it. I deposited a dime and dialed my office. By the time Sinbad was at the corner, not four paces from me, my answering service was on the line. I muttered, "No message," and watched Sinbad hail a cab.

To hail another cab and to follow is not an easy task in New York City. In detective books and movies, trailing cab-to-cab works like the proverbial charm. But in real life, with the constant flowing daytime traffic and New York City drivers, the trek is almost impossible. Besides, no other taxi was immediately available. I couldn't even try to follow. So much for playing paperback detective.

I hung up the phone and walked back down 77th Street. Maureen was still at her desk, this time alone. She wasn't writing, she wasn't reading, she wasn't talking on the telephone. She was sitting, her hands folded and cupped in front of her mouth, her eyes lowered. It took her a second to become aware of my rap on the glass. She looked up and toward me. But her eyes weren't seeing me. I waited. When recognition finally dawned, she reached under her desk and buzzed me in. Was that a new safety addition? I walked into the office.

She didn't rise from her desk. "Didn't Sidney give you enough information?" she asked. Belligerence was the order of the day.

Briefly I was taken aback, thinking Sidney may have called her after my morning visit to him. Then I realized she was referring to the other day. "I want to talk to you, not Sidney," I said.

She hefted the palms of her hands onto the top of her desk and lifted herself out of the chair, as if she had the weight of the world on her shoulders. The ponytail that hung down her back was as taut as the set of her jaws. But the jaws sprang free. "What do you want to talk about?" Weary acceptance. "If it's about Max, there's nothing to tell that you don't already know."

"And if it isn't about Max?"

She straightened up. Her eyes changed from weariness to caution. "What do you want, Cain? Make it quick. I'm a busy woman."

"Do you always work on Saturday?"

"Only when I want to. What the hell do you want?" It was a demand.

"Sidney is the editor. Why should you do all the work?"

"Because I'm better at it." She came from behind the desk. "Look, Cain, if you have something to say, say it. If you have something to ask, ask it. Then leave. And be damn quick about it." A snappy British brush-off. She walked to the door and opened it.

Her English accent wasn't as provocative as Sidney's. In fact, it wasn't provocative at all. But the tone wasn't belligerent anymore, either. Her weariness had returned.

"Why were you going to fire Max?"

"Did Sidney tell you that?" It was almost a laugh.

I didn't answer.

"Sidney and Max were . . . friends, should I say. Why would I fire him?" Even through her weariness, a secretive smile formed over her face. "Sidney liked Max."

So much for Sidney's deep, dark, closeted secret. "Liked?"

"Come on, Cain. You're gay yourself. Am I that stupid? Sidney isn't fooling anyone but himself." Her outward thoughts briefly disappeared inside. Her eyes returned briefly to mine. "He's the fool. Sidney and I haven't had a real marriage for years." Realizing the door was still open, she closed it, but she didn't move back to her desk.

"It's the way we live," she continued by way of explanation. "I prefer it that way, and so does Sidney."

"Do you have a choice?"

"Of course I have a choice. I could divorce him. But why?" She didn't wait for a reply. "I don't need sex to fulfill my life."

"It's a good thing, because Sidney wasn't going to give it to you. Sex, that is. Not when he had a man on hand. Conveniently on hand, I might add."

"Max." She said the word with contempt.

"Another man isn't easy for a woman to take. That is, if the other man belongs to her husband."

Maureen laughed. A long, loud, false laugh.

"Don't be an ass, Cain. I wasn't jealous of Max. If Sidney found someone he could . . . someone who could . . . who satisfied him . . ." She trailed off, then returned from a different direction. "Maybe Max was even good for Sidney."

"*Was* Max good for Sidney?"

"Then again, maybe not," she answered. Her voice wasn't at full force this time. "And their relationship wasn't serious. You should know that. Max played with Sidney because he was convenient. Honestly, don't you people have any shame?"

"You mean, going after a married man?"

She dismissed the idea. "No, having sex on the run, behind desks . . ." She gestured to the door behind her. "In toilets. In trucks. Did Sidney really think I didn't know?"

My question exactly, so I didn't have to answer it.

"Sidney had his fling," she continued. "So what." She shook her head. "But he was a fool. He still is, for that matter."

"He's your husband."

"Yes, he is. And he'll stay that way." A small sadness crept into her eyes. "If that's what he wants, so much the better. It's out of my hands."

"Better for Sidney?" I asked. No answer. "Better for you?"

"Yes, better for me."

"Are you a lesbian?"

A laugh burst out of her small frame. The sound was loud and clear, all sadness gone. "If a woman doesn't want a man, that doesn't necessarily mean she's a lesbian. No."

"Okay. And you weren't jealous of Max. So why were you going to fire him?"

110

"I wasn't," she said strongly.

"Max thought so."

"Max knew better," she threw back at me.

"Sidney thought so."

"That's what I wanted Sidney to think."

"Why was Max afraid to come back to work?"

"Was he?"

"Yes." I didn't know for a fact that Max was afraid to go back to work, but according to his diary, he couldn't or didn't want to go to the office. What was it he wrote? "I can't go back to work." I doubt if it was fear of Sidney's persistence that was scaring Max. And diaries don't lie. If Max hadn't quit his job, he'd certainly been on the verge.

The telephone rang. Maureen hesitated, then walked back to her desk and picked up the receiver.

I looked around the office, this time without utilizing the narrow beam of a tiny flashlight. Numerous books were scattered on shelves, sloppily placed, both the books and the shelves. Most of the books looked as if they hadn't ever been handled. The seats of several wooden chairs were filled with manuscripts or pamphlets or more books. As I peered through the window to the outside world, I wondered how Maureen could work in full view of the street and the passing public. I also kept my ears attuned to the conversation behind me.

"Yes," Maureen said into the phone. She turned her back to me, her voice low. I moved closer.

"How did you know that?" she asked. An explanation was given at the other end. "Yes," she said again. Another pause, then another "Yes." Then, "No, I'll be going." She replaced the receiver, no good-bye.

"Don't you find it awkward to work out of a storefront window?" I asked to satisfy my curiosity.

She leaned her small frame back in her chair, her hand still on the telephone. "Who are you?" she asked.

Her tone was too thoughtful. I tried to lighten it. "Archie Cain, private eye."

She leaned up and asked again, "Who are you?" This time

111

I didn't speak. She suddenly said, "We have nothing to hide. If the FBI wants to spy on us, they could look right in our window." She sat back in her chair, her eyes on me. Her accusing eyes.

"You think I'm from the FBI?"

"It wouldn't be the first time," she said.

"It would be for me. Your informant was all wet," I said, snapping a finger at the phone.

She arose, a triumphant glare, or sneer, on her face. "Okay, you want to know about our setup. Here's next week's schedule. Yes, I am going to Washington on Monday. And I will testify before the Senate Select Committee on the Inner Cities. If you want to know what I'll say, be in hearing room seventeen-A on Monday at ten-thirty A.M. Now get the hell out of here, you bastard."

She stomped to the door and held it wide open, a hand on her hip.

I started to walk out, but I decided I had to ask. "Who was that man who was in here before me?"

"There was no one here."

"Yes, there was."

"Get out," she said.

When I walked past her, she said, mocking, "Using poor Max as an excuse to harass us." She shook her head.

I stopped, her face only inches from mine. Her eyes were dead serious. I moved on by and walked out without a word of good-bye, from me or from Maureen. I wanted to laugh. Her paranoia was overblown and sky high. And whoever tipped her off on the telephone gave her the wrong tip. I wondered if Sinbad had seen me before he hopped a cab. And what the hell was he doing there in the first place? Or was that Sidney on the other end of that phone call?

It was almost noon, and I stopped at a small greasy spoon for a quick burger. While my burger was being boiled in oil, I called Larry.

"You sound like you just got up," I said.

"I did," Larry said. "My God, what time is it?"

"Noon."

"It's Saturday," Larry groaned, almost in despair.

"No shit," I said. "Just double-checking. Tonight, the dance at the firehouse."

"I told you I'd be going."

Larry was not his usual flamboyant self. He never is when the telephone wakes him out of a sound sleep or takes him away from a good fuck. The way he was moaning, I would guess it was not the latter.

"Hold on a minute," Larry said, and the phone went silent. My greased and burned burger was set in front of my seat at the counter. I nodded at the counterman.

"Okay," Larry's voice came back on the line. "At least I know I'm alive. I can't stand to talk with a mouth full of cotton. So what are you doing up so early on Saturday?" A healthy yawn.

"Some people have to work for a living," I said. "And I have—"

Larry cut me off. "Oh, yeah, that reminds me. Can we meet at ten tonight? I want to stop at Drones. I might be able to get a job as doorman."

When Larry wasn't acting in a play off-off Broadway, and for very little money, he does odd jobs. And I mean odd. He was a clown in Central Park for a mime troupe. He was an attendant at a gay bathhouse on the Lower East Side. He was an usher in a movie house on 42nd Street. (But that didn't last long. He was fired for sucking a guy off in the balcony.) He's distributed fliers for a topless bar in Times Square.

"Sure," I said. "No problem. I'll be over your place by ten."

"No, I'll pick you up," he said. "You're always late and I can't afford to sit around waiting for an aging queen to put on her face for the world."

"Me, late? You bitch," I said. "Hell, if you were ever on time for anything in your life, it was probably in the tearoom at the Thirty-fourth Street station during rush hour."

"No, honey. Then I was early." Larry was wide awake and swinging. "To get a front-row seat."

"In the cubicle with the biggest glory hole this side of Brooklyn."

"The bigger the better, honey," Larry whispered seductively.

"But smaller is nicer," I countered.

"You should know," Larry snapped back.

My burger was getting cold. "Suck dick, bitch."

"I can't. I'm all alone this morning. Ah, me, will wonders never cease? This is the first time in years that I've opened my eyes and not seen some gorgeous brown number laying next—"

"Hey, guy, I gotta go." It was my turn to cut off. This could have gone on for hours. Larry's a telephone freak. I'm not. For me the telephone is a tool, not an instrument of pleasure. "Like I said, business. Ten, my place, right?"

"Of course," Larry said. "I've never been late a day in my life. Except for the time Deno was staying with me and his—"

Again, I cut him off with a laugh and a quick "See you later." I laid the telephone back in the cradle, went back to the counter, and feasted on cold greasy burger.

Chapter 11

The flea market on Canal Street was crowded, and not all the people were browsers. Saturday was buying-and-selling day. I walked through the entire three floors, searching for an office to no avail. Glenn's booth with the genuine imitation, but legal, Mahana carvings was less crowded than many of the others. One man was browsing and turning over Glenn's statuettes, but Glenn obviously didn't think him a serious buyer. He was sitting on a folding chair on the outer corner of his booth,

114

reading the *Post*. He looked up and spotted me. I'm not sure he recognized me. He didn't smile or say hello.

"How's it going?"

"How you been?" Glenn replied, laying the newspaper on his lap. "Cain, right?"

"Right."

"Make up your mind?" he asked, nodding at the merchandise.

"Yeah," I said, then added, "No. They're not my style."

"What is your style?" he asked. His eyes rested on my brown leather jacket, the holster hidden underneath.

I wasn't here to cruise. "Where's the office in this fucking place?"

"Upstairs," Glenn said. "Behind the World's Fair booth. Who do you want to see? The manager isn't here on Saturday."

"How about the assistant manager?"

"Yeah, Johnny should be here."

"Thanks, Glenn," I said. I started to leave, turned, and asked, "Do you know Sinbad Imports?"

It lasted only a swift second. But in that second, Glenn's body tensed. He covered it. "No," he answered. "Why?"

"See you later," I said. I winked to show him I knew he was lying.

I again climbed to the third floor. The World's Fair setup was the most striking booth in the entire building, with Art Deco posters from the '39 Fair predominant on the walls and a large metal model of the Unisphere in the middle of a round aluminum table. I sidled behind the booth and, sure enough, there was a door with a small sign that read MANAGER.

I knocked. An annoyed voice from within said, "Yeah?" It was Johnny's annoyed voice. I opened the door and walked in.

It was a grimy office with a desk that had seen better days, many dented and rusted filing cabinets, chairs that were broken, crumbling cardboard boxes overflowing with junk. Johnny was sitting behind the desk and, in contrast to his surroundings, he was as neat as a pin, although he did wear dungarees. But they looked neatly pressed, like they had just

115

come back from the cleaner's. And they still weren't the dungarees that Mr. Strauss invented. A smile lit up his eyes when he saw me. "Archie," he exclaimed. The annoyance I heard in his tone outside the door was gone.

I sat on a wobbly chair facing his desk. Johnny smiled. "It's good to see you. What can I do for you? Don't tell me you're thinking about renting a booth here. Business that bad?"

"No," I said. "In fact, business is good. Too good. I have more customers than I can handle." I thought about the unanswered letter I sent to the heir in California and the thrift shop job I was to start next week and that auctioned painting I was supposed to be checking out.

"I, ah, enjoyed our talk last night," Johnny said. "It gave me a lot of food for thought."

I wanted to tell him that I felt the same. I seldom ever open up to anyone. It was an unusual experience for me. But I wasn't exactly comfortable having told my life story to Johnny, who, after all, was basically a stranger. A stranger with connections to murder. Yet I liked him. Maybe too much. I sat on those feelings, at least temporarily.

Johnny shrugged. "Well?"

I waited two beats. "Max was afraid of you."

"Afraid?" Johnny said, surprised. "Was he?"

"I think he was," I said. At least, that's what Max's diary had implied. And, again, diaries don't lie.

Johnny caught the serious note in my voice. "I doubt it."

"Don't doubt it. He was scared."

"Maybe he was afraid that Davie was jealous of our relationship."

"What exactly was your relationship?"

"Friends," Johnny insisted. "Listen, Archie, we went through all this last night."

"Maybe you weren't lovers, but you were more than friends."

"We never even went to bed together," Johnny said quietly.

"But you wanted to."

"Max wanted to."

"And you didn't?"

I could see the wheels spinning, but he didn't speak. The grinding wheels were reflected in the lock of his jaw. Still no answer, merely a searching stare. "Why didn't you and Max ever make it together? Everybody thought you were, anyway." I thought of Sidney. Johnny returned only silence. "You're afraid, too, aren't you?" I asked.

"Of what?"

"Men."

Johnny shook his head. "No," he said, trying to be offhand in his answer. "And I wasn't afraid of Max."

"Of sex?" I offered as a suggestion.

Again the well-controlled grinding of the teeth. My God, first Sidney, deep and fearful in the closet. Now Johnny. Not in the closet, but not out, either. And fearful nevertheless.

"I . . ." Johnny started to say. I waited. "I . . ." He stopped trying. His body lost confidence. His shoulders slumped.

"Have you ever been to bed with any man?" I asked.

A tiny sharp shake of his head, an admission of homosexual virginity. My initial observation was correct.

"Why not?"

A deep intake of breath. He lifted his hands to stop my words. "Archie, I can't talk about this."

"That's the only way you're going to resolve it," I said.

"It's not that easy." He let a small cynical smile graze his face. "It's not only Max. I mean, it is Max. But that's on a personal level."

"As opposed to?"

Johnny arose from his seat, his eyes avoiding mine. If there was a window in the room, Johnny would have stared out of it, gathering his thoughts. But there wasn't a window. And staring at filthy file cabinets and corroded boxes wasn't conducive to heavy thinking. So he looked at me. What was in his eyes? Fear, certainly. Confusion, maybe.

He finally spoke. "You're a private detective. How far can you be trusted?"

"As far as murder goes, not at all. How far do you want to trust me?"

Johnny didn't have an answer, and I sensed I had said the wrong thing. His eyes left mine and rested on the top of his desk. I tried to bring the mood back. "If Glenn didn't tell me where your office was, I never would have found it," I said conversationally.

Johnny's head snapped up and his eyes turned dark. "Glenn?"

"The dealer on the first floor. I asked him where—"

Johnny sat down, a cloud over his head. The mood did change. From bad to worse. He leaned back in his chair, one elbow resting on the wooden arm, a fist tight against his chin. I felt the need to explain, although I didn't know why, or even what. "I was on a job for a client down here last week and I was talking with Glenn."

Johnny only stared. Or maybe glared. I stopped talking.

"Listen, Archie," he said, leaning into the desk. He didn't get up. "I have some work to do. Have a good one." I was being dismissed.

And I had bungled a chance. I felt that Johnny was about to open up to me. But then he rapidly clammed up. Because I mentioned murder and because I mentioned Glenn. A thought slipped through my mind that Glenn and Johnny were making it together. But I also let that thought slip by. Glenn was too obviously on the make. With Johnny, seduction would have to be slow, subtle, and very private. But this wasn't the time or the place. And I missed an opportunity. I bid him a "Take care," and left him alone. Temporarily.

I wandered downstairs. Glenn's both was still almost empty and he was still reading his newspaper. When I stopped in front of him, he put down the paper and almost smiled up at me. Almost, but not quite. "Change your mind again?"

"Maybe," I said. "Have I seen you before?"

Glenn looked at me askance.

"At the bars?" I elaborated. "G.A.A.? The firehouse?"

Glenn gave off a small snort. "That's not a new come-on,

Cain. If you're trying to find out if I'm gay, I am." He stood up. "Obviously."

Glenn wasn't an unattractive man, with his long blond hair and small slim body, and he wasn't effeminate. People go for types, and at first glance Glenn would have been my type of man. Dungarees, work boots. But on second glance, he wasn't. He was almost too pretty, and certainly too forward.

"Interested?" he asked.

His words weren't loud, but they were loud enough for the man and the woman who were looking over the merchandise in his booth to hear. Glenn's closet definitely had no doors. I didn't say anything.

"Want to go for a late lunch?" Glenn asked.

"I already had lunch. I could do with a coffee," I said.

When the couple left his booth without making a buy, Glenn ran a rope over the entrance and flicked off two lamps. Johnny was standing near the exit when we left. He didn't say anything to either Glenn or me, but he kept his eyes on us until we were out the door.

We only walked two doors down, to a small Mexican restaurant. Glenn ordered a dish with spicy sauce. I ordered coffee. The coffee and Glenn's meal appeared quickly and at the same time.

"Why did you want to know if I was gay?" Glenn asked.

"You're a good-looking man," I said.

"Maybe. But that isn't why you asked."

"Why did I?"

"Why were you down here last week? You weren't interested in any Mahana knickknack rip-offs."

"Wasn't I?"

"Do you always answer a question with a question?"

"No," I said. "Do you?" We were both trying to gain ground on each other and I didn't know why. But Glenn seemed to be more in control of what was happening than I was. He ate his peppered food voraciously, but his concentration stayed on me.

It was my turn again. "How long have you had a booth at the flea market?"

"Why do you want to know?"

"Now who's answering a question with a question?"

"We both are," Glenn conceded. There was a glint of humor in his eyes. Dark humor.

"Those statuettes you're selling are illegal," I said.

Glenn sipped his soda, smiled. "Well, at least it's not a question. But no, Cain, they're not illegal. When I said rip-offs, I meant that they were cheap. Cheap, yes, but not illegal. If you have any smarts at all, you'd know that. Next question."

"Why are you so defensive?"

"Ask," he said. It was an order.

"How long have you had a booth here?"

"Same question. But I'll answer it anyway. Two months." A pause, a mouthful of food. "Ask."

Okay, he wants to play twenty questions, we'll make them good. "Why is Johnny afraid of you?"

"Is he?" Before I could respond, Glenn held up his hand. "Okay, no questions for a question." But he changed his mind. "Did you ask Johnny why he's afraid of me?"

"No," I said.

"He knows," Glenn stated. I waited for him to continue. He did. "Because I know who he is and what he's done."

"Who is he and what has he done?"

"If you don't know, you're a lousy detective."

My face dropped. I hoped it was only on the inside. "How'd you know I was a detective?"

"Why did you ask about Sinbad?"

"Because I wanted to know."

"Don't."

"Don't what?"

"You're stomping around in deep shit, Cain," he said. "You're up to your chin and out of your depth. Don't move, Cain, you'll drown."

"I can swim," I said.

"No you can't. Not in these waters. They're too thick."

Glenn wiped his chin, crumbled his napkin, downed the remainder of his soda. He arose. "You've had your twenty questions. More or less." He flipped open his wallet and laid some bills on the check. I followed him out the door.

I walked him back to the flea market. Glenn stopped me from going inside. "No," he said, quietly but strongly. "This is not some chicken-shit murder you're fucking around with, Cain. Max was only on the edge."

People were climbing the four steps into the old stone building, but Glenn was talking to me and I was the only one who heard him. He held the palm of his hand on my leather chest. "Stay away," he said firmly. When I didn't budge, he added, "But you probably won't stay away, will you?" The answer was obvious. "You're a fool, Cain."

He slipped a hand in his back pocket, brought out a piece of paper, and passed it to me. I took it. Seven numbers. Obviously a telephone number. "Not unless you have to," he said. "And you'd be smart if you didn't have to." He turned, walked up the stairs, and didn't look back.

I slid the tiny piece of paper into my wallet and walked uptown in something of a daze. My mind was a muddle of too many facts that didn't fit. Sinbad at the magazine office, at Sidney's office, where Max worked. Johnny's fear of Glenn, and Glenn's warnings against pursuing facts on Max's death. Even Glenn knowing about my search for the person who slew Max threw me. It didn't make sense. And Sinbad seemed to swim in and around every corner I poked.

At Spring Street I took the subway to 23rd Street. I stopped at the first empty phone booth I came to, took out my wallet, and dialed the number Glenn gave me. There was no answer. I hung up and continued down the street.

Chapter

12

The outer shell of the YMCA reminded me of the building that housed the flea market. Both were large, had stone steps, and giant pillars guarding them.

At one time I was a member of the Y, utilizing their gym. But after a year I let my membership lapse. But I did miss it. The gym was a haven for closeted homosexuals and for the straight men of the neighborhood, and it was often fun to cruise, not knowing if you were making a play for a straight guy or one of your own. It was that hint of mystery that made it exciting. But the gym disintegrated rapidly, not that it was ever in great shape to begin with, not in my lifetime, anyway. Free weights were lost, stink covered the shower walls. When my membership expired, I signed up for karate classes on 34th Street. The karate school didn't have the same cruising facilities as the Y, or the same workout equipment, but it kept me in shape. And at the same time I learned a few defensive moves.

The same obnoxious clerk, well remembered from gay days gone by, sat in the same small cage off to the side. And, as usual, he ignored anyone coming in or going out. I walked around the cage and through the coffee room and slipped a dime in the phone booth. After the fourth ring, the telephone was answered in the usual bored tone. "McBurney YMCA."

"Johnny Grabowski," I said. "I'd like to leave a message for him. Room 541, I think."

"No, it's not," the clerk said, as if I had made a crucial mistake that would set the world afire. "He's in Room 839." His tone noted that he could have added, "See, stupid, you don't know anything." I hung up the phone and walked through the other door, toward the resident dorm.

I watched the bent arrow above the door. The elevator was excruciatingly slow in coming down. By the time it reached my level, seven men were standing, waiting. Me included.

A full gaggle of men stepped off the elevator and we seven stepped on. Eight was the top floor. By the time we reached it, only two of us were left standing and not talking to each other in the tiny and dirty and creaking enclosure. Me and a big sloppy teenage boy with too many pimples on his face and a fat ass. We both stepped off. The boy ignored me, turned the corner, and stepped through the door of what I assumed was the men's room. There was no nameplate on the door, but the odor exuding from it permeated the corridor and I heard the sound of water running.

Room 839 was near the end of the corridor. I tried the doorknob. It shook weakly, but it was locked. The sloppy kid finished his job in the men's room and walked toward me. I tapped on the door of 839. The kid stopped three doors down and inserted a key. He walked into his room and shut the door without glancing in my direction.

The lock to Room 839 was easy to pick. A blind man could have done it with one eye tied behind his back. I closed the door behind me and it locked itself.

The room was much smaller than I had expected. The only furniture was a bed (smaller than a twin), an old bulky wooden dresser with a large cracked mirror atop it, a desk that badly needed repair (Johnny's telephone sat on the desk), and a desk chair overlooking a window that overlooked a courtyard with more windows. I pulled down the shade. The shade was as filthy and as faded as the paint on the walls. The furniture was crammed so close together, anyone with a serious case of claustrophobia would find the room a tomb. There were no pictures on the walls. On the back of the door were hooks, nothing hanging from them. A clean white towel was on a rack on the door. An old TV was screwed to the wall.

Although the bedspread was spotted and probably hadn't

123

been laundered in a year, the bed was neatly made. I sat on it and opened the middle drawer of the desk. There were a multitude of neatly stacked fliers and letters from G.A.A., some pencils, two pens, paper clips, assorted bars of candy, and a bag of peanuts. I pulled open the only other drawer, a large one on the side. Four books were stacked neatly inside. Three were paperbacks: *A Tale of Two Cities, From Here to Eternity,* and *By Jove.* I scanned the back cover of *By Jove.* "The story of perverted love in the shadows of the big city." It was copyrighted 1954. I tossed it back into the drawer. Underneath the paperbacks was the hard cover, a Western by Max Brand. Inside the book was a small thin muscle magazine of men posing in skimpy trunks or jockstraps. It was the sort of magazine that, as a teenager, would take me hours to work up the courage to buy at a 42nd Street newsstand; and after I finally worked up the courage to buy it, I'd travel back to New Jersey, frightened out of my wits that someone had seen me buying a book with pictures of near-naked men. I tucked the innocent pseudo-porno magazine back inside Max Brand, then slid the drawer shut.

A tame collection of books, I thought. Dickens for intellectual stimulation, Jones for middle-class smut, a dated gay novel, and Max Brand for Western masculinity. And a dated muscle magazine. Johnny was deep in the closet, of that there was no doubt. Nor was there any doubt about his virginity. I felt sorry for him. But then again, he was trying, by joining G.A.A.

The bottom drawer of the dresser was empty. The next one held four sweatshirts, all navy blue, and two pairs of gym shorts, also navy blue. The second drawer from the top was filled with Johnny's shirts, colorless and formless. Mr. Conservative. Johnny's socks and his underwear filled the top drawer. Johnny wore the same brand of briefs I did, white and cotton and Fruit of the Looms. There was also a box containing one used jockstrap.

The contents of the closet next to the exit door changed my conservative evaluation of Johnny. But not completely. It was

124

the black leather jacket that struck my eye. It seemed totally incongruous to Johnny's persona and stood out like a sore thumb. Or a dark star. It had zippers galore, empty pockets, and by the sheen of the leather, I would have guessed the jacket had never been worn.

There was also a dark gray suit hanging on a wooden hanger, along with two neckties. Another wooden hanger held a navy blue corduroy sport jacket. Two pairs of corduroy pants, dark colors, hung on wire hangers, along with two pairs of dungarees, not Levi's. A pair of sweatpants and a spring jacket were hanging on the back of the closet door, completing Johnny's wardrobe. As skimpy as my own, I thought.

I pulled the large suitcase from the top shelf. I knew it was empty before I opened it. I tucked it back on the shelf. The remainder of the shelf was empty. A laundry bag half filled with T-shirts and shorts and socks was on the floor of the closet.

There was nothing else to look at. A disappointment. From the looks of the room, Johnny led a dull life. But the more I thought about it and the more I looked it over, I realized that the room was too dull. And largely impersonal. Too impersonal. No photos, no notebooks, no address book. I stopped to look under the bed. A duffel bag. I reached under. The lock on the door clicked. I stood up. The knob turned and the door opened.

Johnny stood in front of me. His eyes were as surprised as mine. I grabbed him by the front of his jacket, pulled him into the room, and slammed the door behind him. It was a loud slam.

"What the hell?" A look of confusion, shock.

"Don't you work a full day on Saturday?" I asked. I half expected Johnny to slug me and I prepared myself. But it never came. He pulled his emotions inside himself, or tried to. His fists were clenched, and a thin vein in his forehead stood out, throbbing.

He stared at me and won control over himself. His fists unclenched, his forehead eased. "Get out," he said softly. "Please," he added, much to my surprise.

I managed my way to the door without touching him, not an

125

easy task in the tiny cubicle. I had my hand on the doorknob, but I hesitated. Johnny wasn't even looking at me. He wasn't looking at anything. That is, his eyes weren't focused. He merely tilted his head slowly in one direction, sighed, then in the other, and sighed. He still wore that silly blue and gold school jacket.

"Trouble?" I said. The quiet of the room made my word a whisper.

"Yeah, trouble." Johnny sighed again, a decisive sigh.

"Can I help?"

A small glance at me, a swift cynical grin that disappeared as quickly as it had appeared. But not a word.

I took a step back into the room. A small step. I didn't want to crowd Johnny.

"No, Archie." Johnny raised up a hand, then let it down as if it weighed a ton. Another sigh. His body seemed to collapse within himself. He was a defeated man. And it wasn't I who had defeated him.

"If I found somebody poking around in my home, I think I'd make something of a fuss," I said, half in jest.

"So would I," Johnny said. He gave off a small laugh that rapidly died.

"But you didn't."

"Doesn't matter. This isn't my home." He said the last words bitterly. "I'm leaving." The decision sounded spontaneous, so was his movement. He brushed against me as he opened the closet door, swinging down the empty suitcase and tossing it on the bed. He opened a dresser drawer and began placing shirts in the suitcase. I watched in fascination. With one drawer empty, he started on the other. I don't know if he was aware of it, but tears began streaming down his cheeks.

"Johnny," I said.

He didn't let me continue. He broke down and began sobbing, at first slowly, then uncontrollably. But he still filled the suitcase. I moved one step closer, laid a hand on his shoulder. He stopped, looked at me. His face was red, his cheeks wet. A man on the verge, not of a jag, but of the verge of a breakdown.

126

"Hold it," I said sharply. Johnny gazed at me with frightened eyes. His body began shaking. I grabbed his other shoulder, pulled him to me, and held him, feeling his limbs shaking, his sobs muffled into my neck. "If it wasn't," he cried between tears and shivers. "If it wasn't . . ."

Johnny couldn't finish his thought. He held me tightly, as if I were the thin thread that held him to the earth. I let him hold. I let him sob. I comforted him by petting his hair, soothing his brow, wiping his tears. "Hey, kid, it's not that bad. Nothing is. It'll be okay."

"Kid," he muttered and offered an odd little laugh.

When the tears stopped, when he was able to control his shakes, he pushed himself away from me. He took a deep breath. "Maybe I should say, 'Thanks, I needed that,' " he said, wiping his face with a towel, stringing his hands through the brush of his hair. A hint of a laugh. He threw the towel on the floor and went back to the closet, pulled his corduroy pants off the hangers, his suit, his sweatpants and jacket off the door and stuffed them into the suitcase, along with the laundry bag. He opened the top drawer of the dresser and tossed his socks and underwear on the bed. The suitcase overflowed. He bent under the bed and pulled out the duffel bag.

"Where are you going?"

"To a hotel," Johnny answered, now very much in control. The tears were gone, wiped away. But the edge was still there, reflected in the vein protruding from his forehead. "I'm sorry you had to see this, Archie. It really isn't your problem." He stuffed the duffel bag, rather viciously.

"Isn't it?"

He zipped up the duffel bag and snapped his suitcase shut. "No, it isn't. It's mine."

The room was empty now. Only me, Johnny, a full suitcase, a bulging duffel bag, and empty impersonal furniture. Johnny pulled off his school colors and hung the jacket on the back of the closet door. He reached in the closet, carefully pulled the black leather jacket off the wooden hanger. He pushed his arms into the sleeves and the jacket slid on his back, giving him a

127

masterful and comfortable look. Although I wasn't sure how comfortable Johnny felt wearing it. When he zipped up the cuffs, I said, "I never saw you wear that jacket before."

"It's time," he said, forcing a smile, then letting it drop.

He walked out the door with the suitcase in one hand, the duffel bag in the other, and his school jacket still in the closet. I followed. He didn't even bother closing the door. I offered to carry the duffel bag. He wouldn't let me. He didn't say a word while we waited for the elevator. When we stepped inside, the elevator was empty. By the time we hit the lobby, Johnny and I were crammed to one side. More than one of the men inside the enclosure had given the two of us more than a passing glance. We made a fine-looking pair. I thought so, anyway. A long-haired man in a brown leather jacket and a crew-cut stud in black.

We were the last to get off the elevator. As we walked the long corridor to the clerk's cage, I asked, "Why the sudden move?"

"I want to talk to you, Archie," Johnny said, but continued his walk. I kept up the pace.

He handed in his key and received cash back for the rent he had paid in advance, no questions asked.

When we were on the sidewalk trying to hail a cab, I asked, "Talk about what?"

"Me," Johnny said. A cab stopped. "Max."

Johnny tossed the suitcase in the backseat. He climbed in with it, the duffel bag on his lap. I opened the front door and sat beside the driver.

"Thirty-ninth, between Madison and Park," Johnny said.

I corrected him. "Perry off Hudson," I told the driver. Johnny didn't argue. We headed downtown and rode in silence.

Johnny didn't argue when I paid the driver, either. I got out of the cab and opened Johnny's door. He handed me his duffel bag and reached over for his suitcase.

I recognized the car parked at the curb, unmarked as it was. Captain Carney was sitting behind the wheel. " 'Bout time," he said.

The cab pulled away. Carney opened his door and stepped out. I set the duffel bag down and waited. Johnny held on to his suitcase.

Carney gave a sharp glance and almost a sneer at Johnny. "New boyfriend?" he asked me. When I didn't answer, Carney added, "Bad choice," and turned his face away from Johnny.

"What do you want, Carney?" I asked.

"A talk."

At one time I might have invited him upstairs, but not this time. Not with Johnny standing there.

"I have some good news and some bad news," Carney said. He tried to sound jovial, but I thought he tried too hard. "For your ears only."

"I'll go over to the Stud for a drink," Johnny offered.

I looked at him. His tears and fears from our encounter at the Y were well hidden. "Okay," I said. "I'll take your things up." I took the suitcase from his hand.

Johnny walked down the street and turned the corner. Both Carney and I watched. I watched, I must admit, with a touch of lust. With the suitcase in one hand, the duffel bag in the other, I entered the building, Carney beside me, and we rode upstairs. Both my hands were full, and Carney didn't offer to help carry my load.

After I set down the bags and locked the door, Carney said, "You're going to have to lay off. No," he quickly added. "First the good news. Max's boyfriend is out."

"Davie? Why?"

"I thought you'd be glad." Again Carney tried to sound cheerful. And again he didn't make it.

"I thought you had him dead to rights, he was about ready to confess." I must admit, there was sarcasm in my voice. I hung my jacket in the closet.

"I see you finally picked up your permit," Carney said, eyeing the pistol under my arm.

"Why did you let Davie go?"

"In a minute," Carney said. He pulled out a chair from the round table. He looked at me, as if asking permission. I nodded.

Carney sat. I lit a cigarette and joined him on the other side of the table.

"How'd you like to come back on the force?" Carney asked. It seemed he held his breath as he asked. "As detective sergeant," he added. "Plainclothes."

"And get the shit kicked out of me again for being a queer cop?"

"Any cop who touches you, they answer to me," Carney said, more strongly than I would have imagined. He was defending me. A surprise. A puzzle.

"What does this have to do with Davie?" I asked.

"Who said it has anything to do with the kid?"

"It does, doesn't it."

Carney leaned up in his chair, resting his elbows on the table. "You gotta lay off," he said. His eyes didn't meet mine when he said the words. But they landed there quick enough after he spit them out.

"Lay off who?"

"Sinbad," he said.

It was a curveball that hit me dead on. "What?" I didn't disguise my confusion. I crushed my cigarette in the ashtray and immediately lit another. "Sinbad?"

"That's right." His eyes were dead serious and immobile. "And I'm not asking."

"What the hell does Sinbad have to do with anything?"

"Just lay off," Carney said.

I was stunned. "He isn't even my client anymore. What's to lay off?"

"The 'lay off' is, stay away from the flea market on Canal Street."

My spine gave a shiver. Glenn didn't want me around there, either. My mind was trying to figure out the connection. Carney mistook my silence for agreement. He pushed his chair back, stood up, and with a grin of obvious relief on his face, held out his hand. "Deal?"

I snapped my mind back to the immediate situation. "What the hell are you talking about, Carney?"

Carney took his hand back. But he didn't sit.

"Why is it so important for me to stay away from Canal Street? Important enough for you to allow an acknowledged faggot back in the department?"

His words were smooth. "Do it, Cain. And don't ask why."

"I'm asking."

"Don't ask. Take the deal."

"And if I don't?"

"It's out of my hands."

My confusion turned to anger, which at the moment was uncontrolled, sputtering to a boil. I arose and crushed out my second cigarette. "Well, whose hands is it fucking in?" It was almost a shout.

"Hey, Cain, I can't explain," he said. His words weren't a whisper, but they weren't a shout either. "You just gotta do it."

"I don't have to do anything," I said. "I don't work for the city, remember." My anger was coloring my words.

Carney's anger also came to the fore, but it wasn't forceful and I didn't even think it was sincere. "You carry a license in your back pocket," he said. "If you want to keep carrying it, you'll lay off."

This was my living we were talking about, and my gut gave a fearful tug. But no matter, I couldn't let it stop there. "Carney, I'd as soon go out and dig ditches than go back to work for the department. It's not you, Carney, it's the system. The system that treats me like shit because I'm gay." Considering the situation, I felt stupid saying that, but it was true. And my spoken militancy calmed me down.

"Whether you come back to work for me or not—as a detective sergeant," he emphasized, "you have to lay off Sinbad." He waited. "Deal?"

I didn't acknowledge Carney's deal with an affirmative, and for the moment I let it ride. "Why'd you let Davie go?"

Carney seemed to noticeably relax, his shoulders drooped a quarter of an inch. "He didn't kill Harmony," he said.

"How do you know that? Did you find out who did kill Max?"

"No," he said. "But the kid didn't do it."

"How do you know?"

"I know, that's all. He has an alibi. His neighbor saw him take out the garbage that night and go back to his apartment."

"That's crazy," I told him. "You would have checked his alibi long before now."

"Nevertheless, it's there," Carney said.

"You're not saying very much today, are you, Carney?"

"As much as I can." Carney walked around me and to the door. "As much as I know." He opened the door. But before he walked out, he asked me, "Will you lay off Sinbad?"

"Maybe," I said. "When I know why."

"If you don't, they're going to pull your investigator's license." Carney didn't sound happy about it. "Think about it."

He started to walk out the door, but I stopped him. "Why did you say Johnny was a bad choice for a boyfriend?"

Carney turned in the doorway. "That's why you'll never make it as a private dick, Cain. You don't see what's in front of you." He paused, his eyes grinning into mine. I could swear he was laughing at me. "Take the deal."

I didn't take it. Carney walked out, closing the door behind him.

But I did think about the deal. I pulled a beer from the refrigerator, slid my holster off my shoulder, looped it over the chair, and laid down on the couch, a pillow propped under my neck.

Sinbad meant nothing to me. He was a client, that's all. An importer who was afraid of competition. But there was more. Why was he in the office of *Current Social Thought*? There was a connection between the Merediths and Sinbad that I couldn't fathom. And Glenn at the flea market, he was the other connection with Sinbad. And he— My puzzlement was interrupted by the buzz. Johnny. Another puzzlement.

I hopped up and buzzed him in. I opened the door and went back to the couch and my thoughts.

After Johnny entered, he locked the door behind him and stood by the table. I had momentarily forgotten about him and his problems. But he and they were here.

"What did the cop want?" Johnny asked.

"He said you're a bad choice for a boyfriend." I again pushed myself off the couch. "You want a beer?"

"Yeah," Johnny said and walked to the living room. "I'm not your boyfriend."

"I know that," I said. I tried to find some signs of recognition in his eyes. "What are you?" I asked. I handed Johnny his beer and sat next to him. "Well?" I prodded him.

Nothing. He sipped his beer. Okay, twenty questions again. "What do you know about Glenn?"

"At the flea market?"

"Yeah."

"Why do you want to know?"

"He says he knows about you and what you've done."

"He told you that? That stupid son of a bitch."

"What did he mean?"

Johnny held up a hand to his face. "Not yet, Archie."

Okay, I thought, we'll try another direction. "What do you know about Sinbad?"

"Who?"

"You don't know him?"

"No."

"Tell me about Glenn."

Johnny got up and walked toward the kitchen, taking his can with him. "I don't think I should." He took a swig of beer.

"You do know, then, don't you?" I arose and followed Johnny.

He turned to me. "Know what?"

"About Glenn," I said. "Tell me."

"I can't do that, Archie."

"Tell me," I said, more loudly than I intended.

Johnny walked away from me and back to the living room. He swept a hand over his lips. "Archie, I have to tell you something." He turned to face me again.

I waited.

Johnny was searching deep inside himself. I could see it in every taut muscle in his frame. He quickly found what he was looking for. "I quit my job yesterday," he said.

"That explains why you came back from the flea market so soon. That's why I went—"

He didn't let me finish. "No, not the job at the flea market." He sat on the couch, not facing me. "That isn't the job I'm talking about. But I'll be leaving there, too." Again, he had to reach inside himself. "First," he continued. "First I have to tell you why, why . . ." He inhaled. I waited. "Why I joined G.A.A."

He looked up at me. I still waited.

"You know, Archie, this is a crazy time we're living in. For the country. Hell, you have that crazy yippie Abbie Hoffman mouthing off about oddball revolution. You have that insane doctor out in California telling his students to take LSD and drop out of society."

"You said it yourself," I told him. "They're oddballs. What has that got to do with G.A.A.?"

"Hell, I know they're oddballs," Johnny said impatiently. "You have the radicals on the campuses demonstrating against the war."

"I'm not exactly for the war myself. What the fuck are you driving at?"

"You have the SDS. The kids bombing buildings, upsetting the established structure. The Black Panthers. You have organizations plotting against the government. You have—"

I had my guard up. I didn't like where Johnny was going. "Get to the fucking point," I said, my voice cold.

"The point is, we have to do something about it." The passion in his voice was as heated as mine was cool.

"We?"

"Yes, we. We can't let them tear the United States apart." His eyes bore into mine, seeking, what? Understanding?

He stopped talking, but he couldn't stare me down. Finally, he blinked. "I'm not a militant." He paused. His next words came out gnarled but understandable. "I'm not even gay. I'm a member of the FBI."

Johnny got off a good shot, but he had prepared me for it. I told him, "I don't believe you."

"It was a job, Archie," he said, a plea for understanding. "We had to infiltrate the group, to see if they were planning—"

"Oh, I believe you're FBI. If I look at you now, it's obvious. Your haircut is a dead giveaway. Not to mention those damn dungarees." I was angry with him and myself for not recognizing it earlier.

"I'm not the only guy with short hair at G.A.A." It was his turn to be confused. "And what's the matter with my dungarees?"

"You don't wear Levi's. Your clothes. You look like you just stepped off a college campus, worming your way around the long-haired demonstrators on your way home. Yeah, it's obvious. Now." I mentally kicked myself in the ass.

"I handed in my resignation."

Another twist. Johnny knew how to get off his shots. Why did he look so pathetic? Better yet, why did I feel sorry for him, the fucking spying-ass bastard? I don't know why.

I sat next to him on the couch. He shied away. "Spying wasn't up your alley?" I asked.

"I don't like that word."

"It isn't inappropriate."

Johnny didn't disagree. "Did Max know about you?" I asked him.

"I don't think so." After a second, he qualified. "Maybe."

"Maybe?"

"He began acting funny toward me the last couple of weeks. And he wouldn't tell me anything about upcoming demonstrations. And he used to confide in me. The last time he gave me any information was on the demonstration at—"

I finished it for him. "The marriage bureau zap."

"You know about that?"

"That's why it went wrong."

"It depends on your point of view. From ours, it went right. The FBI—"

"Is that when Max began to suspect?"

"I don't know. Maybe. Anyway, after that he began to change. But I don't see how he could have found out about me. I think it was something else that was bothering him, Archie."

"What?"

"I don't know, but I wanted to find out."

"Is that why you followed him to the trucks?"

He shook his head and said quietly, "No."

"Why did you follow him?"

"I don't know. I wanted . . ." He stopped. He didn't know what he wanted.

I filled in his words. "You wanted to try." Johnny looked at me. "Sex."

His face was pained. "Yes."

"But you didn't."

The pain was still there. "No."

If I could read eyes, I would say that Johnny's were begging to be believed. But eyes can be deceiving. He turned his away.

"You're wrong about one thing," I said. He looked up at me, afraid of what I was going to say, yet knowing what I was going to say. "You *are* gay."

"No, I'm not," he said quietly, apologizing.

"Then why'd you decide to quit spying at G.A.A.?" He didn't answer. "Why'd you bawl your eyes out at the Y?"

I didn't mean to, but I reminded him of our scene together. But I couldn't forget that moment at the Y, when I held him close for fear he'd fall apart, when he held on to me for dear life. And I couldn't let him off that easy. I put my hands on his shoulders and turned him to face me. He didn't resist my manipulation. And he didn't resist when I leaned over and kissed him. The touch of his lips was warm. They held against mine, but they didn't reciprocate the tender need.

I was aroused. But not my sex. My memory was aroused to way back when, when I could no longer deny it. When I finally admitted to myself that I was gay. When I stopped being

136

passive and dove in. Johnny was on the verge. I let my mouth float away from his, and my hands fell from his shoulders.

"What does that prove?" Johnny asked. His voice was as warm as his lips had been.

I didn't have to tell him what it proved. He knew. "You can stay here for a couple of days, until you decide what you're going to do." I tried a weak smile. It wasn't returned.

"Thanks," Johnny said.

"You're out of one job," I said. "But you still have the flea market. It might help." I saw an opportunity here. Maybe Carney wanted me eighty-sixed from Canal Street, but an ex-FBI man on the inside might help.

"No," Johnny said. "That was part of the job. The bureau set me up for that. I wouldn't have to work too many hours, and there were always a lot of fags hanging out there who I could sift through for information."

"Fags?" I said, smiling. It was the first time Johnny used the word.

"I'm sorry," Johnny said. "When I made my reports, we—"

"That's okay. We're allowed to call each other faggots." I waited for him to agree or disagree with me. He didn't do either.

"What about Glenn?"

He backed off again. "Don't, Archie. That's an entirely different can of worms. I can't talk about that. And it has nothing to do with G.A.A.," he assured me. "Or Max."

I certainly didn't agree with that. But I let it ride for the moment. "You didn't tell me why you stopped being a mole for the FBI."

Johnny just shook his head in quiet confusion. "I wish I knew."

I could tell him. Because he could no longer betray his homosexual compadres or his own feelings. But I kept silent.

I trust people about as much as I trust the weather. And I never let anyone stay in my apartment when I'm not there. Not even Larry. But rules are made to be broken. "I have to

go out," I said. "Will you be here when I get back?" I slung my
holster back under my arm and reached for my brown leather
jacket.

"Yeah, I'll be here," Johnny said.

"Good." I gave him my warmest smile. Not many people
have received it. Not genuinely. "Then take off your jacket and
stay awhile." I turned and walked into my office. When I
returned, Johnny was hanging his black leather jacket in my
closet. "We really have to get you some decent shirts," I said.
His was a washed-out yellow that my father would wear.
Before he could answer or act insulted, I handed him Max's
diary. "I'll be back in a couple of hours," I said.

Chapter 13

It took me forty minutes to get to the Upper East Side. The
name on the bell hadn't been changed—HARDIN/HARMONY. I
pressed the buzzer. Within two seconds I was buzzed in. If that
was Davie up there, he didn't ask who was calling.

When I reached the top floor, Davie was standing at the
door, a pathetic sight. His hair was disarranged and chaotic, his
eyes dazed, his smell acrid. He clutched his worn and faded
terry-cloth robe over his frame. "Cain, Cain," he exclaimed
before I reached the top step. "Thank God."

Near panic seeped through his movements as he tried to pull
himself together. He rewrapped his robe, tightened his tangled
belt, patted his hair into some semblance of neatness. I followed
him inside. He slammed and locked the door quickly behind
me.

138

The apartment was virtually empty of furniture. Even the round oak table was gone.

"I need some money," he said, then waited. But not for long. "I said I need some money," he shouted.

"How much did you get for the table?"

"What difference does it make? The money's gone. I need cash, Cain. *Now.*"

If I didn't hand some cash over, it looked like Davie would pounce. In his condition, it wouldn't be much of a pounce to fend off. I stalled. "Why do you need the money?"

"Jesus Christ," he said, turning away, stringing his fingers through his hair, striding to the living room. He suddenly turned to me. "If I don't, if I don't . . ." He dried up and flopped onto a chair. A broken wooden chair that he obviously couldn't sell for cash. The only chair in the place. But the apartment wasn't entirely empty. Clothes were strewn about, and bed sheets, and shoes, knickknacks no one wanted, magazines. And Davie, lost in the middle.

Davie reminded me of Ray Milland's *Lost Weekend,* battling his bats. He sobbed into his hands. I glanced through to the kitchen. Unwashed dishes and pots and pans lay in the sink. I was surprised he hadn't sold them, too. The small garbage tin was filled and overflowed onto the linoleum. Roaches were having a feast. Even my presence didn't disturb them. I walked through to the bathroom. It was filthy. Pill bottles were scattered on the floor, every one of them empty.

Davie was at the bathroom door, leaning both arms on the frame, his eyes red, teared, lost. And not only for the weekend. "Shit," he said, and backed off. I followed him to the living room. I stood where the wicker couch once sat. Davie paced with unsteady steps.

"I mean it, Cain, I need some money." He again pulled his robe closely around him and again retied it. His voice was under control, but barely.

My words were soft and, I hoped, calming. "I can see that. But I can't help you."

He snapped again. "Those bastards at G.A.A. won't help me,

either. Hell, I let them raise money for me, and now they won't give it to me."

"That was for your defense."

"But I need it," he begged. Then he physically controlled himself, hugging hands to elbows. "I don't know, I don't know . . ."

His eyes lit up as quickly as a firefly in summer. He turned around like a bat out of hell, and he climbed into the bed loft. I heard movement up there, the clanging of glass and metal. I heard the strike of a match. I climbed the ladder and peeked upstairs. Davie was lying down, his back against the wall, his robe splayed open, his body relaxed, as he toked on a joint.

"I forgot about these," he said after inhaling deeply and letting the grass leak into his lungs, his bloodstream, his brain.

The bed of the loft was a smelly and grungy mess, worse than downstairs. Davie clutched a small plastic bag in his fist. I could see at least ten rolled joints inside. The square of fogged glass from the light fixture was at his feet.

Davie was sliding on a moonbeam. His eyes softened, his muscles turned to mush. "Max said he was saving these for a rainy day. Well, we've had a helluva storm." He almost laughed, but he had tears in his eyes, tears of relief. "He kept them up there." He pointed to the encasement of the bare unlit bulb. "Funny." He laughed coarsely to himself.

I maneuvered myself through the opening and sat cross-legged in front of Davie. My head almost touched the ceiling. I was wearing my worn 501's, but I felt they were being soiled by the shit on the sheets. The windows in the front room gave off enough light to give a soft smoky glow to the loft, to match its smell.

"What are you going to do now?" I asked.

"Finish this," he said, toking deeply. The joint was burned almost to his fingers. When the flame died out, Davie laid the tiny roach onto the shelf. I expected him to light another. He didn't. He was hoarding. He kept the remainder clutched tightly in both hands.

140

"What are you going to do now that you're out of jail?" I asked again.

"I don't know," Davie said. His intoxication had given him balance and some sort of reality. "I have to get a roommate to support me."

"Like Max?"

Davie lifted his eyes in a quizzical and comical manner. "Yeah, like Max." The pillow behind his head was a comfortable throne, and for the moment Davie was king. "You ever been in jail, Cain?"

"Yeah," I sneered. "But not on the losing side of the bars."

Davie thought that funny. But his laugh faded as fast as a burned match. "That was my first time. And in a strange way it was wonderful."

It was my turn to laugh, but I didn't.

"No responsibility, no problems . . ." His mind was wandering back to his "freedom" in jail. I let it wander and watched his face. It seemed so at peace, so stoned, so sad, so dead. "I was terrified at first. But . . . but. You know they put me in a cell with another queen. We have our own special section, for gays only."

I knew that, but I also heard it was hell. That wasn't the case. Not according to Davie.

"This black guy," he continued. "He latched on to me. I guess because of my blond hair." Davie strung his fingers through his thin hair like he was Veronica Lake and I was Alan Ladd. The dark roots spoiled the picture. And I'm not Alan Ladd.

"Cable," Davie went on. "He told me to call him Cable. He showed me the ropes. He also said I was his pussy. Imagine!" Davie exclaimed. "I was scared shitless the first time. But, but, he fucked me, and it was okay. He gave me dope, said I was his fuck-boy from then on."

Davie reached into his bag of goodies, slipped out another joint, reached for the lighter, and flamed. After two deep tokes, he offered it to me. I didn't accept it. He continued inhaling and talking.

141

"It was wonderful," he said between tokes. "Cable. What a man! And I didn't even have to do anything, Cain. I had my meals, a bed, and all the dope I needed, television. I was Cable's pussy." He laughed harshly. "I had it made."

"Better than you had it with Max?"

"No, not better. But probably just as good," Davie said, again quickly burning the joint down to his fingers and placing the minute butt next to his previous one.

"What would have happened if you were tried and found guilty and shipped to Attica?"

"Nothing," Davie said simply. "Nothing changes. Cable told me he knew some guys up there. Real high dealers with some great dope. They'd take me on, I'd be their pussy."

I wanted to lash out at him. Ron was right. Davie was a leech. It didn't matter where he was, as long as he could be supported. As long as he had his dope. Jail in upstate New York or an apartment on the Upper East Side. It didn't matter to him, as long as he had his fucking dope.

"Ya know, Cain, I kind of liked it."

I could believe it. I uncrossed my legs and moved to go back down the ladder.

"Where you going?" Davie asked. There was the previous hint of panic on the edge of his voice.

I didn't answer and lowered myself onto the floor. Davie scampered down after me. "You can't go yet. I do need some money, Cain."

I looked at Davie. "You have nothing left to sell. And that isn't going to last forever, is it?" I said, nodding at the hand that clutched the bag like it was a lifeline to heaven.

Davie smiled sheepishly.

"What happens when you run out?" I glanced at the clock in the kitchen. "By six o'clock, I'd guess." It was now four.

"Cain, lend me some bucks, and I'll pay you back."

"With what? You don't even have a job."

"I'll get one." His panic was edging forward.

"Tell me about Max."

"Sure, Cain. Anything. What do you want to know?"

142

I wondered if he had had a bath since he was released from jail. I wondered if he had had a bath since he went in.

"People tell me that Max changed during the last couple of weeks before he was killed."

Before I could even ask a question, Davie talked. "No, he was the same. Nothing different." Davie was being eagerly cooperative, hoping for some sympathy and some money. "Nothing changed. He still bought me grass. And he gave me enough bucks for me to go downtown for my diet pills. No, he didn't change."

Davie's entire life revolved around dope. If Max had changed, Davie wouldn't have even noticed it, not until his dope ran out.

"He told me he was going to quit his job," Davie continued. "But I didn't believe him. He'd said that before. He'd never do that. And he told me I had to get a job. And I was gonna, too," he quickly added.

"Why was he going to leave his job?"

"He had to. That's what he said, anyway."

"Why?"

"I don't know. He said he did something stupid a couple of years ago. Something about immigration. He tried to contact the law school at Columbia. . . ." Davie stopped. "Do you really want to hear about this?" He became eager to change the subject. "Hey, Cain, where do you live? You know if you moved in here, the rent ain't that much."

"Why'd he call Columbia?"

"Ah, they have kind of student law service. You know, I'm not always this way," he said defensively, tying his robe tighter. He waited for me to respond. There was nothing for me to say. "I mean, I may be stoned all the time, but I'm not oblivious." I waited. "I heard him talking on the telephone."

"Yeah?"

"Yeah," he said, annoyance in his voice. "Are you going to give me any money or not?"

"That depends on what you tell me," I said. I just broke one

143

cardinal rule. Never buy information. The seller usually tells you want you want to know, regardless of the truth.

"Well, okay," Davie said, again meekly. "Anyway, he called the law school. And after getting the runaround, he talked to some guy, probably a lawyer. Max asked him what the penalty was for lying in court." He reached in his little plastic bag, wavered slightly, then changed his mind, his hand coming up empty. But he still clung to the bag.

"Lying about what?"

"Max said, he said, he asked them, what if somebody swore that he knew somebody else for five years, but he didn't really know them that long. What was the penalty?" Davie stopped and waited, almost with his hand out.

I waited, too, for more. And there had to be more. He wasn't making sense.

"That's it, Cain," Davie said. "That's all I know." His voice was almost a screech.

Davie was dry. He waited expectantly for his reward. I reached in my back pocket and pulled a ten-spot from my wallet. A small smile appeared on his lips, but he quickly smothered it.

"That won't even get me an ounce," he cried, tears in his voice. But the tears were also smothered. "My doctor costs only seven bucks," he said, almost to himself. He reached out to grab the bill. I let him have it and took two steps to the door.

But I couldn't leave without an understanding. An understanding, maybe not of Max, but of Davie. I wasn't even sure I believed what I heard. "You mean," I said, "you'd seriously consider spending the rest of your life in jail, just to have all the dope you want, and a bed, and meals, and a good fuck?"

"Why not?" Davie asked. And he was serious. I didn't answer. I opened the door and walked out. "Why not?" he yelled again after I closed the door. "What else can I do? I don't have nothing else." The sound of his voice was ugly and almost desperate. I guess I can leave out the "almost."

I walked down the stairs with more fear in my gut than I'd admit. Davie's voice was eerie and it stayed in my ears. Where

144

is he heading? I wondered. I also wondered how I could help him. I'd talk to Ron, I decided. G.A.A. wants to help their gay brothers. Well, here's their chance. Here's a man who needs help badly. Poor Davie. Is he headed for hell? Or is he already there?

My question was answered before I reached the corner at York Avenue. What was it that made me turn around? A sixth sense? Fate? Fear? It doesn't matter. When I looked up, I saw Davie sitting on the ledge of the fifth-floor window. Before I could speak or call or yell, he pushed himself off and almost landed on an old couple walking their dog. The couple screamed.

I ran. The old man and woman were still yelling. I bent to Davie and heard a rattle. Yes, it's real. The death rattle. But less a rattle than a grinding, gasping release—of breath and life. The pulse on the side of his neck didn't exist. There was little blood, but what blood was there dribbled out of his ears and his mouth and his nose.

A doorman from the building across the street came out to see what all the shouting was about. I told him to call an ambulance and the cops. The couple continued screaming, but their screams by now were slightly muffled, at least to my ears. I walked away. I walked to the subway.

Chapter
14

It took me an hour to get back downtown. When I stepped into the station house, my best buddy from uniformed days gone by was on duty at the front desk. He gave me a bright hello. Then I guess he remembered I was a faggot. His face lost its friendly glow. He told me Carney wasn't in today. I left a message for Carney to call me. My best former buddy didn't say good-bye.

When I got back home, Johnny was sitting at the table. His hair was wet and shining. He had on a clean white T-shirt and dungarees, still not Levi's, let alone 501's, and bare feet. Max's diary was open in front of him.

"Confused son of a bitch," he said, noting the diary.

"He wasn't the only one," I said, but I didn't feel like talking about Davie. The thought made me sick to my stomach. "How so?" I asked, pushing Davie into an unused corner of my mind.

"I don't understand a lot of what he said."

I hung my brown jacket on a hook in the closet. Johnny's black leather was on a wooden hanger. "What about this?" Johnny asked, his finger pointing to an open page.

I leaned over his shoulder and read aloud. " 'I can't see Johnny anymore.' What does it mean?" I asked him.

"I don't know, Archie. He never told me he didn't want to see me."

"He didn't say he 'didn't want to.' He said he *can't*. Then he *did* know you were FBI."

"No," Johnny quickly said. "I don't think so. Nobody did." But a wrinkle formed on his brow. "Wait. There was another mole in G.A.A." He looked at me like a kid who'd hit the popcorn jackpot. "Yeah. After Max clammed up on me, my contact told me I wasn't getting enough information on upcoming zaps. He said they approached a member and almost had him."

"Do you know who it was?"

"He didn't tell me. I didn't have the need to know."

"Can you find out?"

He shook his head. "I don't work for the FBI anymore, remember. But . . ." His wheels were turning. "Stern," he said. "He works in statistics. We roomed together at the academy."

"A bedmate?" I said.

Johnny's face flopped. "A roommate," he said, a little annoyed. But his tone changed as quickly as his words. "You know, Archie, I've been thinking. Maybe too much. You're probably right." He was confiding now, not discussing.

"About what?"

"Being gay, maybe." He didn't look at me when he muttered, when he remembered, "I guess I did have a crush on Stern. Christ, I never could have said that two weeks ago."

"You couldn't have said that two hours ago," I said, smiling. "Do you think he has the info on the mole?"

"He has access to information on everything."

"Would he tell you?"

"Maybe. If he doesn't know that I resigned." Johnny reached for the phone. "Shit," he said and stopped. "His department doesn't work on Saturday." Johnny got up and bent down to his suitcase, which was opened on the living room floor. He picked out his address book, sat back at the table.

The telephone rang and I picked it up. Carney was at the other end.

"Hardin is dead," he said.

"No shit," I said, bitter as hell. Johnny looked at me while I related my pitiful afternoon with Davie. Carney listened without interruption. So did Johnny. I told Carney everything Davie told me, except about the overheard conversation between Max and the Columbia Law School.

"He's better off dead," Carney said when I had completed my story.

"Nobody's better off dead," I said. "He just didn't see any other way out. Why'd you let him out, Carney?"

"He didn't kill Harmony."

"I know. Why'd you let him out?"

A pause, then, "Orders," Carney whispered.

"From who?"

"He was getting too much publicity from that damn fag organization who was trying to raise money for him. And from you," he added loudly. "Digging, trying to find out who killed that guy."

That made no sense. "You think I'm going to stop?"

"You have to, Cain."

147

"I don't have to do anything, Carney. Not for you."

"That offer's still open. Take it."

I didn't reply to that. He already knew my answer. He asked anyway. "You coming back, Cain, as detective sergeant?"

"I'll be talking to you, Carney," I said, and hung up.

"Jesus," Johnny said when I still had my hand on the receiver. "Davie, my God. Suicide. I'm sorry, Archie."

"Yeah," I mumbled. "So am I."

"And for dope?" Johnny asked, unbelieving.

"It was his life. Max wasn't," I said. My eyes focused on Johnny's open address book.

"Why'd they release Davie? What did Carney say?"

"Not a fucking word," I said. "Now he wants me to lay off finding out who killed Max. It wasn't a request. It was a fucking order."

Johnny didn't even ask if I would follow the order. He knew better. He took his address book in hand. "I can call Stern at home. He does most of his work there. Works off a modem."

I didn't understand the term. Johnny explained. "A device hooked up to the telephone whereby his computer can talk to the in-house computer, so to speak."

I shifted the phone to his side of the table. "Call him," I said. But I held my hand on the receiver. "Davie also told me something else," I said, "that I didn't tell Carney. Max was trying to get some legal help. He was afraid of jail time." I reached for the diary and read from the open page. " 'I'll be going to jail for a long, long time.' Davie overheard Max on the phone, something about immigration problems. And his job at the magazine. Do you know anything about that?"

"No. We had nothing on Max," Johnny said, and suddenly looked as if he'd been caught with his hand in the cookie jar. "We checked on the background of all the officers in G.A.A. Max was clean. No record, not until he started getting arrested at G.A.A. demonstrations."

"Does that mean that it's not true? Max didn't have any other legal problems?"

"If there was anything out there about Max, the FBI would have had it."

I sat there mulling that over.

Johnny was doing his own mulling. "Immigration," he muttered. "That would be the CIA," he said, almost to himself.

"CIA?" I asked.

Johnny snapped his mind back. He reached for the phone and dialed.

After no more than two rings, the other end was picked up. "Stern?" Johnny said. "Grab here."

I smiled at that. Odd nickname, but it went with Grabowski. I liked it. Johnny caught my grin. He returned it.

"I have problems with G.A.A.," Johnny said. After a pause, he also said, "Yeah, I'm still with that faggot organization." He didn't look at me, and in fact turned to the side, the phone in his lap.

"Listen, something big is coming off," Johnny said. "I need some help down there. . . . Oh, Christ, quit your fucking crying. No, you don't have to rub asses with those queers. You're a desk man. . . . I know you're kidding. . . . Hell, it's not that bad. They're just like everybody else. . . . No, really, they are. . . . No, Stern," Johnny said firmly. "I'm not turning queer."

Johnny looked up at me. I winked at him. He quickly turned away again.

"Listen, Stern. I have somebody else working in there with me. I need his help, but I don't know who the bastard is. . . . No, it can't wait," he said impatiently. "It's coming down tonight." Johnny turned to me, holding his hand over the mouthpiece. He said to me, "I don't know. He's checking. I don't think so." He quickly returned the receiver to his ear. He listened. "Thanks, Stern. I owe you one. Let me owe you two," he quickly added. "What's the latest update on Harmony? . . . Yeah, I know he bit it, but do you have anything else that I didn't know about? . . . Okay," Johnny said, again impatiently. "I know I'm busting your balls. But mine ain't exactly swinging free." After a short pause. "Suck my cock, faggot," Johnny said, and waited.

Johnny looked up at me and smiled, his hand over the mouthpiece of the phone. I was about to speak. He held up a finger. "Yeah . . . Yeah . . . You can't get at it? . . . When? . . . Okay, Stern, I appreciate it. . . . No, I'm in the field. I'll get back to you."

After Johnny hung up, I asked, "Well?"

"Shaker," he said.

"Helen," I said, surprised. "The vice president."

"And when Ron resigns, soon to become president," Johnny reminded me. "But the bureau hasn't got her yet. They do have her on the hook, though. They checked her background, found out she had an illegal abortion four years ago."

"They're holding that over her?" I said.

"Yeah."

"You play dirty pool, don't you?"

"Archie, this country's in trouble. We play any way we can."

"G.A.A. isn't a subversive organization," I said, getting more miffed than I should have. I willed myself to calm down.

Johnny also cooled down. "I know."

We sat across from each other, each of us lost in our awkward thoughts. Johnny broke the silence. "There's another file on Max. One that I didn't know about. I never even knew about it."

"What is it?"

"I don't know. It's locked. Stern doesn't have the code. He might be able to get it. But he has to go through channels. I told him I'd call him back at five. I wouldn't have much hope."

I checked the clock on the wall. Close to four-thirty. "So we wait."

"We wait. What's up with immigration?" Johnny asked. "Any ideas?"

"You said something about the CIA," I told him.

He brushed it off. "It has nothing to do with this. Any other ideas?"

"One," I said. But I didn't share it. I reached for my jacket. "There are some TV dinners in the freezer. Help yourself. Oh, and Johnny, Helen knew about you. She was going to expose you at the meeting this Wednesday."

Johnny was surprised. "How do you know that?"

"She told me. And Ron knows, too. I'll bet you ten to one."

"That's why he's been acting so strange to me lately. How'd he find out?"

"It seems there are spies everywhere," I said in jest. But only half. I slipped my arms in the sleeves of my jacket.

"Where you off to now?" Johnny asked. He stood up and I could again see the wheels turning in his head.

I grabbed him, gave him a quick kiss, and said, "West side, this time."

Before Johnny could react to my little peck of love (well, maybe not love), I reached for the door. When I touched the knob, the downstairs buzzer sounded. I snapped my hand away as if a bee had sunk its stinger into it. Johnny looked at me as if he too had been stung.

My apartment building didn't have an intercom, and I usually didn't answer the buzzer unless I knew who was there. "You expecting anybody?" I asked Johnny.

"Nobody even knows I'm here. Except Carney."

I pushed the button on the right side of the door, directly beneath the poster of Jimmy Dean's Rebel. We both waited silently. We heard the elevator stop and footsteps nearing my door. They weren't Carney's. Not unless he'd taken to wearing boots, as silly a thought as any I've had.

The doorbell rang its tinny ring. I placed my eye on the peeper. Expect the unexpected. On the other side of the distorted glass, Ron's misaligned face looked comical. I opened the door.

He began speaking in stunted gasps even before he crossed the threshold. "Cain, I have to tell you. Davie is dead. He asked me for money, but I didn't give it to him, and—" His words stopped as if he were slammed on the bean. "Johnny!"

Johnny didn't speak. Ron's eyes were popped at the sight. To me, he said, "What is he doing here?" It was less a question than a demand.

I stepped around and closed the door. "He's staying with me. What are you doing here?"

His voice was toned down, but not his excitement. "I came to see you about him." He spit out the word *him* and pointed at Johnny. "You," he said. He said the one word to me, recognition sliced gravely across his face. He added another word, "You, too."

By his accusation you would have thought that Ron was Kevin McCarthy and I had just stepped out of a pod. He backed toward the door, his hands fumbling for the knob behind him, not turning his back on us. "She didn't tell me that." Fear lit up his eyes. Sharp, almost uncontrollable fear, I thought.

He couldn't get the door open.

I felt an explanation might calm him down before he fell into a pile of pickup sticks. I reached out to him. "Ron, Johnny is staying here because he told me—"

Ron pushed me away with one arm, as if I was trying to strong-arm him. I wasn't. I wasn't even touching him. He turned, pulled the door open, and almost knocked himself over with the effort.

I walked out into the hall. Ron didn't wait for the elevator; instead he opened the fire staircase. Before the door closed behind him, he turned to me with hatred in his eyes. "You son of a bitch."

When I went back to my apartment, Johnny asked, "What the hell was that all about?"

I let out a deep sigh. "A guess? Of course he knows you're a mole for the feds, and now he thinks I am."

I didn't give Johnny another good-bye kiss. But I did give him a "chin up" tug on the shoulder.

Chapter
15

At twenty minutes after five I was walking up West End Avenue. A small breeze coming off the river was snapping around the tall brick apartment buildings. Summer was definitely gone, and autumn taking firm hold. I cut down to Riverside Drive, heading toward an empty phone booth. By now, Johnny might have contacted his buddy in statistics, assuming Ron's in- and outburst didn't foul Johnny's brain. Not likely. Johnny's a pro. An FBI pro. I still didn't know how I felt about that. I pulled a coin out of my Levi's and slipped it into the slot. But I didn't dial the number. I was distracted.

Across the street and in the park, two men walked side by side slowly, curving around the hedges. I placed the receiver back in its hook and collected my dime. When I crossed the street and entered the park, the two were still in sight.

A family of four—a man, a woman, two dinky toddlers—was bundled up warmly and strolling leisurely, enjoying the comfort and beauty of the trees half shorn of golden leaves, enjoying the slight breeze, the quiet of the park. I walked with my hands in my jeans, my eyes up ahead, watching the two men. Sidney had stopped. He stood in front of the man who had taken a seat on the bench, Mr. Sinbad.

An odd combination, I thought. But not too odd, considering I had seen Sinbad at the office of *Current Social Thought*. I still couldn't place him with Glenn at Canal Street, but he was there, no doubt about it. But Sinbad and Sidney made a little more sense, not enough to figure out what was going on, but enough to put two similar pieces of the same puzzle into the same corner. Max had problems with immigration and Sidney was an alien resident. And Sinbad, he was an importer. Of what? People or things?

Sinbad lit a cigarette and handed the pack to Sidney. He refused the offer but sat next to him, not too close.

None of the early-evening strollers, mostly older folks, glanced at me as I walked off the cement pathway and into the bushes. Riverside Park wasn't exactly unknown territory to me. Just a little farther up the road was the Soldiers and Sailors Monument, one of the best nighttime cruising areas on the Upper West Side. And the concrete pathway that led to the monument was sided by benches and trees and winding walkways with an abundance of bushes suitable for a quick rendezvous.

But there wasn't much cover behind the bushes now. Fall had taken its toll on the leaves, but not entirely. There was still enough green and wilted brown that hadn't yet fallen. I carefully trod the trampled path in back of the benches. It passed near the concrete wall that ran between the sidewalk and the park. The path was only about a foot wide and certainly off the beaten track. Only men looking for other men in the dead of night usually walked this path. It was daytime now, a lingering twilight, and I certainly wasn't hidden from view. But Sidney and Sinbad were faced toward the river, not toward me.

No matter how carefully I stepped—and I was careful—leaves crunched underneath my feet. I was getting too close, so I stopped. The traffic on the street behind me was a soft grind, occasionally mingled with the roar of a bus. The voices coming from the men sitting on the bench almost in front of me were soft. I mentally blocked out the noise from the street and strained my ears to the bench.

"I don't believe you are telling me da truth, Mr. Meredith. All of da truth." It was Sinbad talking. Was his accent thicker than I remembered it being?

"I wouldn't lie," Sidney retorted. The whimpering in his British accent seemed no different than when I had talked with him when he had whimpered to me. And it was just as sorrow-ful.

There wasn't an immediate reply. Sidney waited. So did I. Sinbad merely gave off a huff, small in sound but deadly in tone. He turned to face Sidney head-on. "You've become dangerous, Mr. Meredith."

Sidney didn't say a word.

"You don't disagree?" Sinbad asked, in mock surprise.

Sidney turned away from him, still without a word. He leaned an arm over the bench. Another small turn of his head and he couldn't miss seeing me. The turn came. Recognition came in the sharp snap of his body. But Sidney didn't sound out. He turned quickly to face the front. The movement wasn't lost on Mr. Sinbad. He craned his neck around to see what had caught his attention. He saw the same thing Sidney did. Me.

The surprise in Sinbad's eyes was brief but definitely there. But there was no surprise in his voice. "Mr. Cain. Enjoying de evening air?"

The sun had gone west. The lingering light left over from the day was dull gray, like steel after it has been burnished.

I walked from behind them, my feet stomping on the dead leaves loud enough to wake the dead. "I always enjoy the evening air." To Sidney, I said, and sympathetically. "How are you doing?"

Sidney didn't speak. He barely nodded.

I waited for Sinbad to talk. He waited for me. Sidney just waited. The wait became pointless for all of us. I took the first step. "Did you find someone else to track down your imitation carvings?" I asked Sinbad. "Someone else to do your sleuthing?" I added. Irony was mixed within the question and Sinbad caught it.

"You're not very good at your vork, are you, Mr. Cain?"

"I'm not bad either. I'm here, right?"

I think Sinbad flushed on the inside. His eyes gave a slight quiver and stayed on mine. I didn't blink. Sinbad didn't either.

Without taking his eyes from mine, he said to Sidney, "Give my best to your vonderful vife."

Sidney didn't speak or move, even when Sinbad pushed himself off the bench. Sinbad's eyes left mine, leaving behind a grimy residue. He spoke to me, but not at me.

"And you, Mr. Cain. I understand you don't have a vife. Do you have a husband?" A slip of a smile parted his lips. "Give my best to him." He gave a barely distinguishable bow. "You vouldn't let me keep you on retainer, Mr. Cain." He waited a bare second, then said, "You could have helped." He turned and walked on.

When Sinbad turned the corner and was out of sight, Sidney immediately spoke. "You fool." His words had more strength in them than I would have thought Sidney possessed.

"Who is he?" I asked.

"You seem to know him," Sidney snapped back.

"Who is he?" I asked again.

Sidney arose. "This is ridiculous," he said, flabbergasted. "Do you know what you're doing?"

I joined him on the sidewalk side of the bench. "No, I'm afraid I don't," I said. "Suppose you tell me."

"How can this happen?" It was a question, but it wasn't aimed at me. It was aimed at himself, or the heavens. And neither one had an answer.

"It started with Max," I said.

"Max?" The one word seemed lost in an echo of confusion inside Sidney's mind. "He was a witness when Maureen became a naturalized citizen."

"Tell me about it."

"There's nothing to tell. That's it."

"Max is dead."

Sidney looked at me like I had struck him with a flatiron. "That has nothing to do with it."

"With what?"

"With Sinbad."

"How about Glenn?"

A question mark plowed Sidney's forehead.

"Sit down, Sidney," I said. I sat on the bench.

He stood over me, but he might just as well have been sitting on the ground. He was trying to be defiant but couldn't succeed. And it looked like his ego was as deflated as one of last year's Thanksgiving Day Parade balloons. "Tell me about Max," I said. Sidney gave up the pretense, sat with head bowed, hands hanging between his knees. "And Maureen."

Sidney didn't stir. He began moving his head from side to side. "I don't know," he said.

"What don't you know?"

"Nothing happened," he said, looking up to me for forgiveness. He spread his hands, palms facing up, almost in prayer, praying for help from a God who wasn't here. "Max was a witness for Maureen when she became a citizen. I told her it was wrong, risky. We could wait. She said she knew better. And she does," he quickly added. "But I didn't see any need. We could wait. I could wait."

His words were forced, but they were also freeing. Each short sentence led to the next, with some cautious probing.

"Wait for what?" I asked.

"Maureen wanted to become a citizen right away. She couldn't wait the five years. You have to live in the country five years before you can become a citizen." He said the words all in one breath. It was as though if he stopped talking, he wouldn't have the courage to continue. His sentences became disconnected. "Christ, when you first came around the office, Maureen called Sinbad and told him that you were there asking questions."

"Is that when Sinbad contacted me?" Sidney didn't respond. He was still lost in his own confusion. "Why?"

He didn't answer the question but forced another thought out. "She couldn't wait. And she was right again, too. She got the job. I told Maureen that Max was going to quit. Max was only being—"

His head snapped forward and down, almost in slow motion. But fast enough for me to see a hole and blood seeping through the back of his skull. I hadn't heard a shot. When I turned my

157

head there was no one to be seen walking the sidewalk on the other side of the concrete wall.

I felt for a pulse in Sidney's neck. I might as well have felt for life in a stuffed animal. I hopped over the bench and ran, taking a running leap and, placing my hands on the pointed concrete barrier, lifting myself over. A woman and a little boy were walking hand in hand, heading south. Two old men, one with a cane, were walking toward me, but not yet near. On the other side of the street, pedestrians were taking their Saturday-evening constitutional. A bus was heading south. Cars buzzed by both ways.

I ran toward the bus. It was stopped three blocks down. A passenger came out the door. The bus picked up speed on the way to the next destination. I followed suit. Three more blocks and, at the next bus stop, I caught it, out of breath. As the door was opening, I pushed into it, climbing the steps in two bounds. I almost knocked a woman over who was departing.

"Can't wait for the bus to stop?" the driver said. He wasn't obnoxious, but rather almost friendly.

I ignored him, my hand gripping the silver rail, my eyes scanning the passengers. Not one person was even vaguely familiar. The driver was asking for my fare when I turned and hopped down the steps. The door of the bus steamed closed behind me. I ran back the way I had come.

I didn't hop the concrete wall this time. I ran back down the path. Sidney was still there, as if sleeping, head bent forward, hands at his side, feet on the ground. There was a small round hole in the back of his head, and leaking out of it was a thick gooey stream of red and yellow.

A few people were walking the path, talking to each other or communing with nature, all ignoring Sidney, who was nothing but a dozing resident in the friendly park. A dozing resident who would never wake up.

I walked to the nearest phone. I didn't rush.

Within four minutes, I heard the sirens. I waited, sitting next to poor Sidney.

Chapter
16

Pictures were taken, the ambulance had been there and gone. A detective was questioning me. I told him the story, of Sidney and me talking, but not of Sinbad. Of course I was frisked, and my .38 was taken in hand. My laminated license was also taken in hand. Detective Bogan was skeptical, and his mood was turning harsh. Mine was becoming just as harsh. His questioning had lasted a half hour, which became pointless because I had given him all the information he was going to get. If he wanted to take me downtown, let him. I was tired.

"Listen," I said to him. "You have it all. You need me again, you know where to find me." I put a hand out for my gun and license.

"Stay right where the fuck you are."

We were sent to our separate corners when Carney made a guest appearance.

"This is kind of out of bounds for you, isn't it, Carney?" I asked when he approached. Somehow, I wasn't surprised to see him there, even though his turf was the Village, not the Upper West Side. Carney acknowledged me, not with a word, but rather with a look that could smash stone. He took Detective Bogan aside. I was being guarded by a handsome young uniformed patrolman. I took out my pack of cigarettes, flipped one between my lips, and offered one to the uniformed man at my right. He shook his head in a very serious rookie recruit's negative salute. Regardless, I smiled at him.

Carney left Bogan standing alone in his corner and came over to where I was standing. He had a present for me. Carney handed me my gun and license. "Let's go," he said. After an okay from his superior, the young studded cop allowed me to pass by him. I walked alongside Carney.

"Okay, give it to me," Carney said.

I gave it to him, leaving nothing out, including Sinbad.

"Jesus Christ," Carney exclaimed. "I told you, Cain. Lay off. But, no, do you listen?"

"I don't need a hearing aid," I countered. "Riverside Drive is miles away from the Canal Street flea market."

Carney didn't disagree with me. "You're fucking up, Cain."

"I'm fucking up nothing," I said. I was getting tired of being accused of something, and I didn't even know what the fuck it was. "I was here. Sinbad was here. And Sidney Meredith was here. Here," I emphasized. "Not even in your jurisdiction. What the hell are *you* doing here?"

Carney stopped at the edge of the park. I could see his unmarked car at the curb. "Listen, shitface. I get orders to cool you down." He was pointing his large index finger at my leather-coated chest. His knuckle was hairy. "And what the fuck do you do? You get yourself dug deeper still."

We were standing in front of the car. "Deeper into fucking what?" I moved his finger from his aim with a quick slap.

Eagerness or anger flared on Carney's face. "Get in there," he snapped, opening the door. I hesitated. "Get in, Cain." He was asking this time, not ordering. I slid inside the car. Carney walked to the other side and pulled himself in behind the wheel. He didn't start the engine.

He leaned an arm over the back of the seat, his other arm resting on the steering wheel. He gulped in a deep breath like he was getting ready to jump out of a plane and was hoping his parachute didn't have any holes.

"Cain. I got orders," he said.

"From who?"

"You goddamn . . ." Carney started to mouth off but swallowed his words. "Okay." He started again. "From the district attorney."

I was about to speak.

160

"From the commissioner," he added. "From goddamn J. Edgar Hoover," he added. He said the last words almost in a whisper.

I was about to speak again, but Carney compounded his words.

"From the goddamn CIA." Still, almost a whisper.

He stared at me, this time daring me to speak but not wanting to hear what I had to say. He needn't have feared. The commissioner, the D.A., the FBI, the CIA. "Why?" I asked.

He faced front, both hands slamming on the steering wheel. "Do you think I know?"

"Do you think *I* know?"

He turned to me again. "You know more than I do," he said, exasperated. "What do you know?" He was asking for information, and I almost felt sorry for him. He looked like an old-time Biblical warrior, exhausted, though not from battling the Philistines, but from the battle of the streets.

"I know that Max Harmony died in my arms. And I know that his lover jumped out of a window. And I know that the man Max worked for was sitting on that bench with me when a bullet flew into his brain. I don't know who offed Max. I know his lover was done in by his own hand. And the odds are pretty good that Sinbad shot Sidney." I was out of breath. I gulped in some fresh air and continued. "What's the connection with the FBI and the CIA? How the fuck do I know?" I briefly thought of Johnny. But just as quickly knocked that thought to that same comfortable unused corner of my brain.

"Cain, all I know is that I got a call from both the D.A. and the commissioner to slow down on the Harmony killing. I did slow down, but I didn't stop. Then I got a fucking call from the fucking bureau to play it easy. When I asked why, I wasn't given a reason. I told them to fuck off, it wasn't a federal case. Before my phone was even cool, I got a call from the CIA. They told me to lay low on Harmony and goddamn Sinbad. I didn't tell them to fuck off. But I wasn't agreeable either."

Carney bowed his head, resting. After too many seconds, he lifted it and continued, frustrated. "I arrested Hardin for the murder. That was it. I was out of it. Case closed, and I didn't even know what the fucking fuss was about. Then I was told there wasn't enough evidence to keep Hardin. We let him go."

"You never really believed he did it, did you?"

"What I believe has nothing to do with it."

"Why'd you let him go?"

Carney gave me a look to kill. "I was told to keep you off the fucking case. You were prying into areas you ain't supposed to. Areas that were out of bounds. As long as Hardin was in jail, you were going to keep hunting."

I was stunned. "And with Davie free, you think I would have stopped?"

"No." Carney almost laughed. "But they did."

"Who are they?"

"The goddamn commissioner called and told me to cut you down to size. The fucking CIA." He almost cried, not in sympathy, but almost in pain.

"Why?"

"If I knew that, I wouldn't be asking you."

When I didn't say anything, the silence became too much for Carney. "Your boyfriend was spying for the FBI in that fag organization."

"I know that," I said. "How do you know it?"

"When Hoover's boys called me, they let me know. They said he'd be looking into the murder of Harmony."

"Did you buy that?"

"No," Carney said quietly. His fingers clawed at the wheel. "I can feel my pension slipping through my fingers," he said. He realized I was still there. "You want a ride downtown?" he asked. He started the car, pulled away from the curb, and headed down Broadway. "I don't know what to tell you anymore, Cain."

"You're not telling me to lay off?"

"Would it do any good?" He eyed me, a small ironic smile on his face.

I didn't answer but returned the compliment.

When we reached Columbus Circle, I asked Carney to let me

out. He pulled in front of the Coliseum. I opened the door. I felt I should thank him, but I didn't know why. I pushed myself out the door and leaned into the car.

"I wish I was young again," Carney said.

I waited a beat, then said, "So do I." I slammed the door, feeling as old as Carney looked.

Carney went his way, I went mine, crossing the circle and walking up the edge of Central Park. A cement barrier similar to the one that enclosed Riverside Park surrounded Central Park. I crossed the street to an empty phone booth.

The telephone was answered after the first ring.

"Johnny," I said.

"Archie. Yeah. I got in touch with Stern."

"Was he able to open the file?"

"Yeah, he opened it," Johnny said. "Get this. Max was a witness when Maureen Meredith was sworn in as a U.S. citizen."

"I know that," I said.

"Did you know this? Max has sworn in a written deposition that he had known Meredith for five years. She couldn't have become a citizen unless she lived in this country for five years and had a witness to prove it. And Max had known her only for two."

"That means Max broke the law. A serious offense?"

"Serious enough," Johnny agreed. "And that's not all. Two weeks before he died Max went down to the immigration office to confess his offense."

"And?"

"The CIA was brought in and told him not to say a word to anyone. If Max talked about it, he would be sent to jail."

Johnny stopped talking. I didn't speak. My mind was grinding many wheels. "You still there, Archie?"

"Yeah, I'm here."

"Essentially the CIA was blackmailing him. If Max stayed silent about his crime, he was free. If he confessed to breaking the law, he'd go to jail. And what's so funny, Archie, that's

163

why he went down there, to confess. But they wouldn't accept his confession."

"Why?" I asked.

"You tell me." Johnny was excited as a kid with a new toy bomb.

"It's almost seven o'clock," I said. "I'll be home by nine. I have one more stop to make."

After I hung up, I realized I hadn't even told Johnny about Sidney and our early-evening and ultimately fatal encounter in the park. Or about Sinbad. Pieces were falling. Whether they were falling into the right places or not, I wasn't sure. But they were falling.

Within fifteen minutes, I was pressing the bell of the Merediths' apartment. I heard soft music on the other side of the door. And I heard the peephole slide back. I was being scrutinized. The door opened. Maureen Meredith, in flannel pajamas and with dry eyes.

"Why am I not surprised to see you?" she asked, not expecting an answer.

I wondered if she had been told that Sidney was now a slab on a table. She didn't leave me wondering for long. "You were there, weren't you? With Sidney. In the park. Just like you were there when Max died." She walked away from the door and into the living room. I followed. "Close the door," she said, then turned back to me.

I kept my eye on her as I eased the door closed. I was glad I didn't have to tell her about her husband.

"Are you satisfied?" she asked. She sat at a small round table at the window. The music was soft, the sound classical. She looked out the window at the courtyard below. "Funny," she said. "Sidney played the stereotype." She turned to me. "Fags commit suicide, don't they?" She nodded to the long drop outside the window. "We have the perfect setting."

"That stereotype has been long gone, killed by Stonewall." I don't know if she understood my meaning. I continued, "Besides, Sidney didn't commit suicide." I walked to the window, looking thirteen floors down onto a brick walkway.

164

"No, he didn't," she said, no note of sadness.

"You knew he was gay," I said.

"Of course, Cain. I told you that before. Or as much as. I knew it even before he did," she said. "Ours was a marriage of convenience. We made a good team. He was a good editor, I was a hard worker who could make the right connections."

"Why was Sidney killed?" I asked.

"I don't know." Almost a purr.

"Why was Max killed?"

"The police are going to have to figure that one out."

"You have no idea."

"No."

"Don't you think it's unusual that Max, your jack-of-all-trades, was killed one week, and your husband the next?"

"Yes. No. Max was killed by a jealous lover. His jealous lover just completed his scenario by killing Sidney. I understand he was released from jail."

"Only one thing wrong with that theory," I said. "Actually, two. The jealous lover didn't kill Max, and the jealous lover took a leap out of his fifth-floor window four hours ago. If he shot Sidney, he fired the gun from heaven." Or hell.

Maureen looked at me, debating whether I was telling the truth or not.

"Yes, a stereotypical homosexual of old," I said. "But his faggotry didn't kill him, dope did." I let that sink in, then added, "Any other suspects?"

I think she decided I was truthful. "You live in a weird world, Mr. Cain," she said, a playful smile on her lips. Slightly incongruous, considering her husband hadn't been dead many hours. "You and your kind take your life into your hands by . . . by cavorting downtown in a rotting pier that I understand will be condemned by the city. And you wonder when one of yours gets killed?" A small laugh, no longer playful.

"Sidney wasn't sitting on a rotting pier," I reminded her.

"He wasn't alone either," she countered.

It sounded like an accusation to me. "Which means?"

165

"Which means that no matter where you faggots have your playground, it's dangerous."

"But not usually deadly."

"It certainly was this time, wasn't it?" She leaned back in the chair, pulled her arms across her chest.

"Was Sinbad a faggot?"

"Who?"

"Your friend. Your friend the importer," I specified.

"I don't know what you're talking about."

"I wasn't the only one in the park with Sidney."

"Who else was there?" she asked. Her body in her pajamas tensed.

"Sinbad was there."

"I don't know any Sinbad," she said, couching her anxiety.

"Well, Sinbad knows you," I insisted.

"Impossible," she insisted right back.

"It's a fact," I stated. "I saw him in your office."

I waited for my words to seep in. I had time. Maureen again crossed over to the window. For a second, I thought she was contemplating the big jump. Sometimes I worry unnecessarily. She turned back to me, determination in her eyes. "Why did you come here tonight, Cain?"

"To offer my condolences," I said. I didn't sound convincing even to myself.

"Why don't I believe you?" she asked. But she didn't wait for an answer to that, either. "You may not believe this, Cain, but I am upset about Sidney's death. He shouldn't have died."

If she was upset, it didn't show in her eyes. They were as clear as a day without smog.

"But I can't do anything about Sidney's death," she continued. "I have to live with it. Or without it."

"You might at least mourn," I suggested.

"Everyone mourns in his or her own way. Did you mourn Max?"

"In my own way," I conceded. "Max was a witness at your naturalization."

166

The sudden change in conversation caught her off guard. She flared at me. "So what."

"He also lied."

If looks could kill, I would be sharing a cloud with Sidney. Maureen stared at me from across the room, her eyes fiery. I stared back, neither of us speaking. Her eyes cooled down. Softly, Maureen finally said, "You can leave now, Mr. Cain. Condolences accepted."

Another pregnant pause and I turned to go. But I changed my mind and faced her again. "You do know that the CIA is on to you," I said.

She didn't change expression, she didn't move a muscle, but her eyes grew bright. "What do you know about it?" she asked, her tone deadly.

"Enough to know that Sinbad isn't likely to stop at Sidney."

Her eyes relaxed. If I could have read faces better, I would have said she was laughing behind those eyes. Maybe I was pretty good at reading people's faces after all, because a small laugh did escape her lips when she spoke. "Get out, Cain. You're a fool."

I left. As I rode down the elevator to the ground floor I had the odd feeling she was right.

Chapter
17

Johnny sat and didn't speak while I told him the whole story of Sidney's murder, Sinbad's flight, and Maureen's superior attitude.

"Put it together, what does it all mean?" Johnny asked.

"I'm not sure. Maybe I'm too close. I can't see the forest for the goddamn trees."

Johnny settled back into the chair, poured himself another mug of coffee. He offered to pour for me. I waved him off and lit a cigarette. The clock said nine-thirty and I realized that Larry would be over by ten. I told Johnny of my plans to attend the dance at the firehouse with Larry. I wandered into the bedroom to change. I wasn't going dancing, but I was going to the firehouse.

"Okay," Johnny said. "Two weeks ago you were at the trucks, you met Max, and you both went to the docks, right?"

"Yeah," I said, stripping off my shirt, Levi's, boots, and socks. Johnny was in the doorway. I kept my shorts on and headed to the bathroom.

"Before you had the chance to . . . have sex . . . to do anything, Max was stabbed, in the dark, at the docks. You didn't know who did it. You didn't see anyone you knew."

"I saw a small figure dressed in black who ran up to the docks just before Max and I went in."

"You never told me that."

"I am now," I said. "And I also saw you there," I reminded him. Johnny was leaning on the bathroom door. I slipped my thumbs into the waistband of my shorts and pushed them down, tossing them on top of the seat to the toilet.

"Yes," Johnny continued, not turning his face away. "I was there. Yes, I was following Max. You know that."

"Do I know why?" I asked and stepped into the tub, adjusting the water, closing the curtain.

"Yeah, you know why," Johnny said, loud enough that his voice was heard over the running water. I think the fact that we were separated by the small curtain of plastic and many sprinkles of water released Johnny's inhibitions. "Yeah," he said. "I wanted to find out what it was like. Not necessarily with Max," he admitted. "But I wanted to. I knew Max wanted me. And I wanted him. But I was afraid."

I stopped soaping my body. Johnny sensed my attention was focused on him. I let the water drain the soap from my body, shut the tap, pushed back the plastic. He was sitting on the closed toilet seat, my shorts on the floor next to his feet. He handed me a towel.

"I was afraid of my own feelings," he said. He wasn't looking at me.

I rubbed myself dry. "Okay, finally you admit it. You had the hots for Max that night. Or any man who would show you the way," I quickly added. "We're veering off the point."

Johnny looked up. I wrapped the towel around my waist and stood in front of him. He smiled shyly. "If you stand around like . . ." He let it lie and smiled.

He was becoming goddamn brave in his feelings. I smiled, too, and stepped out of the bathroom. He followed me to the bedroom. I opened a drawer, tossed off the towel, picked out a clean pair of shorts, and stepped into them.

It was my turn now. We both went into the living room. "I was hired by Sinbad for a useless job. This was after I began digging into Max's death. Sidney told me Maureen contacted Sinbad right after I called at the office of the magazine. And then Sinbad got pissed when I wouldn't continue the job. This was after I visited the Ole Times on Canal Street for the first time."

"And that's where I come in again," Johnny said.

"What was the connection between Sinbad and Max?" I wondered out loud. Johnny didn't have an answer, either. I snapped my mind back. "Let me back up a bit. I visited the Merediths' office and Max's apartment."

"Not exactly legal, I might add," Johnny said, a mild rebuke in his words, but not too harsh, considering he himself had been a spy at G.A.A.

"I found Max's address book and his diary. What were the most significant points we found in the diary?"

"We?" Johnny asked.

"We," I answered.

"Max wrote that he can't see me anymore. Why?"

I offered a suggestion. "He knew you were FBI."

169

"And the only way he could have found that out was from the other mole in G.A.A."

"Helen."

"We'll have to accept that," Johnny said. "We have no other answer. Okay, let's assume Max knew I was FBI. He didn't confront me. He just tried to avoid me. Again, why?"

"He had other, larger, worries on his mind," I said.

"Exactly," Johnny agreed. "Here." He opened the diary to a page that was indexed with a small file card. He quoted. "I can't go back to work. I'll be going to jail for a long, long time."

"According to your buddy Stern, Max was feeling guilty about swearing falsely to Maureen Meredith's naturalization. He wanted to confess his mistake to immigration, but they wouldn't accept his confession. Why not?"

"They wanted to have him under their wing as another spy at G.A.A.?" Johnny asked.

"We're talking about the CIA here," I told him. "Not the FBI."

We both ran out of words. Where do we go from here? I wondered. I had hoped two heads would be better than my own.

"Okay," Johnny offered. "We go back to the flea market. Why was I assigned a job there?"

"You don't know?"

"No, Archie, I do know. This may sound like we're back in McCarthy's 1950s, but that flea market is a haven for homosexuals."

I almost laughed at that. In fact, I did. "Is that news?"

"Don't laugh. Gay liberation may have hit the Village, but most homosexuals are in the closet and would never expose themselves. Homosexuals are still fodder for blackmail."

"So?"

Johnny looked up at me. There was a warning in his eyes when he said, "I wasn't the only organization man working that flea market."

"Glenn," I immediately said. Before Johnny could confirm or deny, I added, "CIA?"

"That's a good guess," he said. I figured Glenn was under-cover, but I wasn't sure from which organization. "I was also told to steer clear of him. This was long before I became friends with Max. Max had nothing to do with it."

"Didn't he?" I asked, more to myself than to Johnny. "Sin-bad wanted me to investigate Glenn. And Sinbad was involved with the Merediths. And immigration. And so was Max."

It was almost ten o'clock. "Larry will be here soon," I said.

I dressed while Johnny talked. "You saw Sinbad at the Merediths' office. And the Merediths were aliens."

"But not illegal," I said. "Except maybe Maureen, since Max swore falsely for her to become a citizen of this country."

"Exactly," Johnny said. "Why did she want to become an American citizen so badly?"

I snapped the buttons on my shirt. My heavy khaki shirt. "Maureen knew some important people in Washington. Her magazine had a following among the political establishment." My mind ranged into a new arena and I was almost afraid to say the words. "She was a foreign spy." Even after I said them, the words sounded ridiculous.

Johnny didn't say a word, but he didn't laugh at the thought either.

"A spy for England?" I said, contradicting myself. "That's downright silly. The Revolutionary War was fought almost two hundred years ago."

Johnny took my words more seriously than I did. "England has spies, too," he said. "James Bond, for instance. And how do you know she's English? Anyone can affect an accent."

That was too much confusion for my weary mind to absorb. I turned another corner. "Why was Davie released?"

"You said it yourself," Johnny said. "Carney told you they wanted you to give up the hunt to set Davie free because you were treading into international territory."

"But I didn't give up."

"So they tried another tack. Carney offered you your job back."

"With a promotion," I added.

The doorbell buzzed. I slipped my holster on. Johnny went to the door and pressed the buzzer.

"That'll be Larry," I said. "Make yourself at home." Johnny offered me the most wonderful smile this side of Bleecker Street.

I returned to the problem. "Where does Sinbad fit into all of this? It still doesn't jibe," I said, pulling on my boots.

"That, buddy, is the sixty-four-million-dollar question."

"And you don't have an answer."

"Neither do you," Johnny countered.

He was right. I didn't. Not yet.

I heard Larry's footsteps in the hall. "We've pounded our brains enough for one night," I said.

I reached in the closet for my brown leather jacket. Johnny's black leather was hanging next to it. Looped over the hanger was a holster to match, filled with a revolver.

Chapter
18

Larry and I began our trek downtown but headed west first.

"Now, who was that?" Larry asked. "You're holding out on me. He's a little young for you, isn't he? He reminds me of a young John Wayne in a gung-ho marine movie, if John Wayne was ever young." Larry was almost swooning.

When I had introduced them, I knew Johnny was put off by Larry's flamboyant performance.

"A friend, that's all," I said.

"Uuuu-huuummm," Larry said, fluttering his eyelashes. "How big is his cock?"

"Is that all you think about?" I asked.

"Is there anything else?" he asked right back.

The farther south we walked, the more crowded Hudson Street became, with male bodies spruced up in their Saturday-night finest, which included wrinkled and worn 501's, polished boots, black leather, and maybe a chain here and there. Larry wore black leather pants and a leather jacket. But they were both designer wear. I think he got them from a modeling job.

The sidewalk in front of Drones had a small crowd waiting to get inside. It was a private disco and you needed a membership card to enter. Larry had the card, and with me at his side, we were passed through the door without having to pay the price of admission.

The music was loud, the dance floor large but nearly empty. It was too early. The real freaks don't come out until after midnight. The manager led me and Larry to a storeroom behind the D.J.'s booth. Larry introduced me to him, but I didn't catch his name. He was a sleezeball from the word go. His dungarees were too tight for his tubby frame, his mustache was too thin for his fat face, and his attitude was condescending. But Larry took his shit. It was embarrassing to watch.

The gist of the conversation was, yes, Larry could be the new doorman on Sunday nights. The manager would try him out for a month. Larry thanked him and wiped his lips. We left.

We walked crosstown, aiming for the firehouse. Larry was subdued. "I'd glad you didn't mention that we were going to the firehouse," he said. "He hates that place."

I didn't say anything.

Larry's calmed nature didn't last for long. It never does. Soon he was cruising and commenting loudly and suggestively on every person, male or female, we passed. I stopped at a phone booth. "Have to make a call," I said and fished out a dime.

"Can't be away from your little Johnny Wayne for two minutes, can you?" Larry said. "It must be love."

I smiled, dropped a coin in the slot, took out my wallet, dialed the number. The phone was answered after the first ring. I talked to Glenn.

173

Larry struck up a conversation with a tall, brown, muscled man who was standing at and hustling the corner. My conversation with Glenn was brief. When I stepped out of the booth, Larry introduced me to Chico. I said hi, but Chico ignored me. Larry asked him to come to the firehouse dance. Chico said, "No, ain't got no money, man." We went on our way.

Larry hung on my arm and whispered in my ear. "I had him last month. You wouldn't believe the size of his dick."

I listened to Larry with one ear. That was more than enough.

After we reached the front of the firehouse, we had to wait in line five minutes before we handed over our bucks.

The D.J. was starting to warm up the night. Only a few couples were beginning a slow beat with their feet on the dance floor. They were all male to male. A few women were on hand on the sidelines, along with more men, more men than you could shake a bottle of amyl nitrite at. But they didn't stay sidelined for long. Like Glinda waving her magic wand, the witching hour began, the time to start the fast dance into morning. The floor became smaller as the crowd became larger.

As quick as the strike of a match, the heat and sweat combined with the writhing bodies, most bare-chested, and the music, obnoxiously loud, made the firehouse an inferno of male sexuality. Larry was in the heat of the crowd, dancing by himself or with the whole room, his body insinuating its rhythm into the other bodies around him. His mind? Who knows where it was. Before we entered the building Larry had surreptitiously dropped a tab of acid. Not too surreptitiously, though. He knew better than to offer me a tab. That was an hour ago, and Larry was now hitting his peak. I watched him grind. He was oblivious to me and to the world.

Beer was being handed out at a makeshift bar set up at the rear in front of the storeroom. The music was luring me on, my body subconsciously reacting to the rhythm of the beat. I grabbed a beer and joined Larry on the floor, letting the beat of the D.J. pave the way. I'm not sure Larry even saw me. His eyes were open, they glowed. I didn't stay on the floor very long. My body may have been willing, but my mind wasn't. I was scanning the crowd, searching for Ron. And even though the firehouse was becoming more jammed by the minute, I was sure Ron wasn't among us.

Fully dressed, I was oddly out of place among the half-naked men. I didn't want to remove my jacket and the sweat was heating up inside my leather, so I stopped and walked off the floor. Larry didn't miss me. I upended my beer and left the empty can on the floor by the wall.

I had my hand stamped and wandered outside. The air was refreshingly cool and welcome. There were pockets of men leaning on cars or milling around, talking or cruising or smoking, both dope and otherwise. I didn't spot Ron. My watch said 12:45.

There were few women on the dance floor inside, and even fewer hanging around outside. But I did spot Helen Shaker standing with another woman near an alleyway two doors down from the firehouse. When I approached them, Helen saw me and offered enough daggers to cut out my heart. She then turned her back. I walked up to her anyway.

"Seen Johnny?" I asked. Her back noticeably stiffened. Her female friend eyed me cautiously.

"I'll meet you inside," Helen said to her. Her friend obliged, but not before bouncing her shoulder against mine when she passed. Helen turned to me.

"No, I haven't seen Johnny," she said. She didn't even attempt a smile.

"Well, I thought you might have, considering you're both working for the same company."

Her teeth were clamped tight, her eyes slits. She spoke through grinding teeth. "Ron told me that Johnny is staying with you."

"He is."

"You're going to ruin it, Cain."

"Ruin what?"

"You know fucking what." She turned to go.

I grabbed her arm. "Ruin what?" My words matched hers in intensity. Her eyes slid down at my hand holding her arm. I released her and said, "Johnny isn't a spy anymore."

175

"Who says?"

"I do," I told her. "But you are."

"Jesus fucking Christ," she exclaimed. This time she took my arm and led me into the alley on the side of a garage. Once we were in the dark, off the mainstream of men, she released her grasp.

"I'm sick and tired of these fucking games," she growled. "What do you mean, Johnny isn't a spy anymore?"

"He quit the FBI," I said.

"You're kidding? When? Why?"

"Yesterday. He couldn't take the hypocrisy."

Helen laughed. It wasn't a sarcastic laugh, but rather almost friendly. "He's gay, isn't he? I mean, I know he pretended to be gay to infiltrate G.A.A. But he wasn't really gay." She paused. "Is he?" There was almost joy in her words.

"He's just now starting to admit it to himself."

"I knew it," she said, triumphant, a wide grin on her face. She took a step closer to me. "And you mean Johnny really quit the pigs?" She didn't wait for an answer, but she knew the words were true.

"How did you know Johnny was working for the FBI in the first place?"

"Come on, Cain. You want me to tell you all our secrets?"

"I didn't realize that G.A.A. was a secret organization."

"It's not." Her tone changed, her grin gone. "No matter what the FBI thinks. Nor are we dangerous or subversive. Listen, Cain," she said, pulling me farther into the alley. "Not all lesbians are out of the closet."

"No kidding."

"Okay," she admitted. "I know somebody at the FBI. She has nothing to do with their fucking spying shit. And she isn't even a member of G.A.A. She works in the office downtown. She would never join our group. She couldn't. If her boss ever found out she was gay, she'd not only lose her job, she'd probably lose her kids. But she helps the cause any way she can."

"And she told you about Johnny?"

"I found out, didn't I?" she said proudly.

I smiled.

"And Johnny really quit?" she asked anxiously.

"Yes."

"That means we can still go through with it, right?" She waited briefly for an answer. I didn't know what the hell she was talking about. She added, "If you don't fuck it up."

"Fuck what up?"

"I'm still gonna spy for the FBI," she said, a sneaky smile on her face.

"You mean you'll spy for the FBI and counterspy for G.A.A.?" There was more than a touch of amusement in my voice.

"Why not, Cain?"

"Indeed," I said. "Why not?"

"I can dish the FBI all the dirt they're looking for." She paused. "Except the truth." A wide grin splayed across her mouth. "They won't stifle our zaps anymore."

"Good luck while it lasts," I said. "Do you still think Max was a spy?"

"Yeah, I do. An inadvertent one. He was too close to Johnny. Whatever he spilled to Johnny ended up downtown. I think Max figured it out and cut him off. Of course, I hinted as much to Max. Maybe that helped. But when he clammed up on Johnny, I guess that's when I was approached. The FBI wasn't getting the goods anymore."

"Aren't you frightened?" I asked.

She stood tall. "Of what?"

"Of going to jail. An illegal abortion."

Her eyes darkened. "My God, does everybody know? Shit, Cain, I was raped by five men four years ago. On the fucking beach." She motioned to some distant dark ocean. "And the cops wouldn't do a fucking thing about it because I'm a dyke. They fucking laughed. I didn't want no kid. My lover at the time, she gave me the money and bought me a round-trip ticket to D.C. That's funny. D.C.," she said, an ironic twist in her voice. "The fucking capital. Some sleaze-ass doctor cut my insides out. By the time I got back to New York, I left behind a bloody seat on the goddamn bus."

"Aren't you afraid of going to jail?"

"It won't be the first time. And it won't be long now, anyway, when abortion will be legalized."

"In the meantime, what you did was a crime. And the FBI is hanging that over your ass."

"And I'll hang it right fucking back," she said, glaring at me, but warily. "I'm not afraid of fucking jail." But maybe she was. There was a certain amount of skepticism in her eyes when she asked, "You won't tell them about me? That I'm counter-spying?"

"I don't even know anybody at the FBI. Who could I tell? Johnny doesn't work there anymore."

A warm smile replaced her frown. Probably the first warm smile I'd seen on her face. A nice addition. "You're not a bad sport, Cain. For a fag."

"And you're not a bad sport, either, Shaker," I said. "For a bulldyke." If she was a man I might have kissed her. "I think you better talk to Ron," I said. "He thinks I'm the devil incarnate."

For a second, Helen seemed startled. We walked out of the alleyway side by side. "Ron called Johnny at your place."

I stopped, spotting Glenn across the street, leaning against the side of a yellow van. I tried to set my concentration back on Helen but kept my eyes on Glenn.

"What do you mean? When did Ron call Johnny?" I asked.

Helen checked her watch. "About an hour ago."

"Why did he call him?"

"He said he wanted to settle things once and for all."

My attention was back full force on Helen. "What things?"

She seemed to cower. "I told Ron that Johnny was a mole."

"I know that. Ron was at my place earlier this evening."

Helen began to bite a fingernail. "He was going to meet Johnny at the docks," she said. "That's what Ron told me. He was going to have it out with Johnny."

"Have it out?"

* * *

Inside the firehouse, the D.J. was hitting his earsplitting and bone-crushing stride. I couldn't even see Larry amid the lights and the smoke and the steam and the men. That was okay. He was on his own. I couldn't wait around.

I muscled my way back through the door. Once outside, I scanned around for Glenn. The sidewalk was now swarming with sweating men and tired men and stoned men and resting men. I wandered through the bodies of shoulder-to-shoulder men. Glenn was near the alley. I walked over to him.

"Small world," I said.

"Not really," he said, his face not cracking even a small smile. "What did you want to talk to me about?"

"Everything," I said. "Why Sinbad? Why Max? Why Davie? Why me?" Glenn looked at me like I had gone mad. I didn't give him a chance to answer. "Something for you to think about. And I want an answer. But not yet," I said. "Wait here. I'll be back." It wasn't a request, it was a goddamn order. I left him standing alone to figure it out, and walked north.

Chapter
19

I didn't find an empty taxi until I hit Houston Street. It was a short drive to Christopher and West. He knew the quickest route and most of the traffic was heading south. The cabbie let me out on the busy corner. Even though I was preoccupied with worry about Johnny, I noticed the cab that pulled up behind me. And another cab behind him. What was this, a fucking parade? I turned the corner and waited to see who was following. When I peered around the corner, I didn't see a face

I recognized. I stepped back out. The cabs were gone. Any passengers they brought were now mingling with the rest of the men of the night.

The air was almost cold, but the weather didn't inhibit the action. The street was now hepped up for autumn. Not as many men as a summer night would bring, but more than enough, and warmly dressed. The men were prepared for a long night of street cruising—with heavy fall jackets. And the weather wouldn't stop them from overflowing into the backs of trucks and onto the docks.

To find Johnny and Ron in the darkness of the piers or in the back of a truck was like searching for a pin in a pile of iron shavings. But I had to try.

I walked up Hudson Street and peered into alleyways tucked off the street. I edged myself toward any darkened truck that had a sign of movement. I worked quickly and mostly by feel and the light from my cigarette. But I didn't feel or see Johnny or Ron. I was running too fast. I walked back to West Street, but it was pointless to go into the docks. The area is too large, and even the light from my cigarette wouldn't penetrate all the corners of darkness.

It was a useless task and I should have stayed at the firehouse. I hailed a cab and hopped in. The cabbie pulled out with a squeal, and as I was giving directions I saw the two. Ron and Johnny. They were sitting on the deck of the concrete barrier of the pier. I yelled at the driver to stop. He did and began swearing. I pushed a bill into his hand to shut him up.

Ron and Johnny hopped onto the concrete and ducked through the torn fence and under the boards. I ran to the docks and was aware that someone else was running behind me. When I hopped the concrete wall, I turned. A figure dressed in black zipped rapidly past me out of the darkness and into the tiny entrance of the docks. I ran to the same entrance and pushed myself through the wire. The darkness was too thick. I stayed in front of the entrance to allow my eyes to adjust. I called out loudly, "Johnny!" My word echoed in the darkness, but no answer. Any noise in the building, whether moaning or sounds of sucking, seemed to have stopped. I yelled again, "Johnny!"

I felt rather than saw a knife reach above me and come down. When the fist with the knife struck my shoulder, I heard a shot. In the cavernous structure, it sounded like a cannon. In an instant, the pier was filled with sounds. Shouts were heard inside the crumbling structure, pandemonium was breaking all around me, feet were scrambling, bodies rushing to the entrance. To keep from being trampled, I fell to the side atop another body. The feet rushed past me, the running bodies poured through the small hole in the wall.

I lay protecting my face with my arms, although I was well out of harm's way. But not too well. There was a sharp pain in my shoulder. The blade had penetrated my leather jacket but hadn't stayed put. Blood was leaking, but not pouring, through the hole. I moved an arm around to feel the body that was beneath me. I pulled my arm back as if struck by a cobra. The body was a woman. The scrambling of feet quickly dissipated. The dock was empty, silent.

"Cain," a voice sounded out. The voice was near and almost a whisper. A voice with an accent. The rotting pier had emptied as rapidly as an orgasm. I felt like I was alone in a world of dirt. I peered into the darkness and saw nothing. Again, softly, "Cain." The voice was unmistakable. And it wasn't Johnny or Ron. I hesitated to answer.

"It's all right, Cain. It's over now," the shadowed voice continued. I didn't answer.

The voice said, "Look."

I twisted my neck to the sound of the voice, to the entrance in back of me, then watched while the man moved to become a silhouette beside the dimly lighted triangular boards and wire. Sinbad. "Here," he said and tossed a pistol into the darkness.

Another voice sounded out. "It's okay, Archie." This voice I knew. It was Johnny's. It was on the other side—the outside—of the tiny entrance hole. "I have him covered."

I pushed myself off the ground but took hold of the arms of

the body beside me, dragging it to the entrance. My shoulder throbbed with pain, and I felt blood spurt from the wound.

When I stepped into the misty light of the entrance cave, Sinbad helped me pull the body out.

Cars still passed on West Street, but no stragglers mingled about. The horny men of the docks had disappeared into the side streets of the night like magic. The magic of a gunshot that spelled "Danger, get out!"

Johnny was standing on the concrete walkway, his gun at the ready and aimed at Sinbad's back. Ron was standing behind him. Sinbad was a new man. He was wearing Levi's, a bomber jacket, and black boots. A gay clone. I almost laughed, but I knew it would hurt if I did.

The body Sinbad and I were carrying was dressed in black, from the slacks to the sweatshirt to a motorcycle cap that was crushed down on her head. Her back was covered with blood. Her front had exploded into a mass of blood and guts.

"Tell your friend to lower his gun," Sinbad said. "Somevon might get hurt."

I didn't tell Johnny any such thing. And Sinbad saw I wasn't about to. He reached inside his jacket. "I saved your life," Sinbad said cautiously. His hand came out of the jacket slowly. In it was a small wallet. He handed it to me. There was an identification photo of him, an official seal, and the letters that spelled out CIA.

Sinbad smiled and held out his hand. I didn't return the wallet.

"What is it?" Johnny asked.

"CIA," I answered.

"What?" Johnny grabbed the wallet but didn't drop his aim.

"Mr. Grabowski. Mr. Cain," Sinbad said. He looked at Ron. "An explanation is necessary." He turned to me again.

"Wait," I said. I was pressing my hand against my shoulder to cover my wound. Blood was trickling through my fingers. My entire side was throbbing. I told Ron, "Talk to Helen. She's waiting at the firehouse. I'll be there in a little while."

"You going to be okay?" Ron asked, his eyes glued to the

blood oozing through my fingers and over the brown leather of my jacket. He seemed almost afraid to look at the body at my feet.

"Go," I said. "I'll see you later." Ron seemed frozen. I shouted, "Go!" Frightened out of his wits, Ron turned and ran across the street, looking back every ten steps, until he disappeared around the corner.

"Talk," I said to Sinbad.

Sinbad looked to me, to Johnny, and down to dead Maureen Meredith. "She killed Max," he said.

"Why?" I asked. I winced when I said it. The throb had graduated to my head.

"We better get you to a hospital," Johnny said, again without moving his aim from Sinbad.

"Let him talk," I said to Johnny. To Sinbad, I said, "Talk."

"Mrs. Meredith killed your friend because he had svorn falsely to a federal judge dat he had known her for five years, vhen in fact he didn't. He had known her for only two. She vanted to become an American citizen very badly."

His explanation was too slow, too thin, and made no sense, and the pain was becoming too intense. "Tell me more," I said through clenched teeth. Johnny took a step toward me. "No, I'm okay," I said. He stayed put, keeping his guard up.

"All right, Mr. Cain," Sinbad said. "More. Maureen and Sidney Meredith were agents for a foreign government."

My face was impassive, except for the pain.

"Don't be fooled, Mr. Cain. Da cold var isn't over. It isn't even thawed. The Merediths created a very successful social policy magazine. An influential magazine. American congressmen read their vords with much interest. Mrs. Meredith vas offered a job on Senator Dorman's staff." He paused. "Dat's something you didn't know, isn't it?" Sinbad smiled slightly but didn't wait for an answer. "She vas going to move to Vashington, closer to power, nearer the source."

His story sounded fantastic. Just fantastic enough to be true. "Why did she kill Max?"

"Your friend realized vhat he had done, being a vitness for

a foreign agent to become an American citizen. And lying, at dat."

"How did Max know she was an agent?"

"He didn't. Perhaps I vorded it wrong. Max realized he committed a crime, a serious crime, a federal crime. The realization of his crime vas his motivation, not her agent status."

Sinbad looked at Johnny, still holding his gun. "You don't need that, Mr. Grabowski."

Johnny didn't agree. Sinbad shrugged his shoulders and continued. "Harmony told Mrs. Meredith he vas going to give himself up. She couldn't have dat."

"If she was an agent, why would she take the chance to become a citizen illegally?"

"Opportunity was dere. Now. Vashington was calling. A top security job—for an American citizen," he emphasized. "She was on her way to the upper echelon. Dat is, until Max decided to become a martyr."

Sinbad looked from me to Johnny and back to me. Then he focused on the dead body. "She killed Max. Perfect crime," he said, gesturing to the entrance of the sex pier. "Da cover of darkness, da eyes of a cat. Another random homosexual murder. Vhat did it have to do with her? Not a thing. Max Harmony just happened to vork for her magazine."

"Max confessed his crime to the authorities."

Was there a hint of surprise on Sinbad's face?

"But dey wouldn't accept his confession," I continued. "Why?"

Sinbad's brow furrowed. "Vhy?"

"Why?"

"If Max turned himself in," Sinbad said, "it vould blow her cover. Vhen Max vent to the authorities, ve had already known about his false statement. Ve knew vhat Mrs. Meredith was doing. Ve have had her under surveillance since she came to dis country. She became valuable to us. Ve fed her information. She passed it on. Vhether da information vas true or false, only ve knew. And ve couldn't have Max interfere. Ve told him to vait."

"You set him up to be killed."

Sinbad shook his head. "Ve could never have known dat Max vould be stupid enough to tell her dat he vas going to turn himself in."

My blood boiled. That is, the blood that was still inside me. The blood seeping out of my shoulder was now clotted by my fingers. The throbbing was there in my shoulder, but it was nowhere as intense as the throbbing in my brain. And that throb was less from pain than from from the story Sinbad was telling me. There were still many loose ends that wouldn't make a complete rope.

"Sidney," I said. It was a question.

"Sidney," Sinbad laughed. "Sidney vas a veak sister."

"Which means?"

"You know as vell as I do vhat it means," Sinbad said. "Sidney vas a mistake. A great mistake. He and his vife made da perfect cover. Until. Until Sidney . . ." It seemed as if Sinbad was searching for the right words. "Until Sidney let his homosexual tendencies control his life. He became dangerous to Maureen. He vas no longer the perfect cover. Vhen dey moved to Vashington, she couldn't very vell have a husband who vould sneak around into dark corners looking for a man to have sex vith. He vas harming her mission." He paused, and in the moonlight I could almost distinguish a smile on his face. "Instead, she brought him down."

My knees began to give out. My body swayed. Johnny moved to hold me up with one hand. Sinbad beat him to it. "Ve should get you to a hospital," he said.

I couldn't have agreed more. But I asked, "Why were you conveniently at the docks tonight?"

"I followed Mrs. Meredith when she left her home tonight. She vas at da firehouse, vaiting for you for da chance to strike again. You vere getting too nosy. But at da firehouse, da opportunity didn't present itself. My presence there wouldn't be noticed. Not with my"—he glanced down to his worn Levi's—"disguise. Vhen you left, she left. She followed you, I followed her."

His words made sense, yet they seemed too pat. But my arm was lead weight and perhaps beginning to affect my judgment. The streetlights also began a slow swirl.

We left Maureen Meredith alone, by herself, lying on the concrete slab when we crossed the street. Sinbad was helping me along. Johnny still had the revolver at the ready, so I'm not sure how much of Sinbad's story he accepted. Sinbad stopped in the phone booth and called the station. When he hung up, I asked, "Why did you hire me to search out those statues at Canal Street?"

Johnny replaced his gun in his holster but kept one hand in his pocket, only a small movement away, if necessary. "To vatch you, Mr. Cain. And hope you vouldn't discover da truth. If you came too close to discovering vhat was going on among the Merediths and Harmony and da CIA, you would have been told da truth. But dat was a last resort. Ve need not have worried. You never even sensed da truth, did you, Mr. Cain? You never even came close." There was a triumphant glint in his eye.

I didn't answer. He was right. Johnny hailed a cab. I heard a siren in the distance.

"I vill be in touch," Sinbad said and recrossed the highway to the docks. The body of a woman was waiting for him on a concrete slab.

A taxi pulled alongside us. Johnny helped me inside. "Saint Vincent's Hospital," he told the driver.

It was only a short drive to Saint Vincent's. In the cab, Johnny helped me off with my jacket and my holster. He wrapped my .38 in the jacket and held both under his arm. At the hospital, the nurse took me inside a small curtain-divided room.

It was almost two hours before the doctor completed his work. For half the time, I waited in the room alone, lost in thought. The doctor washed, medicated, and bandaged the shoulder. The knife had hit no important nerve endings. He asked me how it happened. I told him I fell, but he didn't believe me. He told me to wait there.

186

The doctor left and I called Johnny in. He helped me into my holster and my jacket. A taxi was parked outside the entrance. When we were in the backseat, Johnny gave the cabbie the Perry Street address, but I changed it and aimed for the firehouse.

"Why?" Johnny asked.

I had had time to think while waiting for the doctor. "It doesn't make sense," I told Johnny. "Sinbad and Sidney in the park. Sinbad at their office. Sinbad at the flea market. Sinbad at the docks." Before Johnny had a chance to respond, I changed my mental direction. "Why were you and Ron going to the docks?"

"Ron wanted to go," Johnny said. "He said he had some time to waste until he had to get back to the firehouse before the dance ended."

"From what Helen told me, Ron was out for your blood."

"He was," Johnny explained, "but he isn't stupid. I told him, yes, I was a mole for the FBI. But not anymore. I also told him that Helen was another mole, and then he knew I was telling the truth. He said that, yeah, Helen was a spy—for the FBI *and* G.A.A. The FBI paid her and she didn't give them anything. Nothing that would compromise G.A.A. or any of the zaps, anyway."

"And you became fast friends at the docks," I said, sounding more jealous than I meant to.

He looked at me. "I wasn't going to carry on with Ron, Archie."

"Working up the courage?" I asked, with a small smile of pain.

"Maybe. After we went inside, I heard you call out my name," Johnny continued. "Before I could answer, I heard a struggle, a shot. Then the place went bonkers. Christ, those men came out of the woodwork like cockroaches. But, hell, within two minutes that place was empty. I was outside and stayed there. Then I heard Sinbad talking to you. You know the rest."

There were only three weary men in front of the firehouse.

They looked like they were on their last legs, ready to drag themselves home after a heavy night of dancing and dope. The entrance door was locked. I rapped on it. When I did, my shoulder began a slow throb again. The last three men of the Saturday-night disco moved on slowly down the street.

"Go home," a muffled voice from inside yelled.

"Ron," I yelled back. The throbbing increased. "Cain."

"Why are we here?" Johnny asked.

The door opened. Ron let us in.

"Is he here?" I asked Ron.

He nodded. "He was," he said quietly. "I told him what happened. He's outside. I sent Helen home. How you doing?"

"I'll be okay," I said. The downstairs of the firehouse was empty but a mess, beer cans galore, crushed cigarettes, crumbled napkins. "Everyone else gone?" I asked.

"Yeah. The cleaning crew will come in the morning," he said.

"It is the morning," I reminded him.

"What the hell are we doing here?" Johnny asked again. Ron had the same question on his lips.

"The CIA."

I heard the creak of the door at the same time as Ron and Johnny. We turned together. Sinbad stepped through the door, bolting it behind him. His revolver was aimed in our direction. A silencer had been added. "First," he said loudly, "please place your revolvers on da floor at your feet and move to da side." He stepped out onto the dance floor. We hesitated. He shot. Ron fell, his eyes wide, clutching his side.

"Don't," I whispered to Johnny as his hand inched up to his jacket.

"Slowly," Sinbad said, coming closer. Ron moaned on the cement floor. Good. Where there's moan, there's life. Johnny and I both eased our hands into our jackets and removed our revolvers very carefully.

"On da floor," Sinbad said.

We obeyed, placing the guns at our feet.

"Move," Sinbad ordered, his gun pointing the way.

We moved toward the staircase. Sinbad circled us until he

reached our guns at his feet. He picked each one up and pushed them into the belt of his Levi's. Ron looked up from the floor at Sinbad and groaned in agony, his hand, red with blood, pressed against his side. His eyes were panicky. My stomach turned, and Johnny took a step forward. Sinbad immediately let off another silent shot. Johnny went down.

"You son of a bitch!" I shouted and began to move forward. Sinbad aimed his gun dead center. I halted.

Johnny turned himself over. His eyes were open, blood was splattered on his right arm. I stepped between him and Sinbad.

"It doesn't matter," Sinbad said.

"Why didn't you finish us off at the docks?" I asked.

"At the docks I couldn't use da silencer. I had to scatter da crowd. But den you had da upper hand, and much too quickly. And him . . ." Sinbad nodded to Ron, who was clutching his side, his eyes wide in pain or fear or both. "You let him go."

"Ron doesn't know anything," I said, stepping forward. Sinbad stopped me with an iron glare.

I could see the pressure of his finger easing into the trigger. I tried to stall for time. "You're finished anyway, Sinbad."

"No, Mr. Cain, you are finished," he said. "You know, if you hadn't seen me at da office of da Merediths, you vouldn't be here right now. And neither vould I."

"But we are here, Sinbad."

"No, Mr. Cain. I am not here. Only one man vill leave this firehouse tonight."

A shot rang out behind Sinbad, the lock of the door splintered, and the door was kicked open. Sinbad turned and I dove for him karate-style, feet first, bringing him down, me on top of him. My wrist held his, trying to wrench the gun free. The wound in my shoulder split open. Glenn rushed in, saw me and Sinbad on the floor struggling. He kicked Sinbad in the face with his booted foot. Sinbad clutched at his head, and I rolled off. Glenn splattered the back of Sinbad's head with the barrel of his gun.

I immediately crawled to Johnny. I reached him and held

him. "What the hell's going on?" he asked. His words a pained whisper, his arm dripping red.

Glenn stepped to Ron and pulled him up. Ron struggled to upright himself and groaned. Glenn took him in hand and walked him to the door. I helped Johnny along, as much as he helped me along. Sinbad stayed on the floor, blood making a comfortable pillow for his head.

The street in front of the firehouse was empty. Glenn set Ron down on the sidewalk, leaning him against the tire of a parked car, then moved to go back inside. Johnny was holding his hand over the wound in his arm. No new blood seemed to be seeping through my bandage. Not yet, anyway. But the throb had returned in spades.

I peered around, searching for a phone booth, then remembered there was one inside the firehouse. I left Johnny with Ron and went back inside. The telephone was directly opposite the door. I was about to drop a coin in the slot, but Glenn stopped me.

"Not yet," he said.

"Why not?"

"I'm not finished." I hung up the receiver. He handed me my gun and Johnny's, pushed Sinbad's into his jacket, then placed his hands under Sinbad's arms and dragged him to the corner storeroom, leaving a trail of red. Sinbad was unconscious and gurgling.

"What are you doing?"

"He can't be found," Glenn said, and dropped the body. He began tearing through the trash cans, ripping out paper and tossing it around. He overturned cartons of empty beer cans, ripped up the cartons, tossing them over Sinbad and the room.

I heard the outside door open and my head snapped around. Johnny was standing and leaning on the doorway, his fingers trying to make a careful bandage for his arm, and succeeding. No blood was seeping through the fingers. He looked at me, asked, "What's going on?"

Glenn scurried through the room, tearing up more cartons, finding bags of unused paper napkins and scattering them all

190

over the storeroom, all over Sinbad. "Get out of here," he said to both of us.

"Wait a minute," I said, moving to Glenn.

"No, you wait," he said, crumbling napkins in his hand. "He can't be found," he repeated strongly. "Get out!" he yelled. He reached in his pocket, flicked open his lighter. The napkins in his hand blazed. "Out!" he again shouted. He held a length of cardboard over the flames of the napkins. When the cardboard caught fire, Glenn dropped the napkins and ran around the room, touching his flaming cardboard torch to anything that would catch.

Johnny and I were almost out the door when Glenn tossed the torch into the storeroom with Sinbad.

Glenn rushed out of the firehouse behind us and slammed the door. From our vantage point, no flames were visible. Glenn, out of breath, stepped back to where we were standing. Ron was on his feet, using a car fender for a wall, watching as if in a trance. I handed Johnny his gun. He replaced it in his holster, not without pained difficulty.

"Sinbad was KGB," Glenn said softly and between gasps. "The same as the Merediths. He came directly from Poland, the Merediths via England. Ten to one, the bullet that killed Sidney Meredith was fired from the same gun that killed Maureen; and the same bullet that Johnny's holding in his shoulder." He nodded at Johnny. "Sinbad killed Sidney because he was becoming dangerous to the entire operation. Maureen, because she killed Max and was going to kill you. Their entire campaign was becoming too messy to continue. It wasn't worth it to the KGB anymore. Sinbad had to clean it up as soon as possible."

That was a story. But there was more. "Why did Maureen kill Max?" I asked. I thought I caught a glimpse of red flames under the door of the firehouse.

"Because Max told her he was going to turn himself in."

"That's what Sinbad had said. So it was true. But why would Max have sworn falsely in the first place?" I asked.

"Max was an asshole," Glenn said. His breathing was evened out now. "When he came downtown to confess, he told immigration that he had sworn falsely at Maureen's naturalization hearing merely as a favor to her. He didn't see anything wrong with it at the time. She asked him, he said yes. He didn't know he was committing a federal crime."

"Not until later," I offered. "Rather naive."

"Stupid," Glenn said, then repeated, "a fucking asshole."

Ron cut in, still dazed. He winced and had a confused look on his face. "That happened years ago. It was no big deal. Max told me about that, but he turned himself in to the authorities. He said that everything was okay." Ron's eyes were glazed, his body shaking. He stared at the door to the firehouse as if not believing what he was seeing. Thin streams of white smoke began gliding under the bottom of the door.

It seems we were all entranced. Johnny didn't make a move, either. Glenn just stared. Not one of us made the effort to call the fire department. A sorry dazed lot.

We walked west. Glenn continued his explanation. "Sinbad had to disappear. Even putting aside the Merediths, somehow Sinbad was on to our cover at the flea market. I don't know how. Maybe Johnny said something to Max about working there. And maybe Johnny said something about me." He looked at Johnny, laying the blame at his feet. "So Sinbad had you snoop around down there." He looked at me, laying the blame at my feet. "We couldn't let the KGB discover that we knew about Sinbad and the Merediths. Now," he said, nodding back to the flickering firehouse, "we'll be able to watch to see where they start up again." He took a deep breath, then to me he said, "You messed it up real good, Cain."

"I messed it up, huh?" I said. I had about had it with all the shit Glenn was tossing around. Smearing Johnny in this whole goddamn mess, and myself.

Glenn saw it coming. He grabbed my arm, the one that pained me, and took me aside, leaving Johnny and Ron standing, waiting, in their own pain.

"I thought the fucking CIA couldn't gather intelligence inside the United States," I said, angry.

"You're a fool, Cain," Glenn said, but he could see my boil-

ing point had been reached. "And lower your fucking voice."
He looked anxiously over his shoulder at the wounded. Back to
me, he continued, "The Merediths were foreign agents. KGB.
That's our territory, whether in Russia or the U.S. or wherever
the fuck we say it is, that's where it is." If Glenn was trying to
placate me, he was doing a lousy job of it. "Don't blame Carney
either, Cain. We had to stop you. You were fucking up the
entire scheme."

"I was fucking it up? My fault, huh?" My voice didn't match
his hushed tone. I turned around to look at the destruction he
had caused. "You mean that's my fault, too?" A window on
the ground floor of the firehouse popped out, along with smoke
and flames. "What happened to Max is my fault? And Sidney?
And—"

Glenn cut me off with a shout that surprised me. The end of
his rope was reached, too. "If you would have stopped your
snooping, Cain, it would have made our job a lot easier. And
maybe some people might still be alive."

"Yeah," I said, and felt like an asshole for saying it. But his
guilt trip didn't take and I wasn't finished. "And you and your
goddamn CIA will go on playing your silly-ass games—at the
flea market, in Washington, at fucking G.A.A.—while we the
people go around not knowing what the fuck's going on. Shit,
that's pathetic."

"Believe what you want to believe. But it's necessary work."

"Not in my book," I said. I walked away, leaving Glenn
standing alone. But I turned around again. "What happens
when the Iron Curtain comes down?" I asked. "What happens
then? Your silly games will be shown up to be exactly what
they are. Fucking games." I didn't wait for Glenn to respond.

A late-night cab cruised by. His sign said OFF DUTY, but I
hailed it and was surprised when he stopped for us, considering
that Ron was bleeding from the leg, Johnny's arm was leaking,
and the inside of my jacket was warm with my own fresh blood.
I told the driver to go to Saint Vincent's Hospital. The hospital
was becoming a regular stop.

The doctor almost popped a gasket when he saw the three of us. He demanded to know what happened. This time I told him to call Carney.

Chapter
20

Three hours later, when Johnny and I cabbed back to Perry Street, having first dropped off Ron at his place, the sun had long been in the sky. I pulled down the shades in the bedroom and tried to undress, not an easy task with a new white bandage wrapped over my shoulder and around my chest. It took some effort and will to finally unlace and pull my boots off, step out of my 501's, and let my shirt fall to the floor. I felt grungy, and my underwear looked it. But a shower was out of the question. I fell back on the bed. It would have been nice if Johnny had fallen alongside me. But he didn't. He struggled to undress himself and stayed in the living room.

I watched him through the doorway, lying on the couch, a sheet covering his body, a pillow behind his head. He wasn't sleeping, either. Too much exhaustion had knocked sleep out of our minds. I was debating whether to get up and go down to the firehouse to assess the damage. I suggested it to Johnny. He went along with the idea but made no effort. Neither did I.

"You knew that Glenn was with the CIA, didn't you?" Johnny asked.

"Not at first. He never told me. When he warned me away from the flea market, he also gave me a phone number. I called him before I went to the firehouse. He met me outside the dance. I wanted to have it out with him, to find out what the fuck was going on with Sinbad. But then Helen told me that

194

Ron was after your blood. I told Glenn to wait for me, then I went to find you."

"I knew the CIA was at the flea market," Johnny said. "Glenn. But I swear to Christ, Archie, I didn't know they were involved with Max. That son of a bitch."

"Yeah," I said, too weary to debate the point. And I believed him. "But I suppose it was lucky for us that Glenn did wait at the firehouse."

"Yeah, lucky for us," Johnny said.

"Lucky for us," I said again. But what about Max? I thought. Max wasn't so lucky. He was a pawn in a game he didn't even know he was playing. At least Davie died by his own hand, his own choice. And Sidney was playing in an avenue he knew was deadly. But Max, poor, innocent, naive Max.

Johnny's brain must have been on the same wave as mine. He asked in the quiet of the darkness, "Archie, do you think you and Max would have gotten together? I mean, as lovers."

"I don't know," I said. "I doubt it. For me, Max was just another trick at the trucks." Just another trick at the trucks, one of too many, I thought, and kicked those thoughts in a corner of my brain that was becoming too crowded with thoughts I didn't want to think about. "What are you going to do now?" I asked Johnny.

"Start over. Somewhere. Maybe become a private dick, like you." He gave off a short, tired, and friendly laugh.

"I could use some help," I said. "I have a contract for guard duty at a Midtown thrift shop for two days a week, starting next week."

I leaned myself up on an elbow. Johnny did the same from the living room. "I have to find a missing beneficiary out in L.A.," I continued, "and I have to check on a painting that was auctioned off uptown. And I haven't called in for my messages for three days now. There's bound to be more jobs." I hesitated. "Wanna help?"

Maybe it was the glare from the sunlight trying to peep through the shades on the windows, maybe it was my active imagination, but I thought I saw a quiet glow in Johnny's eyes. "Yes," he said.

Johnny lay back down. So did I. My eyes were on his when we both fell asleep.

When I awoke, light was no longer filtering through the torn shades on the windows. We had slept the day away and another night had fallen. I inhaled a healthy aroma of hot coffee. I moaned when I lifted myself out of bed, but managed to walk to the kitchen table. My shoulder ached. I felt old and looked worse.

Johnny poured me a mug of coffee. He looked great, bandage on his arm and all, and I told him so.

"Yeah," he said, "in shorts that should have been in the laundry two days ago, and smelling like a pig."

"You need a shower," I suggested.

"So do you."

We helped each other. Johnny used masking tape and a couple of plastic ages to cover my bandage, then let me alone in the shower to do the best I could. I did the same for him and his arm.

By the time Johnny was finished, I was wearing a clean set of white briefs and was stepping into a fresh pair of Levi's.

"Where you off to?" he asked, a towel around his waist, his hair wet and shining like a porcupine in the morning dew. "It's Sunday."

"To the firehouse," I said.

"Not alone," he told me.

I offered Johnny a pair of my Levi's and he accepted. I turned my back to finish dressing, giving him his privacy.

My jacket would have to be cleaned and repaired, what with a slit in the chest and blood encrusted on the leather. And Johnny's black leather needed a new sleeve. We donned flannel shirts and hooded sweatshirts and walked to the firehouse. The night was cool, autumn letting us know winter was coming.

The ruins of the firehouse were still smoldering. One firetruck stood on the side, with two uninterested-looking firemen keeping any onlookers beyond the barrier they had set up. And the

196

onlookers were there, in small groups, members of G.A.A., some crying.

Johnny and I didn't even try to cross the line.

"So ends G.A.A.," I said. I didn't shed a tear, but I felt like it.

"You think so?" Johnny asked.

"It's as dead as Sinbad." But I amended my statement. "Well, no, the Gay Activist Alliance will still exist. And gay liberation can't be stopped. But it'll never be the same. Neither will G.A.A."

We didn't stay long at the site of the former headquarters of gay liberation. When we walked west I'm not even sure Johnny noticed that our hands were intertwined.

2²⁵

Gen 0830M TD